Also by Michael Steffan

A Novel

**North Pacific**

On the eve of World War II, Joseph Vaenko - an American-born son of Central European immigrants – struggles with faith, love, and identity, until a fleeting encounter with a Japanese American woman one morning at Mass forces him to confront the silence of God, the boundaries of culture, and the demands of the heart.

Non-Fiction

**Initial Burden**

A vivid naval history of the Korean War's opening days and weeks at sea, when a small number of U.S. and British warships faced nuclear tensions, air and submarine threats, surface actions, and more – while demonstrating the vital role of sea power in the modern world.

# In Pascal's Shadow

## A Novel

Michael Steffan

Paperback ISBN: 979-8-9875921-3-7

eBook ISBN: 979-8-9875921-4-4

Printed in the United States of America

Cover Art by Michael Steffan. The photo, showing Wright Park in Tacoma, Washington, was taken by the author and digitally enhanced using Prisma photo editing software.

*In Memory of*

*William Isaac Parrett 1927 – 1989*
*and*
*Leona Mildred Parrett 1932 - 2003*

"All great misfortunes are bearable except those which touch the soul."

Blaise Pascal - *Pensées*

# 1.

## *"...too profound for words..."*

*It is dawn. A wave breaks near the shore and rushes powerfully up the beach, straining to see how far it can advance. When the surf finishes its run and reaches its zenith, the cosmos holds its breath—silence, and stillness too profound for words reign. Then, the remnants of the once-mighty wave murmur and whisper as it retreats to the sea, filled with a sense of wonder and awe.*

Thomas Klement, aware that he had closed his eyes and was in that middle state, neither asleep nor quite awake, felt the late morning sun on his face as it crept into the room through the apartment's front windows. Smiling to himself, he felt pleased to have experienced the moment. He tried to remain in that state. He truly missed those times on the ocean beach. But no matter how hard he tried, and as seemed always to be the case, his mind could not hold on to the awe-inspiring dawns of his youth. Instead, it drifted to thoughts of the afternoons on the same beach, where swirling winds and crashing waves conspired to create a dark symphony of disorder, confusion, and the apparent indifference of nature.

Thomas opened his eyes. Glancing at the clock on the wall, he thought he still had a little time before leaving for work. His chair was comfortable, with two wide, flat arms where he could rest books and papers. Beside him stood a side table and a lamp. In front of him, an oversized ottoman held even more books, papers, pens, and pencils inside its hinged lid. There was a small couch against the wall to his left. Above the couch on the wall was a clock with a ticking second hand. A table in the corner held a portable television with rabbit ears. Under the windows, two low bookcases held an eclectic assortment of titles. Was the room messy? Well, that depended on whom you asked. Thomas smiled again and took a sip of cold coffee from the cup he had placed on the side table when he sat down earlier.

The thoughts that came to him while *resting his eyes* had surfaced over the last few years. The moment of stillness and the sense of immediacy were firmly established in the recesses of his mind. Did the dream have meaning? Thomas knew he would not resolve that question at that moment, so instead, he pulled himself up and out of his chair, pausing only to grab the coffee cup before heading for the kitchen. There, he poured the remains into the sink and set the cup on the counter.

The apartment was small. In addition to the compact living room, it included a bedroom, a bathroom with a sink and stand-up shower, and a kitchen with a stove and sink, leaving just enough space for a small refrigerator and a table for two. The *flat*, as it was sometimes called, was located on the third floor of a four-story apartment building. A realtor would likely use the term *cozy* to describe it generously. Whatever the apartment lacked in size was more than compensated for by its beautiful view of the park across the street and its close proximity to his place of work.

Once again, Thomas checked the time, brushed his teeth, put on his jacket, grabbed the paper bag, his wallet, and keys, and stepped out the door. He walked slowly, enjoying the midday sun, which was pleasantly warm but not hot.

## 2

# "A small community...a thousand souls..."

Thomas arrived at the store with ten minutes to spare. He walked to the back room, removed his jacket, placed the homemade sack lunch he had prepared earlier in the day in the refrigerator, and checked the schedule to see who would be working with him that afternoon. It turned out to be James, a friendly 20-year-old who attended the local community college. From there, he walked to the store's front counter, where he greeted Sharon, who looked at her watch matter-of-factly and told Thomas that he could sort the mail and that she was about to leave. As Sharon purposefully retrieved her coat and exited the building, Thomas looked at the mail she had handed him.

Then, James approached the counter, greeted Thomas, and asked, "Thomas, someone told me, I think it was George (George Renko, the owner of the bookstore), that you grew up by the ocean. Is that true?"

Thomas smiled and said, "It is true. I did grow up by the ocean."

"Really," James replied, shaking his head slightly. "That must have been fun. When I was growing up, we would go there on vacation for a few days or the better part of a week, but you actually lived there year-round?"

"I did. However, the year-round aspect of living there might not be as great as it seems. After all, the Washington State coastline is in the North Pacific, and it's not exactly like Southern California. I mean, it's great in the summer, but the rest of the time, there was a lot of rain, and the wind could be stronger than you might imagine. But overall, I have good memories."

James persisted. "Did you get to go fishing?"

"Yeah, I was able to work a couple of summers on a salmon troller. I also, on my own time, was able to cast for sea perch from the beach."

James seemed to have many more questions, but upon noticing a somewhat bewildered-looking customer upstairs in the stacks, he said, "I'll catch you later," and bounded up the steps.

Later that afternoon, reflecting on his conversation with James, Thomas reminisced more about growing up by the ocean. He was born in Aberdeen, Washington, on June 21, 1951, but his home was in Grayland, a small town on the Washington State coast just south of Westport. Grayland, a small community of around a thousand souls, was located between the entrance to Gray's Harbor to the north and

Willapa Bay to the south. There wasn't much there. During the summer, the area saw a surge in business from tourists, campers, and sports fishermen; however, most of the work for those who lived there year-round came from the local cranberry cannery operation.

Growing up near the ocean beach offered him and many of his friends summer work opportunities due to the tourism it attracted. He also recalled his time fishing on a salmon troller, where he operated gurdies, baited hooks, and cleaned and belly-iced fish, as well as working on a crabber, where he baited, laid, and retrieved crab pots. His mother never liked it when he worked out on the water, as it brought back troubling memories. He graduated from the only local high school, Ocosta, and made many friends throughout his years of public education.

The circumstances surrounding his immediate family set him apart from most of his friends. His father had died in a fishing accident a couple of months before he was born, which had been devastating for his mother. After that, it was just the two of them. She worked at the cranberry cannery, and they only had each other for company. That part worked well. She loved him dearly, and he loved her. They were friendly with many neighbors and fellow cannery workers, but ultimately, it was just the two of them.

One aspect of his childhood that stood out to him was his mother Alice's practice of their Catholic faith. She

8

taught him to say his prayers at night before going to bed. When something went wrong, he remembered seeing his mother look to and make the sign of the cross toward the large crucifix that hung on the wall in her bedroom. She insisted they pray the rosary during any crisis while he was growing up.

Every Sunday morning, he and his mother would take the family car, a gray 1950 Chevy, and drive to Aberdeen to attend Mass. Afterward, Alice would go to the church hall to chat and drink coffee with other parishioners, while Thomas would head to a classroom to learn the tenets of the Catholic faith. He recalled that around the time he was in 4th grade, he learned the Latin responses to the priest's exhortations and prayers during Mass, and shortly after, he became an altar server. On the return trip from Aberdeen to Grayland in the afternoon, Thomas would explain everything he had learned that day, while his mother would smile and encourage her son. As time passed, he became increasingly aware of his love for the faith, which provided him with intelligent and reasonable answers to his questions and a solid framework for his young life. Alice Klement was proud of her son.

As Thomas recalled his childhood memories, James reappeared with an elderly woman. "Thomas, this lady has a few questions. Could you assist her?" Thomas nodded and engaged the woman in conversation.

As he walked home from work that night, he reflected on his earlier thoughts. He had never truly recognized how delicate life could be. His father embodied that reality, didn't he? After seventeen years of this existence, he felt secure in everything he knew: the community where he had grown up, the changing seasons by the Pacific Ocean, his beliefs, and his understanding of the world. Then, one day, everything changed when his mother suggested the possibility of moving to Astoria, Oregon, in the next couple of years. Alice went on to explain to Thomas that her sister, Aunt Carol, had recently been diagnosed with Parkinson's disease. She said that someone would have to look after her and provide care in the future.

At that time, Thomas was in his junior year at Ocosta High School and had only begun thinking about what he would do after graduation. Encouraged by his mother, Thomas took the Scholastic Aptitude Test (SAT) and scored well. With that score and his high grade point average, he applied to several regional colleges. In his senior year, he was somewhat surprised to be accepted by Portland State University in the *Rose City* and Rainier University in Tacoma. The deciding factor came when Rainier University offered him a partial scholarship. That, combined with some available grants, resolved the competition in his mind. His mother preferred that he choose Portland State University, arguing that it would be closer to Astoria than Tacoma.

Of course, Thomas could have stayed in Grayland and likely worked at the cannery or perhaps done some fishing, but the idea of being on his own out there in the world, making his way in life, intrigued him. It also frightened him a little.

When school ended, Thomas remembered saying goodbye to all his friends, especially his girlfriend, Tami. She was headed to California, where her recently divorced mother had purchased a home in Santa Monica. He knew from the moment she told him that their relationship would not survive the long-distance separation.

Thomas and Alice decided that with his graduation, it was time for the long-planned move to Astoria to happen. Thomas helped his mother pack everything she wanted to take to Astoria, discarding certain items and giving others to neighbors and friends. Then he rented a U-Haul van and drove her and the selected belongings to Oregon. There, he spent a few days helping her settle in and enjoying some quality time with his aunt Carol. After about a week, he called his friend Aaron back in Grayland, to whom he had given his car keys. Alice had chosen not to take the car with her because Carol owned a nice car, and there would be no need to keep the aging Chevy. Aaron then drove to Astoria and picked Thomas up. Back home in Grayland, he gathered his possessions, and in Aaron's car, they headed for Tacoma. Thomas left the old Chevy behind for Aaron to sell.

Upon arriving in Tacoma, Aaron stayed with him for a few days at a motel along the I-5 freeway, which runs through the southeastern part of the city, while Thomas searched for a living arrangement near the Rainier University campus. He quickly found rental accommodations, a single room and a separate bathroom, in a residential home, a daylight basement apartment with a door that opened to the street, just four blocks from the university. Then he reimbursed his buddy Aaron for gas and his help and waved goodbye as his last link to Grayland and his childhood drove off. The life he had known up to that point—all eighteen years—faded away and vanished, not unlike Aaron and his car disappearing down the street.

That was, what, seven years ago? Thomas shook his head. Looking back, he concluded that his decision to come to Tacoma had been straightforward, along with reasonable aspirations for his future. What struck him after a short while was that reality might not have received the memo.

## 3.

# "She was slight..."

Time marched on. One day, at ten minutes to one, Thomas arrived at work after the brief walk from his apartment. It was another beautiful day in the Pacific Northwest, and Thomas paused on the sidewalk in front of the store, staring at the building. He had discovered the store while studying at Rainier University. Commencement Bay Books, a new and used bookstore, was relatively large and spanned two storefronts. Tens of thousands of titles were stacked vertically and horizontally across the main and second floors. The second floor was approximately one-third the size of the main floor and was accessible by a broad set of open stairs that rose in the center of the store. One could look up from anywhere on the main floor and see the exposed second floor filled with thousands more books. To a booker (someone who gets excited about this sort of thing), the store was a delight.

As he hung up his jacket in the back room and placed his lunch sack in the refrigerator, the store owner, George Renko, walked in and said, "Good afternoon, Thomas. I'm glad I caught you before I had to leave."

Thomas returned the greeting and asked George what was going on.

George Renko, who had initially opened the bookstore over twenty-five years ago, spoke with a distinct Central European accent, having immigrated to the United States in 1940. He expressed his desire for Thomas to sort through the three boxes of books that had arrived that morning and put together an offer. Thomas nodded, assuring George he would take care of it. George added, "Once you're finished, could you please put them back in the boxes and move them to the back room?"

"Sure," Thomas replied. "Do you want me to leave the offer on your desk?" George smiled and nodded in agreement. "Okay, then I'm off to the dentist. I really dislike going to see him. Maybe if I miss the bowl a few times—the one with the swirling water where I'm supposed to spit—he'll hurry up and finish with me. I think that will be my plan." He raised his finger as if he had decided on his strategy, smiled as if he felt good about it, and then headed out the door.

Thomas had a deep fondness for George. The man had offered him a job at a time when he felt lost about his future. Was George a bit eccentric? Absolutely, that was part of his charm. He infused a little bit of the *old country* into the streets of Tacoma. Thomas had worked for George for nearly three years as the night manager, with his shift running from 1:00 p.m. to 9:00 p.m. His responsibilities included managing the store in the afternoons and evenings, counting the money in the till, locking it up in the safe, and securing the premises at night. It was the ideal position, given his circumstances and recent experiences. George had taught him the business as if he were his own son. Thomas Klement was always happiest when he was exploring and rummaging through any bookstore, and Commencement Bay Books provided him with that opportunity every day.

It was just after 5:00 p.m. when business picked up slightly, as a handful of people who worked downtown made their way into the store on their commutes home by car or bus. A bus pulled up in front of the store, and a man and a woman got off. They both entered the store at the same time, but it was clear they were not together. Thomas watched as the gentleman headed straight to the mysteries and thrillers section, while the younger woman, likely in her mid-twenties, approached him. She was slight, wore black-rimmed glasses, and had dark hair twisted up in a high ponytail, giving it an attractive flair.

He greeted her. "Hello, how may I help you?"

She smiled. "I'm looking for a specific title." Glancing at a small piece of paper in her hand, she read aloud, "It's called *Desperate Characters* by Paula Fox." She also noted that it was published in 1970.

Thomas knew it wouldn't be in the new fiction section, but he quickly found two available copies as he walked over to the general fiction section, alphabetized by author. He picked up the one that seemed the freshest and handed it to her while she followed him down the aisle.

"Thank you," she expressed with gratitude.

Thomas returned to the front counter, leaving the attractive woman to examine the paperback book. A few minutes later, she approached the counter and handed the book to Thomas. "I'll take it," she said, pulling out her purse while Thomas rang up the sale, placed her money in the register, and counted out the correct change for her.

She went on to say to Thomas, "I saw Shirley MacLaine in the film adaptation of this book. I had been reflecting on how lonely she was in the story, which created a lot of emotional tension. I decided I needed to see how closely it adhered to or diverged from the book."

Thomas expressed his understanding of her point, noting that film adaptations frequently strayed too far from the original books, often changing the core emphasis of the written story.

"Yes," she agreed, smiling again.

They began discussing specific books and their movie adaptations, feeling surprisingly comfortable with each other as they became more relaxed and intrigued by each other's thoughts. Finally, she asked, "Did you attend either Pacific Lutheran or Rainier?" Thomas smiled and replied that he graduated from Rainier a few years ago.

She mentioned, "I thought I recognized you, but maybe not. I went to both colleges – it's a long story." She smiled, "I'm not trying to pry. I enjoyed our conversation and wanted to keep it going a bit longer."

"I truly enjoyed our conversation! I'm Thomas, by the way."

"And I'm Cynthia."

"Well, Cynthia, I hope we can do this again soon. Enjoy the book."

Cynthia nodded and watched Thomas respond to another woman's question, this time regarding 19th-century poetry. As she headed toward the exit, Cynthia thought she would indeed return to the bookstore to continue her conversation with Thomas.

# 4.

# "...a distinctly secular worldview."

That night, after a small and unremarkable late dinner, Thomas sat in his chair in the living room. It was nearly 10 p.m., and he was about to turn on the TV when his thoughts drifted to memories of his time at Rainier University.

He recalled feeling alone at first, "Not too much different from my current situation," he said aloud. Smiling to himself, he remembered the initial months of learning the mechanics and routines of university life. He worked diligently during those early years and decided that pursuing a real income would be the best path for him to follow.

A significant memory from his college days revolved around his faith. Upon arriving in Tacoma, he discovered a large Catholic church not far from his daylight basement apartment. He was taken aback by what he saw there. The changes initiated by the Second Vatican Council, held between 1962 and 1965, were finally, fully, and even experimentally implemented in the United States. It was here that he was introduced to the likes of the so-called *folk*

Mass. Instead of a choir in the loft at the back of the church, he was now *treated* to young people with guitars, tambourines, and other instruments set up front, just off to the side of the sanctuary where the main altar was located. The priest conducted the liturgy in English instead of Latin, replacing the beautiful Latin hymns from the former Mass with folksy songs sung in English. The last straw for Thomas was one Sunday when a barefoot young woman danced to the music in front of the musicians as part of a *liturgical program* during Mass. Thomas didn't know what to think. He couldn't process what felt like upheaval and a lack of reverence for the Mass as he knew it. Ultimately, these outward changes had a significant impact on him. He was told this new approach was supposed to appeal to young people like himself. Sadly, it did not. This led to his eventual decision to stop attending Mass. It did not change his beliefs, but it did suppress them. This troubled Thomas, but did not lead him back to Mass either.

After declaring his major in Business, he discovered he could take some elective choices unrelated to his field of study. In his junior year, he took a history class titled *The History of the Second World War in the North Pacific,* inspired by a book of the same name written by a deceased professor at Rainier University, which he enjoyed. He took a few philosophy survey classes and an introductory poetry class during his senior year.

He enrolled in the Introduction to Poetry class because he was captivated by the instructor, Professor Ellen Morse, who was likely in her mid-30s and quite attractive. Listening to her present material would, at the very least, be enjoyable. At that time, he thought, how difficult could it be to string together a few *couplets* for an easy, good grade? However, Professor Morse delivered an intriguing and engaging course that revealed to Thomas some hidden values of poetry. One involved exploring a topic he needed to understand and expressing it in a poem. Surprisingly, he found that presenting a subject in poetic form helped him retain the essential ideas related to the topic. He realized he had to work much harder than he initially intended, but he felt the effort was worthwhile.

He looked forward to the philosophy survey classes because he wanted to see how the thoughts of historical and contemporary philosophers aligned with his own ideas about life and the religious beliefs he had been taught over the years. The first philosophy class was a straightforward introduction to the subject, which turned out to be quite dry and not very challenging. Professor David Street taught the second philosophy class, focusing on many hot-button issues and questions in the modern era. Professor Street was well-known for sparking lively discussions among his students on a range of philosophical arguments, topics, and ideas. Street was described as a passionate orator dedicated to his philosophical positions. *David,* as some female students referred to Mr. Street, was likely in his late 30s, with plenty of swept-back black hair and a trendy, fashionable beard. Street introduced Thomas to a distinctly secular worldview. At this point in his life, now that he viewed his religious beliefs as outdated, Thomas adopted independence and reason as the cornerstones for navigating a complex and thoroughly modern society. The class had a significant impact on the young man from Grayland, Washington.

Thomas had made some friends at college, which led to invitations to parties. At the parties, he drank beer and socialized with other students. He also met and interacted with a few women during his junior and senior years. He spent time with each of them—over coffee, lunch, studying at the library, or simply sitting in the sun and chatting. However, he never invited either of them to his flat, a choice that seemed to reflect his non-committal attitude toward women at the time.

Thomas earned a Bachelor of Arts in Business Administration from Rainier University. However, there was a problem: upon graduation, he was not motivated to seek new loans or grants for postgraduate studies. During his senior year, with the university's assistance, he had arranged two job interviews: one with Boeing and another with the Port of Seattle. Securing a good job had been the plan ever since he decided to attend college. However, something didn't feel quite right. Somehow, his university experiences and four years of higher education had drained his drive to *make a lot of money*. At the last minute, he canceled the potential job interviews. His *job* on the college's grounds maintenance crew also ended, meaning he would have to give up his daylight basement accommodations, and he still did not own a car.

He lay in bed in his flat, staring at the cracked lines on the ceiling. He pondered his disinterest in pursuing a career that his degree could offer him. He felt the absence of family connections and mourned the loss of the Church life he had experienced as a child. Thomas sensed his lack of purpose. It was as if he were treading water, struggling with his uncertain and fragile values and beliefs. He slept poorly, tossing and turning and waking frequently.

Despondency weighed heavily on the young man from Grayland. *Gray land,* he mused—a fitting description.

The next day, filled with a sense of distress and realizing he had only a few more days in his flat, Thomas recalled riding the bus to the Stadium District at the edge of Tacoma's downtown area. There, he entered his favorite store, Commencement Bay Books, where he had spent countless hours browsing the large selection of used books over the last few years. During that time, Thomas also formed a friendship with the owner, George Renko. As Thomas counted his last dollar bills along with the change in his pocket to see if he could afford a used copy of *The Radetsky March* by Josef Roth, Mr. Renko approached him and asked if he had a moment to talk.

George launched into a discussion with Thomas, explaining to the young man how many hours he had to work, the toll it was taking on him, and his advancing age. The store owner shared how much he had enjoyed having Thomas, one of his favorite customers, visit the store over the past few years. George mentioned that he particularly liked their debates on the merits of different authors. Then, seemingly out of nowhere, he asked if Thomas had ever considered the possibility of working at the store. George didn't wait for a response. He offered him the Night Manager position (1:00 p.m. to 9:00 p.m.), with Sundays and Mondays off. Of course, George didn't know that Thomas was about to be evicted from his apartment or that he had no job prospects after canceling his job interviews. With surprise evident on his face,

Thomas quickly said yes, thinking this must be like receiving manna from heaven. The money was far from what he could have earned at Boeing or the Port of Seattle, but it was sufficient to prevent him from having to live with a friend or, alternatively, to be homeless.

# 5.

# "...does it not consume you?"

Did the new position he secured at the bookstore resolve the issues in Thomas Klement's life? In a word, no. The rest of the puzzle surrounding this job opportunity fell into place when Thomas found an affordable apartment across the street from Wright Park, just a three-block walk to his new job at the bookstore. After moving into his new apartment, he felt this must be what he was meant to do, at least for now.

Wright Park was an incredible escape from everyday work life in Tacoma. Situated in the Stadium District on the northwest edge of downtown, the 27-acre park (five city blocks by two city blocks) featured expansive lawns, trails, and a large pond. It also functioned as an arboretum, showcasing around 600 large trees representing over 100 species throughout the grounds. Additionally, the Seymour Botanical Conservatory was located on the park site. Three thousand glass panes covered the conservatory's towering, twelve-sided dome with two protruding wings. A koi fishpond inside the dome provided the perfect touch to the beautiful setting.

Thomas started working at Commencement Bay Books the following week. He borrowed enough money from his college friend, Zack Rowland, to cover the first month's rent and the security deposit. By the end of the second month, he had repaid the loan to Zack and felt like he was now a part of the Wright Park neighborhood.

Now, nearing three years into his new life, Thomas had developed daily routines that one could set their watch to. He was surprised by how quickly time passed. During this period, George had given him a couple of raises to help with living expenses. Still, up to this point, Thomas had not purchased a car. He had thought about it but never fully committed to the idea. Where did he need to go? Yes, he needed to see his mother. He had done that between his sophomore and junior years at Rainier University and on two occasions since he took the job at Commencement Bay Books. He took the train from Tacoma to Longview, Washington, and then boarded a bus for the trip along the Oregon side of the Columbia River out to the coast and Astoria. He planned to do it again soon. His mother seemed happy, yet one could see his aunt Carol gaining that distinct hollow look that comes with Parkinson's disease.

Regarding his life situation, he had discussed it with some of his friends from Rainier. Thomas couldn't quite pinpoint it, but something in what some of his friends mentioned during these conversations left him feeling uncertain and somewhat confused. He appeared unmotivated. Why didn't he want to get out there and earn some real money? His response was always, "Why, just for the sake of money? I don't think so. I enjoy my world. Although it is small, I love the area where I live. I feel comfortable." His buddies would ask, "What about women? Don't you want to find the right woman and get married?" Thomas would immediately agree with this notion but then ask rhetorically, "How much money is enough to get married? Then, once you commit to making more money, does it not consume you? Doesn't it become your master?" They would then reply, "Well, it will take a very special person to fit the bill for you, Thomas Klement," followed by laughter. Thomas would also laugh, and they would move on to another subject. Yet the unresolved questions lingered in his mind.

# 6.

## "I met a guy."

It was Wednesday night at Commencement Bay Books. Thomas was engaged in a conversation with Susan, another clerk who was closing with him that evening. Susan, a pretty young woman with large, round glasses and light brown hair, was telling Thomas about her boyfriend. "His car is in the shop. He said it would be ready this afternoon, but he just called and the shop said that it would now take until the next day." She looked upset. "He basically told me I was on my own as far as getting to my apartment tonight." Susan, hands thrown up in the air, looked exasperated and slightly shaken.

"How far is your apartment from here?" Thomas asked.

"I guess about a mile or two," Susan responded, appearing as if she had never considered that question before.

It certainly was not on his top ten things to do list for this evening; nonetheless, Thomas asked, "How about if I walk you to your place after we close up?"

Susan's face brightened at once. "That would be wonderful, Thomas. Are you sure you don't mind?"

Why Susan's boyfriend didn't walk down here to collect her was not a path Thomas wanted to go down. Instead, he said, "It's no problem, really."

She smiled once more and said, "Thanks."

"Let's get the shelves in order so we can get out of here on time, alright?"

They both headed off in different directions, straightening the books and re-alphabetizing them as they went.

It turned out that Susan lived a little over two miles from the bookstore. During their walk, Susan told Thomas that she usually worked during the day with Sharon. She went on to tell Thomas that she had switched with James today because he had a thing to attend. Thomas finally got her safely to her place and saw her enter the apartment building, waving back at him and saying, "Thanks again," before blowing him a kiss. He smiled, turned around, and headed back toward the park.

On his walk home, Thomas stopped at The Rail to Sail Public House, known to the locals as The Rail. The name dated back to when Tacoma was celebrated as the "World's Lumber Capital." Timber from the forests of the Cascade Mountain Range was sorted or milled in Tacoma before the logs and lumber were transported Back East by rail or loaded onto large sailing vessels for shipment across the Pacific.

Thomas entered the establishment, found a seat at the bar, and ordered a pint of lager. Even though it was close to 10:30 p.m., he ordered a single-piece fish and chips to accompany the beer. The bartender handed him the pint and told him his order would be up shortly. A boxing match was underway on the television, and the sound was turned down. The set hung on the wall behind the bar. He glanced out over the small sea of tables, mostly full of regulars who all seemed to be having a good time. A jukebox in the corner competed with the din of the crowd to be heard.

He didn't recognize anyone and turned again on his barstool to be greeted by a terrific-looking young woman with long dark brown hair standing there with his order and sporting an arresting smile. Thomas said, "Hi," and motioned for her to place the plate and condiments in front of him on the bar.

She said, "Hi there," as she arranged the order in front of him. "Need anything else?" She smiled again, making him feel a little weak.

"No, that will do. Are you new here? I don't think I've seen you before. I'm Thomas," he said, fumbling basically to remember his name.

She smiled for the third time and said, "Everyone calls me Minnie."

"Minnie," he said, with a slight surprise in his voice.

"My name is Minerva," she said, playfully placing her hands on her hips. "My mother chose it because she liked an actress who was performing around the time I was born." Raising her hands in exasperation, she blurted, "Nobody is named Minerva. I guess I'm one of a kind."

Thomas thought, dear God, she is truly one of a kind; of that, there is no doubt. "Minnie, I'm pleased to make your acquaintance."

"Well, Thomas, maybe when things slow down a bit in here, I'll come back, and we can get to know each other a little better. What do you think?"

"Sounds like a great plan to me. I'll be waiting."

"Good," she said, giving him a wink, then quickly moved to respond to hands raised or waving from the tables clustered just a few feet from where they were at the bar.

Thomas consumed his fish and chips, watched a bit of the fight on TV, and ordered another beer. Just after 11:30 p.m., Minnie reappeared, true to her word. "Hi, Thomas. I just finished my shift. Do you still want to talk?"

As he visually took her in, the word striking was his first impression. She was fit and shapely, with brunette hair cascading down onto her shoulders. She was, he decided, the cutest young woman he had ever seen. Everything about her was captivating. Moreover, her expressive face fascinated him, as it seemed to convey an emotional transparency he hadn't encountered in other women he knew. He could have gone on, but he realized he needed to say something. "I'm glad you remembered me, and I'd love to talk," he said earnestly.

"Great," Minnie replied. "How about we grab that empty table over there? It'll be quieter." Thomas slid off the barstool, carrying the remainder of his beer, and followed Minnie to the indicated table. Minnie had a glass of water she had gotten for herself before approaching Thomas. They sat down and took a moment to simply take each other in.

Thomas broke the silence with the coolest icebreaker he could think of, "Are you from Tacoma?"

"No, actually, I'm from a small town up on Hood Canal. It's called Union. I think about 500 people live there. You know, of course, that Hood Canal isn't a canal but a fjord. Whenever I tell anyone that, they respond by saying they thought fjords were only in Norway." She laughed. "Seriously, like I had to learn in school, a fjord is a natural body of water created by glaciers, while a canal is an artificial body of water made by humans."

Thomas' eyes widened, and he said, "I did not know that."

Minnie smiled and said, "You're welcome."

Thomas said, "It seems like we have something in common. We're both from very small towns. I'm from Grayland, which is near Aberdeen and Westport. I believe we had nearly a thousand residents."

Minnie switched gears: "I wanted to make something of myself. I couldn't see myself in Union for the rest of my life. So, I moved here to Tacoma because I have a cousin who lives here. It was a good deal for me. I escaped from the little town where everyone knew everyone else and knew what everyone else was doing. I got a job here about three weeks ago, and I've really enjoyed meeting so many new people."

Thomas shared his recent life with Minnie. "I moved to Tacoma around seven years ago. I graduated from Rainier University in 1976. I am the night manager at Commencement Bay Books."

Minnie interrupted him, "I know where that is! I've been there once. Nice store. I didn't see you, but of course, I didn't know you then either. I think it was last Friday, around noon, before my shift started at the Rail. I guess it makes sense that you weren't there since you just told me you were the night manager," making air quotes and smiling.

"So, how are you liking Tacoma so far?" Thomas asked.

"I like it. You're kidding, right? There's nothing to do in Union. Don't get me wrong, I'm sure if I were in my 50s or 60s, it might be a nice, quiet place to retire, but I'm 25. Tacoma offers a variety of shopping, dining, and entertainment options, including movie theaters. I love movies."

Thomas loved her voice and her energy. "I love movies too. Maybe we could go together sometime?"

"Oh, absolutely, that would be fun. This kind of conversation doesn't happen in Union, first because you already know everyone, and second because you have to drive to Shelton or Olympia to see a movie." They both laughed, becoming more comfortable with one another. The conversation continued.

As the two of them realized they were into each other, they discovered deeper aspects of one another. Minnie found that Thomas had paused his immediate future, was happy living in the Wright Park neighborhood, and enjoyed working at the bookstore. He learned that Minnie was a part-time writer who had contributed articles to the weekly Union newspaper and had also begun writing short stories.

The lights at The Rail were raised and lowered. No, they both thought. It couldn't be almost closing time, but it was.

Thomas said, "Oh, Minnie, I'm really sorry. I didn't mean to ramble on. I had no idea it had gotten this late."

"It's not your fault, Thomas. Once I start, there's no stopping me."

They both laughed and gazed intently at one another.

Finally, Thomas asked, "How are you getting home?"

"I have my cousin's car. She lets me use it in the evenings."

"Where is your cousin's place?"

"She lives a few blocks from that spectacular high school and football stadium."

Thomas was well aware of the high school, originally built as a chateau-style hotel, that sat majestically on one side of the naturally hewn Stadium Bowl, offering a stunning view of Puget Sound. "I know it well," Thomas replied. "I guess we could talk again sometime. I'd like that," he said in a more earnest tone.

"I'd really like that too, Thomas. I'm working nights for the rest of the week. Feel free to stop by any time after you close the bookstore."

They exchanged phone numbers, and he walked her out to her car.

As he walked home, thoughts of her consumed him until he locked the door and noticed the clock reading 2:40

a.m. "Wow," he said aloud. It had been a long time since he had stayed up this late. "It was worth it," he murmured quietly.

When Minnie reached her cousin's house, the rustling as she changed into her nightgown and took a sip of water before going to bed awakened her cousin Charlotte, whose room was right across the hall. Charlotte stared at her alarm clock for a moment and then said blearily, almost shouting, "It's after 2 a.m."

"Sorry, Charlotte," Minnie replied.

"I thought you said you were getting off work before midnight."

Minnie hesitated, then, with some noticeable excitement in her voice, said, "I met a guy."

There was a pause, and then Charlotte replied, "I want to hear all about him in the morning."

They giggled together as Minnie switched off her light and pulled the covers up.

# 7.

## *"You must show respect..."*

Over the next few weeks, Thomas visited The Rail after closing the bookstore on several occasions. He and Minnie enjoyed each other's company, and Thomas finally asked her out on a date. They went to the movies on their first day off together. After that, they took walks in Wright Park and explored the botanical gardens at the conservatory on the upper side of the grounds. They met for lunch at a popular café.

After Thomas had walked Minnie to her cousin's house several times, she asked him where he lived and expressed her desire to see his place. The next time they met, Minnie asked Thomas to show her his apartment. He walked her over to his place by the park. Then, she inquired if he could give her a tour. Thomas said, "Sure."

Minnie liked his place and told him so. She laughed upon seeing *his* chair, which had broad, flat arms supporting various papers and books. "That is so you, Thomas," she said with a hint of amusement.

Both had the day off, and in the early afternoon, they went out to pick up some takeout to bring back to his place. After finishing their meal, they talked into the early evening. They sat on the couch, and a little later, as their emotions intensified, they kissed. It was surprising how quickly their ardor ignited. They became lost in each other, entirely overwhelmed by the attraction they felt. They engaged with one another passionately, losing all sense of time. Then, as if struck by lightning, Thomas suddenly realized where this passion might lead. He had certainly *made out* with different girls during his time at Rainier University, including Tami from his Grayland days, but in each instance, he managed not to take that final step. He recognized that if he and Minnie continued down this path, their relationship would reach a point they had yet to discuss. "Minnie," he groaned, "we need to talk."

With a look of surprise, Minnie softly yet confusedly asked, "What do you mean?"

"I guess I'm saying we should discuss this before we go too far. I know I'm right on the edge." He hoped she understood what he was trying to convey.

She moaned and said, "Come here, Thomas. Kiss me." She wrapped her arms around him once more, trying to recapture the momentarily interrupted emotion and passion.

Thomas paused once more. Now breathing heavily like him, Minnie shifted her body and, regaining her composure, said, "You're being serious. Don't you love me? I love you. I've loved you since the moment we met."

Slightly taken aback, Thomas said, "Minnie, you're the most beautiful girl I've ever met, but we shouldn't rush into this."

Now, surprisingly embarrassed, Minnie sat up and shot Thomas a glare. As she tried to smooth her hair and clothes, she said, "How could you…" She looked at him again and began to cry.

"Minnie, please don't cry. I promise I'm not trying to upset or embarrass you. I just want you to understand what I'm saying."

It was too late. Now standing, Minnie paused for a moment and began to cry again. She grabbed her jacket and hurried to the door. She turned to Thomas, who was following her. Again, he said, "Please don't go, Minnie."

However, before he could reach the door, Minnie turned, opened it, stepped outside, and slammed it shut behind her. He opened the door and heard her say, "Just leave me alone," as he watched her run down the hall and the stairs into the early evening dusk.

Thomas closed the door, feeling devastated. He contemplated running after her, but he knew that would only lead to fighting and arguing in front of the entire neighborhood. He didn't want to put her through that. He felt like a total jerk. He had embarrassed her with his doubts about what had just occurred—or what hadn't occurred. He reflected on how he might have handled the moment differently. He had strong feelings for Minnie and wanted to make love to her, believing it would be the most incredible experience of his life. But who knew what that truly meant? What if she got pregnant? What would that mean for their relationship?

"Oh my God," he whispered, recalling his former parish priest, Father Baker, the good priest who had taught Thomas the faith during those post-Mass classes on Sundays in Aberdeen while he was growing up. Why? Why would I think of him? Then, he remembered precisely what Fr. Baker had said about premarital relations. He had talked about balancing passions and desires with reason. The good father had attempted to lighten the serious lesson by comparing his point about balancing to the title of a then-current and extremely popular television series, Mission: Impossible. He recalled all the teenagers laughing and getting the reference. After the teens finished laughing and grinning at one another, Thomas thought about his then-girlfriend, Tami. They struggled with this dilemma and somehow managed to resolve it without the disastrous result he and Minnie had just experienced. He recalled the priest concluding and emphasizing his lesson by calling out the boys in the class. Raising his voice to capture their attention, he said, "You must show respect," lowering his voice slightly, "to women at all times." Thomas shook his head, amazed at the clarity and power of Fr. Baker's message from almost a decade ago. He also thought about how it hadn't been until the last decade or so that young people had started "living together" before deciding to marry—a practice that had been taboo just a short time earlier.

One thing Thomas noted that Father Baker hadn't addressed was how powerful the heat of the moment could be. To Thomas, that made perfect sense when dealing with teens. I've never been with someone and felt the way I did at that moment. I have no idea how I managed to stop and say what I did. Damn, what is she going to think of me? I never should have shown her my apartment. How do I face her? What can I say? I mean, if we really care about each other, as we both seem to claim, it's the right thing to do— to talk about it.

Thomas woke up a couple of hours later than usual the next day and immediately called Minnie. Her cousin Charlotte answered the phone and said that Minnie had just left. She thought Minnie was going shopping before heading to work at The Rail. Thomas thanked her and asked her to let Minnie know he had called. At around 5 p.m., during his shift at the bookstore, he told James he had to run an errand but would be back shortly. He walked to The Rail and looked for Minnie, but she wasn't there. He asked Jake, the bartender, about her, but he thought she had the late shift that night. Thomas thanked him and returned to the bookstore.

After work, he returned to The Rail looking for Minnie. He sat at the bar and ordered a beer. He scanned the room and saw her serving food and drinks at a table. Their eyes met when she glanced up. After finishing with the customers at the table, she returned to the kitchen. A few minutes later, Minnie appeared in front of Thomas.

"Hey," he said softly, a worried expression on his face.

"Hi, what do you want?" she replied in a similarly subdued tone, lacking any emotion.

"I'm here to apologize for last night."

"Why? You don't need to apologize."

Thomas' expression faltered. He knew she was just as angry with him as she had been the night before. "Of course, I want to apologize for what happened last night. I never thought you would get that upset with me. I'm sorry. I truly am."

"I don't know what to say, Thomas. I need to get back to work." Then, as Minnie began to turn away, she glanced back at him and asked, "Are you still going to Astoria in the morning?"

"Damn, that is tomorrow, isn't it?" stammered Thomas. Given the events of the previous day, he had entirely forgotten about his long-planned visit to see his mother and aunt.

As Minnie walked away, she icily remarked, "Have a good time." Thomas watched her vanish once more into the kitchen. He considered this the worst possible outcome of his visit tonight. After waiting a bit longer and not seeing her return, he finished his beer and left.

At home, he sat in his chair, trying to make sense of the situation. He had never seen Minnie like this before. To make matters worse, she had reminded him of his travel plans for the following days. He had spoken to his mother a few days earlier, and she was so excited that Thomas would finally visit her again after such a long time. He remained in the chair, brooding for another hour about whether he should cancel the trip for now before finally going to bed.

He woke up early the next morning and decided to visit his mother, as he had promised to do. He thought that perhaps, after a week of reflection, Minnie might be more open to discussing the circumstances of their situation.

He got out of bed, packed a few belongings, took the bus downtown, and boarded the Northern Pacific train heading south.

# 8.

# "... if it wasn't already a fait accompli."

Thomas arrived in Astoria later that day. Having stewed about Minnie the entire trip, it was comforting to be doted on by his mother and aunt. The time spent with Alice and Carol was long overdue. Mom seemed older to him now, which she indeed was. It had been a couple of years since he last saw her, and the lines on her face had deepened. However, she remained a beautiful woman by anyone's standards. His aunt Carol had gone from showing some early indications of Parkinson's Disease to more manifest signs as it slowly continued to take her life. Thomas was troubled by this reality, but he was uplifted by observing that his aunt faced the illness with such quiet dignity. Overall, his assessment of their situation was that both women seemed happy to have each other for day-to-day needs and each other's company. When his stay ended, Thomas vowed not to wait that long again to visit them.

Upon returning to Tacoma at the end of the week, Thomas resolved to see Minnie the following day. The next morning, he did his laundry, went grocery shopping, and picked up his mail from the past week at the post office. He arrived at work on time and was brought up to speed on everything that had occurred while he was away. In the evening, he and James closed the store, and Thomas walked down the street to The Rail.

With great hope, he entered the pub and took what was becoming his usual seat at the bar. When they saw each other, to Thomas' great disappointment, Minnie still looked visibly upset. He tried to engage her in conversation, but she gave him the cold shoulder. She spent a lot of time at different tables laughing and mingling with other customers, mostly men. When the two finally interacted, she seemed distant and uninterested. Thomas endured it for as long as he could, but ultimately left without either of them saying goodbye to the other.

At home that night, his thoughts were filled with the real possibility that he might lose his relationship with that amazing woman if it wasn't already a fait accompli. Thomas reflected further and devised a plan that, if unsuccessful, would undoubtedly lead to his embarrassment. He reasoned that he needed to perform an act of humility, which could potentially pave the way for their reconciliation.

During his lunch break at work the next day, Thomas visited the florist across the street from the bookstore. He was assisted by a friendly woman, likely in her forties, who seemed to take an interest in Thomas' puzzled expression.

He told her he wanted a manageable bouquet of flowers for a young lady, which essentially conveyed, *I'm sorry.* The florist smiled and said it would be easy, as if she had heard this request a time or two before. She led Thomas over to the counter, explaining that the best approach was to combine passionate red and pure white roses with a touch of baby's breath mixed in. The resulting bouquet would melt any woman's heart and resolve any misunderstandings from the past. He nodded affirmatively, and she assembled the bouquet in just a few minutes. As he paid, he thanked her for her help and then returned to the bookstore, where he stored the flowers in the back room until closing time.

Again, he arrived at the pub and sat three spots down from his usual barstool, which was currently occupied. He placed the flower arrangement on the bar and ordered a pint of lager. The beer arrived as he began to survey the tables. The rock group Nazareth's ballad "Love Hurts" (didn't he know it) was playing on the jukebox. His eyes finally rested on a table in the far corner. He strained a bit to see better and, to his confusion, spotted Minnie leaning over a guy sitting at the table with her hand on his shoulder. He blinked and looked again, and to his bewilderment, Thomas recognized the man as none other than David Street, the philosophy professor at Rainier University. He took a big swig of his beer, fixing his gaze on Minnie and Street. The two of them laughed while Street entertained two other young men and a woman, likely seniors from the university, with his charm and unwavering confidence. Thomas didn't know what to think. He sat there, staring, completely transfixed. As Thomas would later characterize it to himself, the nightmare came to a crashing end when Minnie, already draped over Street's shoulder, turned her head, and he watched as the two kissed. Then she straightened up and said something to him. The others laughed, and then she moved toward the kitchen.

Thomas felt lost, unsure of what to do next, and feeling completely self-conscious and uncomfortable. He glanced at the bouquet. He set the untouched beer down on the counter, picked up the bouquet, stared at the flowers for a moment longer, and then let them drop to the floor. The guy who had taken Thomas' usual stool turned and said, "Hey buddy, you dropped your flowers." Thomas never heard him and barely remembered how he walked home.

In the weeks that followed, Thomas felt as alone as he could be. He tried to avoid thinking about what had transpired that night at The Rail, yet his thoughts always returned to the images of Minnie and Street together. In his mind, he just couldn't reconcile Minnie and Street as a couple. David Street was married, and Thomas knew this because he had seen the philosophy professor's wife several times after Street finished a class or lecture he had attended. She was attractive, likely five years or so younger than Street, who was probably nearing forty.

Klement threw himself into working at the store, so much so that George corralled him one day and told him to take it easy. All of Thomas' energy expenditures made the rest of the staff anxious. They all wondered and worried about their good friend and night manager. George took him out for a cup of coffee and a chat the second week, trying to figure out what might be bothering him. After George reassured him that he was only concerned about his well-being, Thomas let his guard down slightly. He asked George a broad question, and what he thought was a general sort of searching inquiry. "George, what are your guiding principles?" He waved his arm in a general manner in front of him. "What I'm saying is, do you have some philosophy of life that helps you resolve things that happen, you know, out there in the world?" Again, Thomas gestured toward nothing in particular.

George was trying to follow Thomas' reasoning, but had to admit to himself that he was hanging on by a thread. He hesitated momentarily and said, "Thomas, I arrived in this country just before the war began. In the end, all Europeans were shattered by the brutality and devastation the conflict left behind. Over the last thirty years, I have built a new world. It is my world. Granted, it is small. But it is mine. My bookstore is my world. I built it and have maintained it. Within its confines, I am in control, and it, in a sense, protects me from those things I cannot regulate."

There was a pause. Thomas said, "George, I really appreciate you sharing your thoughts with me. I've just been in a situation that I really don't want to discuss, and it has made me question how the world works." He paused for a moment and then continued, with George giving Thomas his full attention. "The older I get — and I realize I'm still quite young — the more the world reveals itself to be less than I had hoped for."

They continued their conversation over refilled coffee cups, making little progress in addressing Thomas' broader questions but demonstrating evident growth in their continually developing friendship.

Over the next few days, Thomas tried to come to terms with the fact that Minnie had moved on from their relationship. Although he accepted this as reality, he struggled with the thought that she had feelings for David Street. In what world was that even possible? He knew Minnie was strong-willed and sometimes impulsive. Yet, she was also confident, independent, and undeniably passionate. Had he ruined his chance with her? Had his questions and concerns surfaced at the worst possible moment? Obviously, yes. These thoughts plagued him day after day.

A few weeks passed. Then, one day, a city bus pulled up in front of the store right on schedule. Thomas saw the beautiful woman from about six months ago with dark hair and glasses disembark and enter the bookstore. What was her name—Cin, Cindy, Cynthia—that's it. A few minutes later, their eyes met. Both smiled, and a pleasant conversation followed. From their chat, Thomas learned that Cynthia worked as a bookkeeper for a local stationery and supply store downtown. He assisted her again with a book she was searching for before James asked for some help with another customer. As he patiently aided the second customer, Cynthia completed her purchase and waved to Thomas, saying she hoped to see him again soon.

## 9.

## *"The thought seemed deep…"*

The phone rang. It was 9:30 p.m., and he had just arrived home from the bookstore. Thomas answered and recognized Zack Rowland's voice.

"Tom, what's going on?"

"I just got home from the store, Zack. What's on your mind?"

"I'm headed to a party and want you to come."

"Where?" Thomas asked his old college buddy.

"It's at Steve Janson's place. You remember him. He used to hang out with us in the Student Union Building during lunch. He lives up toward 6th Avenue, not too far, really—maybe eight or nine blocks from your place. I'd really like you to come. I'm sure it'll be a great time, and many young ladies will probably be eager to meet you." Zack laughed. "What do you say?"

Thomas, never much of a party guy, instinctively wanted to tell Zack he would probably pass on the invitation, but appreciated it nonetheless. However, something inside prompted him to consider, why not go? He realized he often just sat around and dwelt on things that drove him crazy. Maybe I should go. At least he could say that tonight was different from the numerous nights he spent sitting in his chair in the apartment. Then, to his own surprise, Thomas exclaimed, "Okay, sounds good."

There was a pause on the other end of the line, and a slightly surprised voice said, "Great, I'll be over to pick you up in 15 to 20 minutes. Please be waiting out front."

They arrived at the party just after ten. Steve, a nice guy he knew from their college days, was genuinely pleased to see Thomas. The two talked about anything and everything for about half an hour.

Thomas had nursed a beer since his arrival and was about to grab a second when he noticed his friend Zack lighting up a joint in the hallway. Zack passed the *doobie*, as he called it, around to some friends, including two young women. As the second woman finished her hit, holding her breath, she extended it toward Thomas as he made his way to the kitchen. Thomas paused and saw that the small group of people gathered there in the hall was watching him to see if he would take a puff. The woman holding the joint turned her head slightly and, with a smile as if to say, "Come on, try it," raised it a little higher. At that moment, Thomas somehow connected the situation to the disastrous event involving Minnie, smiled at her, grasped it from her fingers, took a deep drag, and held his breath. After exhaling, he handed it back to Zack. They all passed it around once more, with Thomas getting the last toke.

Thomas continued to the kitchen and took another beer from the fridge. He walked into the living room and sat at one end of the couch. The petite young woman who had handed him the joint had followed and sat down beside him. They introduced themselves to one another. Pam was a salesperson at a women's clothing apparel shop at the Tacoma Mall. Thomas told her he worked at Commencement Bay Books and had attended Rainier University. She mentioned she was also a student at the local community college.

After that, Thomas began contemplating how life, or something, emerged from the ground like a tree. You know, it grew. The thought seemed *deep* to Thomas, and he tried to hold onto it for as long as he could. When the thought— or idea, or concept, whatever it was—faded, he noticed he was now alone on the couch. The young woman had moved on. Thomas sat there for a while, attempting to gather his thoughts. It wasn't working. He then realized that he had, as some of his buddies would say, gotten loaded.

"Damn," he muttered to himself. Try as he might, he couldn't think clearly. He grew frustrated with himself for feeling unable to control his thoughts. For the next hour or so, he attempted to engage with some of the partygoers while sitting on the couch, but he didn't remember much of what passed as conversation between them.

Thomas finally got up, noticed he had only taken a few sips of his beer, and returned the bottle to the kitchen. Without searching for Zack, Thomas left the party through the front door, made his way to the main street, and walked back to his apartment. Upon arriving, he headed straight to bed.

Thomas woke up around eight. He immediately recalled the previous evening and how he had felt while high. As he lay there, his thoughts seemed to be his own, not muddled with an admixture of strange ideas. Thomas remembered being so upset the night before because he had been unable to control his thoughts. Now he felt relieved at feeling like himself again. What had driven him to smoke dope last night? What was his life turning into? How many train wrecks could he handle?

## 10.

## *"He looked deeply into her eyes…"*

When Thomas finished breakfast, he poured himself another cup of coffee and headed for his chair in the living room. His thoughts drifted to Minnie. He remembered how sensual she had been before his unplanned attack of conscience had overridden his intense desire for her. He ached for that unique person who came from a town half the size of his own small coastal hometown. He recalled her describing Union as a little town on a fjord within the confines of Puget Sound.

As he slowly drank his coffee, Thomas was struck by the thought that maybe, just maybe, all was not lost and he could repair his and Minnie's tattered relationship. Perhaps if he talked to her outside the atmosphere of The Rail, she might listen and feel more comfortable sharing her thoughts with him, which could make her more open to discussing their feelings for one another. The idea seemed worth trying. After all, he had survived her walking out on him and slamming the door and, among other things, crushing his feelings as he stood in The Rail with a forgive me bouquet while Minnie kissed another guy. He was sure his dignity and self-esteem were now gone. What did he have to lose? He tidied up the apartment for about fifteen minutes. Out of nowhere, he said aloud, "What are you waiting for, Klement?"

The walk to Charlotte's place took twenty-five minutes. It really wasn't that far, but Thomas walked slowly, contemplating how to start the conversation. Upon arriving, he took a deep breath and knocked. He waited. Just before he could knock a second time, Charlotte opened the door and, recognizing him, said, "Hello, Thomas." He offered a small smile and nodded in her direction. She opened the door wider, inviting him in. He stood awkwardly just inside the entryway, and sensing the tension in the air, Charlotte said, "I'll go tell Minnie you're here," before disappearing around the corner. He heard muted voices, and a minute later, Minnie appeared. As always, she looked fantastic, Thomas thought to himself.

"Hi," Thomas said in a quiet and slightly subdued voice.

"Hello," Minnie replied uncomfortably while furtively glancing out the window on the upper half of the door behind Thomas.

"I wanted to see if I could catch you somewhere other than work so we could talk without all that craziness at the pub." While he spoke, he noticed Minnie's eyes dart toward the window once again.

"Thomas, I'm not sure what to say. This probably isn't a good time. I have some plans, and I'm running late. My ride should be here any minute. Maybe another time, but not now," Minnie said with urgency. As she spoke, she grasped the door handle and opened the door slightly as if to hurry things along.

Thomas was crestfallen. He took Minnie's cue and stepped out onto the porch. "I'm sorry. I just thought that if we could talk, maybe we could clear some things up. I guess I've already told you that," he said, wearing a strained look on his face.

"Well, this really isn't the best time to talk. I'm sorry, Thomas, but as I mentioned, I have plans and need to finish getting ready. Maybe we can talk another time. I'm not sure, but definitely not now," she said with finality.

Thomas could clearly see her stress level rising. He looked deeply into her eyes while she spoke, and he thought he detected some conflict, yet he was unable to figure it out. He also realized that it was time to move on. "Alright,

Minnie. I'm sorry. I probably should have called first. I'll be on my way."

Minnie gave Thomas a forced smile and walked back into the house.

It happened again, he thought. I come up with a plan, and it falls apart. I believe I'm fooling myself. "You blew it with her," he muttered under his breath—"No more of this." I can't go through this again. Can someone please tell me to get a clue? Damn, I feel stupid…and yes, crushed. It won't happen again.

After walking a few blocks, as these dark thoughts continued to swirl in his mind, Thomas caught sight of a blue '69 Chevy Camaro (one he had seen on the campus of Rainier University a few years ago, owned by David Street) pass by him, headed in the direction he had just come from. With his hands in his pockets and his head down, Thomas didn't look back. Keeping his head down, he stayed the course toward home.

## 11.

# "It was surprising how... it made him feel."

Thomas' latest crash and burn scene with Minnie was now a week behind him. It was a Sunday morning. He had eaten breakfast at The Harvester Restaurant and carried some coffee in a sturdy paper cup as he left the establishment and headed for Wright Park. Once there, he sat on a bench facing the duck pond, enjoying the rich taste of good black coffee while watching the ducks moving about the expanse of water. He had risen early that morning, sleep seemingly a scarce commodity after the Minnie affair. He felt a bit lost. Thomas finished his coffee and decided to take a walk. After disposing of the cup in a receptacle, he headed off in the direction of downtown.

The young man from Grayland couldn't deceive himself about his feelings. Thomas, struggling to regain his composure after Minnie's last rejection, recalled his conversation with George about the bookstore owner's philosophy of life, which hadn't really helped him with his issues. In fact, it reminded him of his own poorly considered approach to life. It was a strategy of not only avoiding getting caught up in the larger world and its myriad issues, primarily related to money at the time, but now had him seeking shelter from the storm in a comfortable and beautiful environment, such as the Wright Park neighborhood where he lived, and the comforting confines of Commencement Bay Books. Weren't both he and George, in some ways, avoiding participating in the larger world? Neither of them appeared to have any guiding principles to help them navigate through life - something that would ground them.

Instead of walking to St. Helen's Avenue, which angled and sloped down toward Broadway, the City's main commercial street, Thomas turned down a side street a couple of blocks earlier. A few more blocks into his walk, he came across a small church. Upon further investigation, he discovered that it was a Catholic church, Holy Trinity.

He saw locals slowly entering the church. Thomas looked at the sign on the stone edifice next to the front doors and saw that Mass would begin in about ten minutes. He had not been to Mass since his sophomore year in college. He had nothing really to do, so he said to himself, "Why not?" Thomas entered the church and looked around the vestibule. There, he saw a placard noting that the church had been built in 1899. He proceeded into the nave, reflexively genuflecting toward the tabernacle on the high altar and taking a seat in a pew near the back of the church.

The church looked and felt to Thomas as a church should look and feel. A few minutes later, Mass began.

The priest was likely close to George's age. His homily was both good and straightforward. Most notably, he celebrated the Mass with a true sense of devotion. There was no group of parishioners singing in front of the church, nor were there any distractions to disturb him. The consecration was as reverent as possible, marked by the bells that signaled this most important of moments. That being said, there were still the new post-Vatican II responses by the people to the priest Thomas had been told were supposed to help the faithful in the pews "participate" more fully in the Mass. For Thomas, many of the rote-like, somewhat banal responses seemed to fall short of that lofty goal.

During the time to exchange the sign of peace, participants did so quietly and with dignity, saying, "May Christ's peace be with you." There was no excessive waving of hands, big hugs, or running up and down the aisles to greet people, unlike his previous college days experiences.

When it was time for communion, Thomas remained seated in his pew. It had been a while since he had confessed his sins.

The priest and altar boys processed out of the main doors when Mass ended. There, the priest turned and began greeting the parishioners as they left the church. Thomas stayed after Mass for a few minutes, knelt, and recited a few familiar prayers. He shook his head, realizing it had been a while since he had done that. It was surprising how much at ease it made him feel.

Upon leaving the church, seeing that all the parishioners had departed, he was left face-to-face with the older priest. Over six feet tall with silver hair slicked back, a distinguished, proud nose, and a gray goatee of a beard, the priest resembled a retired Viking. He reached out his hand and introduced himself, saying, "Hello, I'm Father Ron Sinclair. I don't believe we've met."

Thomas clasped Father Ron's hand and said, "Hello, Father, my name is Thomas Klement. I discovered your church during my walk this morning."

Father Sinclair smiled and told Thomas, "The church was originally built here because of its proximity to what is now Stadium High School. Originally, the school was going to be a hotel that the Northern Pacific Railroad was building before it moved its headquarters operations to Seattle, thus, as some would say, ending Tacoma's proud use of the *City of Destiny* as its sobriquet."

"Father, I truly enjoyed your homily this morning, and I want you to know that you celebrate a very reverent Mass."

Father Sinclair was taken aback by Thomas' remarks and replied, "Well, Thomas, I'm at a loss for words other than to say thank you very much. May I offer you a cup of coffee or tea, along with possibly a doughnut and some conversation downstairs in the church hall?"

Thomas said, "Well, I was planning to walk downtown this morning to find something to do, but why not?"

Both men descended the steps on the side of the church and entered a modest yet comfortable space where tables and chairs were scattered about. Two tables were set up at the front, one displaying doughnuts, paper plates, and napkins, while the other held cups and two silver urns. One urn contained coffee, while the other held hot water for tea, each equipped with a spigot for easy dispensing. Tea bags were neatly arranged beside the second urn.

Father poured himself a cup of coffee, and Thomas did the same. Both, displaying strong wills, avoided the doughnut table. The old priest introduced Thomas to a few people at a nearby table and then gestured for Thomas to follow him to the other side of the room, where he paused in front of a solitary, equally senior gentleman and, addressing Thomas, said, "I'd like you to meet a dear friend of mine, Richard Dart. Richard, this is Thomas…" He looked at the young man. Thomas extended his hand to Richard and said, "Klement, Thomas Klement."

Thomas shook hands with him, and they exchanged greetings. Father pulled out a chair and sat down. Thomas did the same. He looked at Father's friend for a moment and exclaimed, "Richard, I think I know you from The

Harvester Restaurant, my favorite breakfast spot. I've seen you there on many occasions. I believe you are usually reading the newspapers." Thomas and Richard both smiled. "I'm the night manager at Commencement Bay Books and have also seen you in the store more than once," he said in an upbeat voice.

Richard nodded and, in a quiet voice, said, "This is true. I do frequent both locations," while maintaining a reserved manner.

Father Sinclair jumped in and added, "Thomas, Richard is not the most exuberant of men. It's just his way. I couldn't figure out if he liked me or not for the first six months I knew him, but that's just him."

Richard smiled slightly.

Over their coffees, Thomas learned that Richard had been a lawyer before retiring to the Wright Park neighborhood. Since then, he has written several serious papers and articles on the history of different church doctrines for respected Catholic journals. He had also authored articles for the local archdiocesan newspaper. As for Father Sinclair, he was nearing the age of retirement for priests in the diocese but had expressed a desire to continue his ministry as long as his health remained good. The parish has always been small, with just a few hundred parishioners, but as Thomas witnessed, the parish life at Holy Trinity seemed vibrant and alive.

The three of them talked for about thirty minutes, with Father getting refills for everyone. As the gathering was coming to a close, Father asked Thomas if he might visit Holy Trinity again. Thomas paused thoughtfully and then told him he would seriously consider it. With that, all three men stood up. Thomas shook hands once more with each of his new friends, and then they went their separate ways.

## 12.

## "Sorry you couldn't join us..."

A couple of days later, about an hour before closing, Thomas used exaggerated hand gestures to explain to James how he wanted a display set up for the new book arrivals. As this teachable moment was coming to a close, Thomas' friend Nate walked in. Nathan Wilson was one of Thomas' friends from his university days. The two shook hands. Thomas turned back to James and said, "You get the idea, right?"

James replied, "Yeah, I think I understand the idea, but would you prefer the display in front of the doors as you enter or to the left of the staircase?"

"It makes the most sense to set it up near the front doors," Thomas said, gauging the available space and the display table.

"Got it," James said as he set off to complete the task. Thomas turned back to Nate and asked, "Sorry, how have you been, buddy?"

The two stood at the foot of the large staircase as Nate, without any prompting, began to update Thomas on their mutual acquaintances. They laughed and reminisced about events from their time at Rainier. Nate Wilson had also earned a business degree and was now working in his father's shop, fabricating parts for Boeing. Thomas recognized that Nate's father was involving his son in the operation from the ground up, preparing him to take over the business one day. It was a good arrangement, one that also included his father co-signing a loan for the house where Nate lived.

Thomas interrupted the conversation a few times to assist a customer, not wanting to disrupt James' work on the new display. After his encounters with Minnie, Thomas felt relieved to have a break from his solitary thoughts about her.

It was nearly nine when Nate, glancing at the clock on the store wall, said, "Tom, how about you and I get a bite to eat and something to drink after you close the store?"

Thomas smiled at the prospect of having some company and said, "Sounds good."

After assisting James briefly with the display, they closed the store. Later, while waving goodnight to James, Thomas walked down the street with Nate. It was then that Nate said, "How about we go to The Rail? I've been dying for one of their burgers."

Thomas hesitated. "Are you sure you don't want to walk up to…"

Nate cut him off before he could finish his thought. "No, man, I've been thinking about that burger all day. They are to die for. It has to be The Rail."

Thomas could tell Nate really wanted to go to The Rail. He wondered if this was one of Minnie's nights off. He imagined it might be, and seeing the look on Nate's face, he finally said, "Sure. Okay." Nate's face lit up again, and the two of them made their way to the pub known for its to-die-for burgers.

They walked into the pub. The two friends decided to sit at a table rather than at the bar. Once seated, Brenda, as indicated on her name tag, approached their table and took their orders. Nate, naturally, ordered the special burger with fries along with a locally brewed lager, Heidelberg. Brenda then turned to Thomas, who replied, "Same thing."

While waiting for their orders, they engaged in small talk and surveyed the crowd. The smooth music emanating from the jukebox was an oldie, "(Til) I Kissed You," by the Everly Brothers. Thomas felt pleased, as Minnie was nowhere to be seen. The food and beer arrived minutes later, and the two savored their burgers and fries. After finishing, they each ordered another beer.

As the pub grew noisier, the music from the jukebox became louder and more upbeat, with Bad Company's hit single "Good Lovin' Gone Bad." Nate and Thomas engaged in a conversation about their mutual friend, Zack Rowland. Nate began telling Thomas how Zack had changed since their college days. While listening to Nate, Thomas noticed a small group heading toward the empty table next to them. He tried to focus on what Nate was saying, but then he noticed that David Street was in the group, and Minnie was with him. Street sat directly across from their table, with Minnie beside him and another couple. With a look of recognition, Street glanced at Thomas and said, "Klement, is that you?"

Thomas, trying to hide his discomfort, said, "Yeah, that's me."

"Thomas, right?" Street asked while recalling the circumstances of their acquaintance. "A survey class on secularism and philosophy, correct?"

Thomas nodded once more and said, "That's right."

Equally surprised, Minnie alternated between staring at Thomas and looking away. Then, she leaned into Street and said something to him. Street glanced at Thomas and then back at Minnie, his eyes widening as she spoke in a low whisper to him.

Thomas simmered with anger. He wanted nothing more than to get up and smash Street in the face. He couldn't get over the idea that the smug philosophy professor was, for all intents and purposes, cheating on his wife. Forget that. He was with Minnie, and Thomas just couldn't take it anymore. He started to rise from his chair when Nate, sensing that something was about to go terribly wrong, grabbed Thomas by the shoulder. He spoke under his breath to Thomas, basically telling him to calm down. With this intervention, Thomas was able to ease up just enough to tell Nate that he wanted to get out of there. Mr. Wilson quickly chugged what was left of his beer and gave Thomas a look of readiness. They both stood.

Street looked at Thomas and asked, "You leaving?"

Thomas slowly nodded in the affirmative as he and Nate began moving away from the table.

"Sorry you couldn't join us," Street said in a tone that was slightly less than friendly.

Thomas shot one more glance at Minnie. She wore that same conflicted expression in her eyes that he had noticed when they last spoke on her cousin Charlotte's porch.

As Thomas attempted to decipher her facial expressions, Minnie appeared to notice.

Thomas caught her glance and turned away as they headed for the exit. Once outside, Thomas thanked Nate for being a friend and for going along with his sudden decision to leave. Nate asked for more details, and Thomas explained that he had dated the girl with the guy he was talking to for a while, but they were no longer together. He didn't tell Nate anything about Street other than that seeing Minnie with another guy was really hard.

Feeling like a jerk once again, Thomas took Nate to The Deep Harbor Tavern, just a few blocks away. There, he bought Nate another beer, and the two discussed more positive topics.

## 13.

# "…where Tacoma kept… its heart."

It was a Saturday. Thomas had just started working. He, James, and Susan, who would be there until five, were handling some brisk business, moving around to assist customers and ring up purchases. At around two-thirty, the surge had passed, and Thomas was about to head upstairs to check on a burned-out light that a customer had reported after making a purchase. Then, to his delight and surprise, he saw Cynthia, his new favorite book aficionado. Something about her seemed different today. Then it struck him as she approached the cash register—she wasn't in her work attire. Instead, she wore jeans. He realized he had only seen her in business suits and dresses before today. With a smile, he welcomed her, saying, "Great to see you, Cynthia."

She smiled broadly and said, "I'm so glad you're working today. I was hoping you'd be here."

"How can I help?" Thomas asked with almost palpable excitement.

"Well," she replied, pulling out a piece of paper from her back pocket, "I'm interested in reading some recommendations I received from my cousin who lives in Virginia. Please don't laugh at me, but they are romantic historical novels set before, during, and after the First World War in Europe. I need some escapism, and my cousin says I can't go wrong with her choices. Can you help me?"

"Child's play," he said with a smile.

Together, they headed for the stacks. Twenty minutes later, they emerged with four novels that had passed the test after Cynthia's scrutiny and inspection. Thomas rang up the purchase and placed the books in a sturdy paper bag. While handing the bag to her, he spontaneously asked if she had time for a cup of coffee at the café next door. Cynthia, surprised yet delighted, said, "That sounds lovely. Let's do it."

Thomas caught James's attention and explained his plan to him. James said he would inform Susan, but he reassured him not to worry. They had it under control. With that, Thomas and Cynthia walked over to the café.

They settled into a booth. Cynthia ordered tea, while Thomas, of course, ordered black coffee. Cynthia was the first to jump in, asking Thomas to share his life story with her. Thomas smiled and offered her a five-minute summary. He noticed he stumbled once, only partially explaining how he became the night manager at Commencement Bay Books. Upon finishing his admittedly short biography, he gave Cynthia a look, wondering if she might want to share her story with him. Cynthia told Thomas that her last name was Innes (pronounced "In-iss") and that she was of Scottish descent. She had been born and raised in Tacoma, specifically in the North End of town.

Cynthia continued with animated thoughts about the neighborhood. "The city doesn't always count the Stadium District as part of the North End," Cynthia said, "But trust me, everyone who lives here does." She gave a little nod, the kind that said, "That's the gospel truth." She couldn't hold back, "Wright Park is our backyard — those old trees, the glass conservatory — it's the lifeblood of the neighborhood. The brick apartments, the storefronts, even that imposing castle of a high school overlooking the bay... it all gives the place its character. And the cafés, pubs, and little shops keep it alive, lived-in, like a mix of old charm and new energy. To me, there's no better place to be. The Stadium District is as North End as it gets." She brought her petite fist down onto the table playfully to finish her point.

Thomas found himself watching Cynthia more than listening. The way she spoke about the neighborhood — with affection, certainty, almost a kind of devotion — told him as much about who she was as it did about the area. Thomas smiled. It was the same story he'd heard from his friends at Rainier University who had grown up here: North Enders always said the North End, including the Stadium District, was where Tacoma kept its history — and its heart.

She mentioned she had attended Pacific Lutheran University because her parents moved to Lacey, near Olympia, about half an hour to the south. However, for various reasons, one of them being "her soul was in the North End," as Cynthia explained, she completed her finance degree at Rainier University a year before Thomas graduated. She took the job as a bookkeeper and got her own apartment across from Wright Park.

As Cynthia paused to sip her tea, Thomas once again noticed his strong attraction to the slim, dark-haired woman, who carried herself with such confidence. He could tell from her composed demeanor that she was highly organized. Simply put, she intrigued him.

After addressing the preliminaries, the two fell into easy conversation that only ended when Thomas noticed the time and realized he needed to return to the bookstore. Once he had paid for the tea and coffee, and they were preparing to leave, Thomas boldly asked for and received Cynthia's phone number in return.

## 14.

# "...they had danced around the edges..."

There was a knock at the door. It was early evening on one of Thomas' rare days off. When he opened it, Zack stood there with a big smile and said, "How's it going, buddy?" Once inside, Zack removed his coat, draped it over the back of a kitchen chair, and immediately checked the refrigerator for a beer. He found one, took the bottle opener from the silverware drawer, and popped the cap off. After Zack took a big swig of his beer, the two settled into conversation.

Over the past year or so, Thomas had noticed a change in his college days buddy. Zack had adopted a more celebratory persona after graduation, a new identity that had persisted to this day. He lived with a couple of other friends and had yet to settle into a steady job. Since graduating, he has tried his hand at selling new and used cars at a few different car lots. The hours he worked covered his share of the rent but left little extra. During this time, he mastered the art of mooching off his friends. All his buddies, including Thomas, would say, "Well, that's Zack."

Thomas sighed inwardly, opened the fridge, and took out a bottle of Tacoma's "Heidelberg" beer. He leaned against the counter while Zack sat at the kitchen table. They talked for a while about a black 1970 Ford Mustang that had been traded in a couple of days earlier at one of the car lots where Zack worked. He mentioned to Thomas that the car would be perfect for him.

Thomas responded, "I hear you, but as I've told you on many occasions, I just don't really have a need for a car right now."

Zack, not giving up, continued to describe some of the extras on the car while downplaying the possibility that the previous owner had *beaten* the Mustang in any way. The car was in fine, if not incredible, shape, Zack extolled, and somewhat of a steal given what they were asking for it.

Thomas took another sip of his beer, then gently shook his head and said, "Zack, it's just not going to happen right now."

Zack, who had nearly finished his beer, shifted gears and asked if Thomas wanted to join him at another party he planned to attend later that evening.

Thomas asked for some details, including whose house it was, who was going, and so forth. Zack told him and added that he believed there might be some good drugs there. Thomas listened and wondered why Zack thought he would be excited about the drugs at the party. As Zack droned on about some new guys he had met, a small bulb flashed in Thomas' brain. He realized that a fundamental difference between himself and his buddy was that he went to parties because girls would be there, while Zack, more recently, had been more focused on what drugs might be available at a party. Thomas tried to press Zack on why he was so interested in drugs.

Zack instantly replied, "Because it's such a rush, man!" He laughed and added, "You've got to be kidding," as if Thomas were the one who didn't really understand the situation.

"I don't know, Zack. I'm just not that into getting high."

Zack looked at Thomas, confused, and replied in a monotone voice, "Seriously, what do you have going on that's better?"

"Oh, come on, Zack, you know what I mean. Where is being high all the time going to get you?"

Zack said with a little more edge to his voice, "So, tell me where your life is going to get you."

Thomas glanced at him for a moment and chose to let his friend's comment slide. "Look, Zack, I'm your friend, and what I said is just my opinion. We're buddies, and I care about you. I really do. I just feel uneasy about things like that. I'm not trying to give you a hard time."

Zack's expression softened slightly. He finished the last of his beer, stood up, and placed the bottle in the sink. "Well, I guess I'm going to head out for the party a bit earlier than planned. Are you sure you won't join me?"

Feeling uneasy for some reason, Thomas said, "Nah, I think I'll pass."

Zack replied in a forced, conciliatory tone, "Your loss, man."

The two friends stood there for a moment, unsure of what to do next. Then, Thomas said, "Thanks for thinking of me and stopping by. I guess I'm just a lightweight when it comes to that stuff."

Zack smiled faintly, gave Thomas a light punch on the shoulder, and said, "See you then."

Thomas walked him to the door and watched as Zack headed down the stairs. Back in his chair in the living room, staring at the dark outline of Wright Park, he thought that they had danced around the edges of the issue. As the evening stretched on, Thomas reflected on Zack's nonchalant attitude toward substance abuse and his own hesitance, which clearly highlighted the potential rift developing between them. When he decided it was time to turn in for the night, he realized that Zack, like himself, had no real long-term plans or goals to focus his thoughts and energy.

## 15.

# "... a shadow of uncertainty..."

It had been a difficult time, Thomas thought. Really, not much had gone right for him in recent months. The tension with Zack and the breakup with Minnie left him questioning why nothing seemed to be working in his life. He had always viewed the world as a tough place, intimidating if you thought about it. He never knew his father. When he was young, the Cuban Missile Crisis occurred, bringing the world to the brink, and then a year later, Kennedy was assassinated. Then came Vietnam. People suffered from starvation in every corner of the world. For years, the war in Vietnam and the draft hung over all young American men.

Friends, relatives, and strangers endured and succumbed to terrible diseases like cancer. If there was one thing he failed to fully understand from his faith formation, it was the problem of evil. Now, as a young man, he ventured into the world, more or less casting aside the guidance of his faith for what he learned on his own and the general higher secular education to which he had been exposed. What was he doing wrong? Would his life be, as Thomas Hobbes, the

17th-century English philosopher, described it, "solitary, poor, nasty, brutish, and short?"

He continued to brood over the topic. In college, when Thomas decided to stop attending Mass, he quickly realized that the fundamental principles he had relied on throughout his life were those he had learned from the faith he had tried to follow. Once the outward practice of attending Mass was abandoned, the core beliefs that had shaped his life to that point quickly faded from his thoughts. Surprisingly, the teachings on premarital relations unexpectedly resurfaced one evening in his apartment.

Now, after graduating and experiencing a taste of the real world, he had hitched his wagon to Modernity. To answer life's most important and essential questions, a person needed to rely on reason, empirical observation, logic, you know, and science. One should be grounded in the present. Modernity implied individual autonomy. What mattered in life was personal freedom and individual rights. Responsibility became a much less-used word in this new world. Regarding morals, the modern world has taught that many values can be subjective rather than objective, contrasting with what the church has always taught.

During Thomas' lifetime, the concept of subjective values was most clearly illustrated by the introduction of *the pill*. This progressive innovation had "freed women" to explore and regulate their sexual lives. This freedom, this emphasis on individual rights, had diminished, if not eliminated, the notion of personal responsibility. That was clearly most evident among men his age. Modernity championed the self above the divine. These thoughts increasingly roiled Thomas' mind each day. A good night's rest had been replaced by a troubled night's lack of sleep.

Well, now he thought things were going to change. It had been almost a week since he had gotten the phone number of that attractive woman with the most interesting ponytail. He called Cynthia one night after work. She answered. Thomas introduced himself, and to his relief, she recognized him and was genuinely pleased that he had called. They engaged in small talk for a few minutes. Then Thomas asked her if she would be interested in going to a movie, taking a walk in the park, or even grabbing a bite to eat sometime. Cynthia said she would love that. They decided to see a film, *Three Days of the Condor*, featuring Robert Redford and Faye Dunaway, at the Temple Theatre, which was a short walk from the bookstore.

They met at the bookstore two days later and walked to the theater. The movie turned out to be a taut thriller that both of them immensely enjoyed. They slowly made their way to her place, occasionally stopping to discuss some aspect of the movie while trying to spend as much time together as possible. As it turned out, Cynthia's apartment was just a block and a half away from his. Attempting to respect first-date etiquette—whatever that was—he told her he had a wonderful time and hoped they could do it again. Cynthia echoed his assessment of the evening, and just as he was about to turn and leave the steps of her apartment building, she reached out and kissed him on the cheek. This elicited a broad smile and a thank you from Thomas. During the short walk back to his place, it occurred to him that he suspected he would sleep well that night for the first time in quite a while.

The following week, they were back at it again, going to see the movie *The Drowning Pool*, starring Paul Newman and Joanne Woodward, at the Rialto Theatre downtown. Cynthia asked if they could take the bus downtown instead of walking, to which Thomas readily agreed. In this film, Paul Newman played a detective who unravels a blackmail scheme. Once again, the movie proved satisfying, with Cynthia especially enjoying Mr. Newman's performance. The movie experience was greatly enhanced when Cynthia leaned her head on Thomas' shoulder and chest during the show's second half. When the picture ended, they kissed before getting up to leave. After the movie, they caught the bus that went directly past Cynthia's apartment building. This time, she invited him inside, and Thomas followed her through the front door, into the lobby, where they rode the elevator up five floors, walked a short distance down the hall, and finally into Cynthia's apartment.

Thomas noticed that his place couldn't compare to hers. The apartment itself was wonderful. She had decorated it beautifully, creating a great ambiance. The living room, larger than his, featured a couch, loveseat, and chair, with a coffee table in the center. Floor and tabletop lamps, artwork, and a couple of oriental rugs strategically placed enhanced the room's appearance. The windows offered a different view of Wright Park, presenting an interesting perspective.

Cynthia brewed some herbal tea, and they sipped it in the spacious living room. They talked about her family, how her parents had divorced, and how her father was now remarried and living in Seattle. Her mother had also remarried and now resided in San Francisco. She mentioned that she didn't see them much, while Thomas shared his parents' story and upbringing in Grayland. They discovered that neither of them had siblings. Once the tea was gone, Cynthia slid closer to Thomas, and they kissed for the second time that night. Cynthia glanced at her watch and surprisedly exclaimed, "Thomas, it's after midnight."

Thomas, who had also lost track of time, asked, "What time do you have to be at work tomorrow?"

"Usually, I go in around nine, but tomorrow, I should be there by eight or so because I need to file some tax compliance documents. I told my boss it would be done and in the mail by noon for the postal service pickup at about 1 p.m. I'm sorry, Thomas. I don't want this to end." She leaned in one last time, and they kissed again.

Thomas got home around 1:00 a.m. after a short walk around part of the park's perimeter. He mused about how much he liked Cynthia and how much he enjoyed her company. As he left her apartment, he recalled her saying, "Let's get together again soon." She was so cute, he thought. Yet, as he slipped into bed, feeling happier than he had in a long time, a thought flickered through his mind. If pressed, Thomas would almost label it a *twinge* since it came and went so quickly. He couldn't quite articulate it, but it felt like a shadow of uncertainty that lingered in the depths of his consciousness. There was something, a subtle enigma regarding Cynthia, that he just couldn't unravel.

## 16.

## "I was such a fool."

After closing the bookstore on a Thursday night, Thomas walked home, reheated some leftover canned beef stew from the night before, and ate. After washing the pot, wooden spoon, glass, bowl, and fork, he was drying his hands with a kitchen towel when he heard a knock at the door. Not expecting anyone, he walked down the short hallway and opened the door. To his surprise, Thomas found himself face to face with Minerva *Minnie* Cadieux (Ka-doo).

"May I please come in, Thomas?" Minnie asked in a whisper.

He stared at the woman who had, not that long ago, broken his heart. Speechless for a moment, Thomas somewhat regained his composure and, in a calm and slightly lowered voice, said, "Minnie, come in." He held the door open for her, and she entered the apartment. Reflexively, Thomas asked for her jacket, and she removed it, handing it to him. He hung it on a hook in the hallway, and they both proceeded to the living room.

Minnie looked around the room for a few seconds and then turned to face Thomas. She stared at him for a few moments, and then, as if a faucet had been turned on, she began to sob. Stepping forward into Thomas' arms and holding him tightly, she said, "I don't know where to begin."

Thomas held her, saying nothing as Minnie struggled to find the right words. "There's so much I want to say, Thomas." She sniffled. "I want to talk about that night we were together here. That night," she repeated, "I can't get it out of my head. Thomas, I felt so foolish when you stopped us from making love. I've thought about it ever since. I suppose, on some level, I was mortified that you didn't want me. You were saying stop, and all I wanted was to make mad, passionate love to you. Oh God, this is so embarrassing!" She stepped back from Thomas for a moment and tossed her hair back. Then she approached him again, leaning into him and wrapping her arms around his neck. She rested her head on his chest and began to cry once more.

Thomas said, "Let me get you some tissues," as he stepped back. He walked over to the ottoman and removed a handful of tissues from a Kleenex box. He handed them to her, and she wiped her eyes before blowing her nose.

"Now I'm embarrassed again," Minnie said, searching for a place to dispose of the tissues. Thomas took them from her and tossed them into the wastebasket on the other side of his chair.

"Minnie," Thomas said in a more intimate and personal tone. "Why don't we sit down and try to sort this out?"

"Thank you, Thomas," Minnie replied as she settled into his chair. Thomas moved toward the ottoman, gathered some books and papers that were on top, opened the lid, and placed them inside. Then, he took a seat facing Minnie. He handed her a few more tissues as she looked once again, on the verge of tears.

"Thank you, Thomas," she said once more, wiping her tears yet again. She took his hands in hers and began in a shaky voice that she had slightly regained control of, "Thomas, I know I told you I was from a really small town up on Hood Canal. It was a big step for me when I moved to Tacoma, even though it's not New York, Los Angeles, or even Seattle. There was so much for me to see and do. I met a lot of people. I had a great time. I decided that no matter what, I wasn't going back to Union. Then I met you. I fell for you instantly." She showed a hint of embarrassment. "I could not have been happier. Then we had…" She paused for a moment, *our disagreement.* She looked at Thomas with her large, dark brown eyes and said, "I wasn't prepared for what happened. I've thought about it a lot, Thomas, and I see now that your need to talk wasn't the disaster I made it out to be. In fact, I believe now that it was absolutely the right thing to do. Back then, no way." She shook her head from side to side.

"Would you like some water?" Thomas asked. Minnie nodded. He stood up, walked to the kitchen, and returned with a glass of water, then sat again on the ottoman, knee to knee with Minnie.

After a couple of sips of water, Minnie said, "Thomas, when I left that night, I hated you. All I knew was that I wanted to hurt you as much as I had been hurt. Then I met David Street. I mean, I know he's older, but he was so nice, and everyone liked him. He was always the smartest guy in the room. He knew everything. He was a professor. He was a big deal and wanted to be with me." She paused again, took another sip of water, and then added with emphasis, "He came on to me big time, and I let him!" She lowered her head and whispered, "It was only later that I found out he was married." She began to tear up once more. "I couldn't believe my ears when he told me." Her voice trembled, "I was such a fool." Minnie began to cry again.

The pain of Minnie's words cut through Thomas like a knife. As Minnie poured her heart out to him, he remembered how expressive and exuberant she had been when he first met her. Yes, she had seemed somewhat insecure, coming from a small town and trying to *make it* outside her rural environs. Minnie was definitely impulsive, but that made her a lot of fun to be around. You never knew what would happen next. This also showed in her occasional impetuousness, but that came with her vibrant personality. Oh, and lest I forget, she is such a beautiful woman. Perhaps all of these factors contributed to her falling into unexpected situations. As he looked at her, he sensed that she had been through a lot. He thought back to the times he had tried to make amends with her and how hard she had rebuffed his attempts. Then, out of nowhere, she showed up, professing her love for me and wanting to talk it out. Thomas closed his eyes and said to himself, "That's Minnie."

Minnie rose from the chair and began pacing in the small living room. "What do you want to do, Minnie?" Thomas asked.

She simply looked at him.

Thomas couldn't help but notice how much more worldly Minnie appeared since their first meeting. He rose from the ottoman. Minnie, who seemed to have composed herself in the last few minutes, now wavered and began to shake slightly.

"I want to help you if I can, Minnie," Thomas said, sensing that she had more on her mind.

Out of the blue, Minnie said, "Thomas, I have to leave. I can't stay here right now. I've got to go." She walked down the hallway, grabbed her jacket from the hook, opened the door, and turned back to Thomas, who had followed her. Struggling to breathe now, Minnie looked directly at him and said in a pained voice, "Thomas, I'm pregnant."

## 17.

# *"He breathed slowly and listened."*

Again, as she had during her last visit to his place, Minnie rushed down the hall, down the stairs, and out of the apartment building, while Thomas reached the door and stood slack-jawed in the doorway. One more time, that beautiful young woman from Union had vanished from his presence. Now, they both faced a reality for which neither was prepared. Thomas closed the door slowly, left only with the echo of her parting words.

After a moment, Thomas made his way to the living room, seeking the comfort of his chair. He sat down, recalling Minnie's sad words, "I was such a fool."

He stared blankly at the now dark sky over the park. The phrase "I'm pregnant" haunted his thoughts. Thomas had never felt more completely shocked. His world, though small, had been turned upside down.

His eyes watered. Thomas wiped them with the back of his hands. Dear God, this hurts. He heard himself speaking as if to a lost friend. How could this have happened? It stung him as quickly as he processed the thought. Stop it.

Can't you remember the anguish on her face? For just a moment, can't you think about what Minnie is going through instead of yourself? Have you considered how, if you had managed the situation differently, she might not have fallen for that despicable clown, Street? You knew Minnie was younger than you and out on her own for the first time. You remember her saying she loved meeting new people and was determined to make it in her new and exciting world. Well, she made a mistake. Is this not as you learned in faith formation growing up - *a fallen world?*

What does this mean? Thomas rubbed his forehead with his fingers. She is with child. No, it's not yours. Minnie says she loves me. Why didn't she accept one of my apologies a while back? Why did she work so hard to hurt me? She claimed she was drawn in by the idea of being wanted by a *big deal* university professor. You know this guy had to be smooth. He drove a cool car and impressed her with his knowledge. She told me I embarrassed her. Being with Street was her way of showing me that she could achieve almost anything she wanted. Does any of this make sense? Well, of course not. Unfortunately, it seems now that this is how life really is.

The guy who believed he could handle any problem now ran a hand back through his hair, feeling that this whole situation was overwhelming. He stood up from the chair and brewed a small pot of coffee. After pouring a cup, he returned to the living room. He resumed his thoughts. She says she loves me. Does she mean it? Does that even make sense? What if she does? Am I ready for something like that? She is carrying a child that isn't mine. What would that mean going forward if everything worked out? What does it mean financially? I would need to seriously consider finding a job that pays more and would be sufficient to support a family. Everything would indeed change. The apartment is too small for three people. We would need to get a house, either by buying or renting. We would need a car. We would have to move from the Wright Park neighborhood because home prices in this area are, to put it mildly, expensive. Essentially, my life, which has tried not to focus on money, would become consumed by it.

Thomas took a big gulp of slightly cooled coffee, holding the cup with both hands. He shook his head.

What about Father Sinclair? Could I talk to him about this situation? As Thomas contemplated what a conversation with Father Ron might be like, he reflected on how good it felt to start attending Mass at Holy Trinity on Sunday mornings. He had spoken to Father Sinclair a few times now and felt pleased with his decision to reengage with the faith of his youth.

Hold on a second. This entire situation wasn't centered on him. It was all about Minnie. How did she feel about being pregnant? What did she want to do?

And then, something that had been second nature to him until just a few years ago occurred. Thomas began to pray. He asked God for guidance on what to say to Minnie. He prayed that he could help her in any way possible – even, he grimaced, if she didn't want him involved. He prayed for strength so that, even if the whole situation went south, he would at least be able to comfort Minnie. Lastly, he prayed for wisdom to do the right thing. Thomas paused and closed his eyes. He recalled walking on the ocean beach at Grayland, where it felt like the whole world surrounded him in all its majesty. He breathed slowly and listened. Then, opening his eyes, he thanked God for listening to his petition and made the sign of the cross slowly and deliberately.

He went to bed that night, determined to talk to Minnie in the morning.

## 18.

## "As always, ... I'm one step behind."

Thomas tossed and turned most of the night. He woke up the following day with a big question on his mind: What about Cynthia? Did he have feelings for her? He had to be honest with himself. Yes, he did. How did these feelings compare to how he felt about Minnie? These are impossible questions, he told himself. However, as much as he didn't need the knowledge then, he realized he had feelings for both Minnie and Cynthia. Damn, it wasn't his fault that one was a bit headstrong while the other was slightly mysterious.

Of course, today was today, and he needed to talk to Minnie. Thomas got up, took a shower, had a bowl of cereal, and drank a cup of coffee. He placed the dish, spoon, and cup in the sink before hurrying out the door. His plan was to walk over to Charlotte's and catch Minnie before she left the house for the day.

It was raining as he made his way from the apartment near the park to the other side of Stadium Bowl, where the homes offered spectacular views of Puget Sound. After getting drenched, Thomas arrived at Charlotte's. He knocked on the door and patted down his wet rain jacket while waiting for someone to answer. Moments later, Charlotte appeared in a robe and slippers, opening the door. Her hair was not quite ready for the day. Thomas said, "I hope I didn't disturb you, but could I speak to Minnie?"

Charlotte looked at Thomas with unexpectedly compassionate eyes and said, "She's not here. Would you like to come in? Perhaps I can help."

Thomas replied, "No, I don't think so…" when Charlotte interrupted him, saying, "I know all about Minnie's situation."

With that, Thomas relented and followed Charlotte into the house. She led him into the kitchen and motioned for him to sit at the nook table. Sitting across from him, she said, "Thomas, I don't know how to tell you this, but Minnie is gone."

Thomas gazed at Charlotte incredulously as he raised his head and shoulders, replying in a shocked voice, "Really, I just saw her last night. What do you mean?"

"Yes, Minnie told me she was going to see you," said Charlotte, shaking her head. "She and I have been talking for days about her situation. Minnie came home last night after seeing you and called a friend. They talked for quite a while. After the call, she packed a few things. I asked her what was going on, and she told me that she was going to spend the weekend with a friend of hers whom she had met at The Rail. I believe she met her through David Street— that loser," Charlotte added to her statement in a disdainful tone. "So, the two of them became friends and did a lot together. I think her name was Vicki. That's it, Vicki Prentis. Anyway, she showed up here around 8 a.m. this morning, and as Minnie was leaving, she said she'd be back on Sunday. With that, she was gone."

Surprised, to say the least, Thomas remarked, "As always with Minnie, I'm one step behind."

Noticing Thomas' distress, Charlotte asked, "Would you like a cup of coffee?"

Feeling adrift, Thomas said, "Thanks, I'd like that," still in what could only be called bewilderment.

Charlotte stood up from the kitchen table, took a cup for Thomas from the cupboard, got the pot of coffee, and filled the cup. "Sugar?" she asked.

"No, black is fine," said Thomas.

When she returned to the table, Thomas accepted the steaming black coffee and asked, "Do you mind if I ask how she's been?"

"Well," Charlotte began, "First, I want to tell you that when my cousin Minnie asked if she could live with me for a while, I was surprised. After all, I'm nearly ten years older than she is, and we didn't really know each other well except during our time together at extended family get-togethers in Union. Anyway, she really begged me, and in the end, I figured that having her with me was probably a better idea than her trying to find her own living arrangements. It was evident that she was coming to Tacoma whether I helped or not. You should know that from being around her, I suspect." Charlotte paused, sipped her coffee, and continued, "As you can imagine, Minnie's been in a state since she found out she was expecting. She told me all about this *lout* David Street. I mean, when she told him she was pregnant, he said that wasn't good because he was married. Can you believe that?" With that, Charlotte pulled a pack of cigarettes and a lighter from her robe pocket and said, in a hesitant voice, "Do you mind if I smoke?"

Thomas shook his head to indicate that he didn't mind.

Charlotte paused, lit a cigarette, and continued. "Well, you can imagine how Minnie felt after hearing what that man had to say." She took another puff and a sip of coffee, then, with focused eyes, she raised her voice and said, "I remember she said they were in his car when she told him about the baby. Then, when he said it was basically her problem, she slapped him across the face, got out of the car, and walked back here." A satisfied look crossed Charlotte's face as she shared this with Thomas. "I was proud of her for what she did." She added, "Like I said, we've been talking about it 24/7 for the last few days."

"You know, Thomas, Minnie really fell hard for you. I had to listen to her talk about you all the time." Charlotte rolled her eyes. "She loves you. That is certainly clear to me. Minnie told me yesterday she was going to go see you and tell you everything."

"That's why I'm here this morning, Charlotte," Thomas interrupted. "I thought we were going to keep talking. She was pretty shaken up when she left my place, and I thought it would be good to resume our conversation this morning. Again, that's why I'm here."

Charlotte stood up. She retrieved the pot of coffee from the stovetop and refilled both cups. "Thomas, this has just been devastating for Minnie. All her hopes and dreams were shattered by the poor choices she had made. But I must tell you, she's a great gal with a heart of gold. She is just sometimes so strong-willed and independent. She wants to prove to herself and everyone else that she is competent." Charlotte made a face and said, "It's somewhat obvious that she tries to hide her lack of confidence."

Thomas and Charlotte continued their conversation until they finished their coffee, and she had smoked a second cigarette. Thomas thanked her for explaining as best she could what was going on with Minnie.

As he walked slowly back to his apartment, the rain stopped. Thomas contemplated what might have been between them if events had unfolded differently and how difficult this situation must be for Minnie. The entire sequence of events that shaped his and Minnie's relationship up to this point left a trail of questions and unspoken words. He shook his head and genuinely wished Minnie had not gone off with a friend.

## *19.*

# *"... accomplishment washed over him ..."*

As Thomas walked up through the Stadium District, he changed his mind about going home and instead walked to Holy Trinity Catholic Church. Since his discovery of the church a month or so ago, he had been attending Mass on Sundays but had not taken communion. Ten minutes later, he opened the front door to the old stone building. Daily morning Mass had ended, and the only people still in the church were an older couple in a pew, kneeling in prayer near the altar. He genuflected and slid into a pew on the other side of the nave in the small church. He knelt, made the sign of the cross, and began to pray. He asked God to help Minnie with her situation. He focused and recited the three standard Catholic prayers: the Our Father, the Hail Mary, and the Glory Be, before sitting back in the pew.

As he sat in the silence and stillness, looking at the crucifix on the wall behind the high altar, Thomas reflected on his recent return to the Church. Growing up, it had been easy. Mass was the same each time. Christ's once-and-for-all sacrifice was made *present* to those in attendance. His ear had been attuned to the inflections and rhythms of Church Latin. He knew how to follow along in his English/Latin missal through the various parts of the liturgy.

Thomas didn't know precisely when it had begun—this quiet tension he felt every Sunday—but it had become harder to ignore over the years since the introduction of the new Mass. The new Mass had promised renewal, greater participation, and accessibility. And maybe, in ways, it had delivered for some. But sitting in the pews, he sometimes felt like a man attending a familiar ritual that had lost its thread.

The English responses were easy enough to say, but they often struck him as a bit hollow - words spoken because they had to be, not because they rose from within.

But the Mass wasn't all about himself: it was about Him.

Holy Trinity wasn't perfect, but it steadied him. There was something about the way the priest moved—unhurried, almost contemplative—that reminded Thomas of what he hadn't quite lost. He stayed for that, because it gave him just enough - a place where the Lord was the focus and not an attempt to make it about us.

Now, after more than a decade since its introduction, at least this small Catholic community had found a way to make the new Mass more reverent again. At Holy Trinity, Thomas was now able to focus on Christ's sacrifice on the cross and receiving the Lord in communion.

He had tried, in recent years, to follow the modern path—science, progress, personal freedom. It had all sounded proper, possibly even noble. The world often spoke about rights, but rarely about responsibility. At the time, he had not minded. It was easier.

But now, kneeling here, his hands folded more out of habit than certainty, those same ideas felt like a poor fit. They didn't help much with heartbreak, guilt, or the tangled duties of love. They offered no guidance on how to forgive or how to stay when walking away seemed easier.

He wasn't turning his back on reason. But he was starting to see its limitations—how it gave answers to questions he wasn't asking anymore.

As he sat in the church that morning, he recalled Father Baker from Aberdeen's advice about showing intellectual concern or "balancing passions and desires with reason." That priest had been spot-on about him and Minnie. Although they had not managed their situation correctly at the time, the priest's advice pointed to a certain wisdom that, under different circumstances, might have dramatically altered the present situation.

Thomas moved forward in the pew and knelt again. He prayed, "Dear Lord, please help me navigate this terrible situation and assist in comforting Minnie. Thank you, Lord. Amen."

He rose from his knees, genuflected in the aisle, and made the sign of the cross, his eyes lingering a moment on the tabernacle on the high altar. As he moved toward the back of the church, he didn't expect to see anyone, but there stood Father Ron, straightening up the literature, holy cards, and the like in the vestibule.

They exchanged quiet greetings, the kind that fill the space after Mass but carry little weight. And then, suddenly, without planning it, Thomas felt a pull—strong, almost urgent. It had been what, five or six years? Too long. He hesitated, uncertain whether it was embarrassment or grace rising in him. But the desire was there—clear as anything— to confess.

He smiled faintly. Days before Minnie's revelation, he'd even begun sorting through his sins in his mind, like a man clearing out a drawer he hadn't opened in years.

Taking a breath and suddenly speaking with what must have been God's grace, asked, plainly and directly, "Would you hear my confession, Father?"

Father Ron blinked, then nodded. "Certainly."

They walked quietly back into the nave of the church and then entered the sacristy. Darkness enveloped Thomas. Father sat down on a chair while Thomas knelt on a kneeler that was set a short distance from the priest. Then, both men made the sign of the Cross, and Thomas spoke the truth of his sins. Not all of it was easy. But it was honest, and it was time.

The priest gave him a small penance, offered the prayer of absolution—and it was done, just like that.

Thomas felt it, almost tangibly: the grace of it, the strange lightness it transmitted. Yet he wasn't naïve. He knew it wasn't a magic fix. There'd be work ahead, a long road of trying to stay turned toward God. But now, at least, he was facing in the right direction.

As Thomas and Father Ron stepped back into the stillness of the church's nave, they shook hands, and the priest excused himself. As Mr. Klement headed out of the church, he was already looking forward to presenting himself again at the altar for communion - maybe even tomorrow.

As he walked away from the church, Thomas briefly considered discussing his current life events with Father, but felt uncertain about how to bring it up, so he allowed the moment to slip by without addressing it. Thomas also reminded himself to be sure to read the chapter of John's Gospel that Father Sinclair had given him for penance and to meditate on it. As he neared home, a sense of accomplishment washed over him, despite not being able to meet with Minnie. Yet, at the same time after everything he had done right this morning, a sense of foreboding began to encompass him.

## 20.

## "What was the word?"

The next day, at Commencement Bay Books, Thomas priced used volumes at the register counter, allowing James and Susan to assist customers and stock shelves with the new titles that had arrived late the previous evening. He noticed that business seemed a bit slow for a Saturday afternoon. He had just dealt with a salesman who was offering fire extinguishers for what he claimed was half off. Thomas told him that the fire department had recently inspected the store's extinguishers, and they had been tagged and dated as being in good working order. Finally, after telling the salesman that he would take his card and pass it on to the owner, the gentleman obliged by handing over a couple of business cards and thanked Thomas for his time.

From behind, Thomas heard a soft, gentle "Hello." He turned to see Cynthia looking particularly attractive in a blue blouse, jeans, and sandals.

"Well, hello to you, Cynthia. What brings you into the store today?"

Cynthia smiled and said, "I was doing a little shopping," holding up a paper bag from the local fabric store. "I stopped by because I was wondering if you had eaten your lunch yet?"

"In fact, I haven't, and I was just thinking about getting a bite to eat at the café next door. Are you interested?"

"That's why I asked, silly," she said, all smiles now.

"Great. Let me tell the gang here where I'll be, and we'll go." Thomas walked over to James first and then to Susan. He quickly grabbed his jacket and, with a gesture of deference, held the door open and allowed Cynthia to lead him out of the store.

Once settled in a booth at the café, the two exchanged pleasantries and ordered food. Thomas had a grilled ham and cheese sandwich with a side salad and coffee, while Cynthia opted for just the side salad and a glass of water. Thomas truly enjoyed her company, and they talked about little of substance. Still, they maintained eye contact, sharing the feeling that they were the only ones there, despite the bustling café being filled with customers. By the time they finished their meals, they had agreed that Thomas would come over to her apartment the following week to watch a movie together.

After Thomas returned to work and Cynthia headed to one last store on the block before going home, he thought about how well they got along and how great she looked. He especially loved how she held her own in discussions on just about any subject. He genuinely looked forward to spending time with her the following week.

He had frequently noted to himself that his relationship with Cynthia was different from that with Minnie, a fact that seemed as true today as ever. Minnie had—how best to describe it—an intense and unpredictable spirit, while he would characterize Cynthia as possessing a mysterious allure. As Thomas straightened a table full of significantly discounted books, he pondered these thoughts and realized he once again viewed Cynthia as someone of unknown qualities. What was it?

As he counted the till, put the money away in the safe, and turned off the lights, Thomas continued to think about Cynthia. Again, what was it? What was the word? She seemed—I don't know—delicate. Yes, that's a good way to describe her. She's fine—she's almost fragile. Where are you going with this analysis, Klement? I don't know. I'm just trying to figure her out. I'm intrigued and drawn to her.

As Thomas left the store and headed home, he put aside thoughts of Cynthia for a while, recalling that he wanted to stop by The Rail to talk to Jake, the bartender. Ten minutes later, he walked into the pub and found Jake—where else—but behind the bar.

Both men greeted one another with a nod and a smile. Thomas asked, "Jake, do you know a friend of Minnie's named Vicki?"

"Minnie's great. She has made a lot of friends since she's been here," said Jake. "She has such a wonderful personality. I don't mind telling you that Minnie has been fantastic for business. She's attractive, and people feel really at ease with her." While wiping down the bar, Jake paused for a moment and said, "Is this Vicki short and pretty cute with long, almost white hair?"

"I really don't know," Thomas replied, feeling frustrated with himself for not asking Charlotte to describe her.

Jake, after thinking for a moment, said, "So, while I wouldn't bet my house on it, I think this Vicki you mentioned is probably the one I'm thinking of. She comes in a few times a week. Opinionated," he said, wrapping up his thought.

"Thanks, Jake," Thomas said. "Since I'm here," he continued, "I might as well grab something to eat." Jake smiled and asked, "What will it be?" "How about fish and chips with a bottle of Heidelberg?"

"Coming right up," said Jake as he moved down the bar.

Thomas enjoyed his meal and finished the bottle. He looked around the place, as he had many times over the last three or four years, paid his bill and tip, and headed home. He thought about Minnie and hoped she was okay. He so wanted to talk to her. And while he continued to think about the puzzle that was Cynthia, for some strange reason, he also thought about this Vicki person.

## 21.

## "Then the years slip by..."

Commencement Bay Books was open on Sundays from 11:00 a.m. to 5:00 p.m. George, Sharon, and sometimes Thomas worked the six-hour shift, allowing Susan, James, and some other temporary help to have the day off. Today, Sharon worked until two and left for a family get-together, leaving only the store owner and his night manager to cover the last three hours.

Business had been steady in the early afternoon, but around three, it began to slow down. By three-thirty, it was essentially just the two of them. As usual, George sat in his office, reviewing daily sales and managing expenses. He positioned himself next to a window, which he opened slightly while working, allowing the smoke from his pipe to drift out into the alley behind the store. At one point, he walked over to the door and, noticing Thomas out on the store floor, asked him a question. "Why haven't you finished preparing your part of the financial reports?"

Thomas rolled his eyes and said, "Come on, old-timer. You know I need the sales figures for the whole week before I can finish those reports."

George smiled, looked again at the paperwork, shook his head, and replied in a more measured tone, "Yes, I suppose I am getting older. Thank you for pointing that out, Mr. Klement." Then he grinned and muttered, "Next time, I'll ask Sharon."

Thomas heard his comment, began laughing, and said, "You always liked Sharon better."

Both men were laughing now. They enjoyed each other's company. George walked over to the counter and continued the conversation. "My back hurts, my joints no longer work so well, and my eyes are worthless," George said. "I'm going to be 75 here soon. Everybody I know who's my age has long since retired or died or retired and then died. The problem is, I don't know what I would do with myself if I didn't have the store to come to every day. The bookstore was my identity when I began the business. In that regard, nothing has changed."

Thomas nodded in agreement.

"Life goes by quickly, Thomas," the old store owner said seriously. "And then what?" Without waiting for a response from his younger friend, George continued, "Life happens, we participate, and then it's over. When I was younger and new to this country, I believed anything was possible. It filled me with a sense of power. Power, because it was up to me to define what meaning, if any, my life would hold. I, George Renko, would be in charge of the value or importance attached to my life. Then the years slip by, and you wake up wondering how many mornings you have left." Thomas thought George seemed a little watery-eyed.

"It's not fun, Thomas." The aging store owner ruffled his thinning hair with one hand as he leaned against the counter.

Not knowing what to say to George, Thomas finally replied, "You don't really believe that, do you?"

"Unfortunately, that seems to be where I am today, Thomas."

The bell on the door tinkled, and Thomas turned to greet a family as they entered the store, each making a beeline for their favorite sections. Behind them came a middle-aged man who immediately asked Thomas to point him toward the location of a copy of Milton's *Paradise Lost*. Thomas pointed upstairs and led the customer to where the book would be located if they had a copy. To the customer's delight, Thomas found three different copies and left the man sizing up each one, trying to decide which to purchase.

Leaving the customer to his analysis, Thomas walked over to the philosophy section and stared at the alphabetized-by-author tomes. He observed the six floor-to-ceiling book units containing the store's inventory of philosophical works and wondered how George was doing. It seemed his employer had laid out exactly what was on his mind that afternoon. George never pulled punches. Thomas worried about the man who had given him this opportunity and decided to go downstairs to cheer him up and to pray for him the following Sunday at Mass.

As Thomas descended the stairs to the main floor, he saw George staring out the large front windows of the store at ominous dark rain clouds moving toward the Stadium District and the Wright Park neighborhood from the southwest.

## 22.

# *"Not to change the subject..."*

Early the following day, Thomas stopped by The Harvester Restaurant for a bite to eat. To his surprise, he spotted Richard Dart, the parishioner Father Ron had introduced him to the day he had first attended Mass at Holy Trinity. Dart was sitting alone in a corner booth, reading the newspaper and sipping coffee. Richard looked up, smiled, and greeted Thomas as the younger man approached the table. "Please, join me," he said, gesturing to the opposite side of the booth. Gladdened by the invitation, Thomas slid into the booth across from Richard and settled in.

The two exchanged further greetings, and then Norma, one of the waitresses, approached the table and asked Thomas if she could get him anything. Thomas glanced at Richard, trying to figure out what he was up to. Sensing Thomas' thoughts, Richard mentioned he had just ordered and was waiting for a Belgian waffle. Thomas turned to Norma and said, "I'll have two eggs over easy with bacon and a cup of black coffee." Norma scrawled the order on her pad and replied, "Thank you. I'll get the coffee and be right back."

True to her word, Norma quickly returned with a cup of black coffee for Thomas. As she stepped away from the table, Thomas noticed Richard was reading the Seattle Post-Intelligencer, the local morning newspaper. Tacoma's own, the Tacoma News Tribune, was an evening publication, available for delivery in the afternoon. Richard folded the newspaper and set it aside.

"So, Richard, what do you enjoy doing when you're not writing articles?"

"I'm sure you'll be surprised to hear that I like to read," Richard said earnestly.

"Well, that makes sense given what I know about you," Thomas replied, adding, "What kinds of things do you like reading?"

"I enjoy philosophy and some theology. Oh, and to be honest, I have a soft spot for novels," Richard answered.

"Really?" Thomas blurted out. "What kind of novels?"

Richard smiled and replied, "I enjoy novels that weave Christianity into the overall story. For instance, English authors Evelyn Waugh and Graham Greene explore faith and different Catholic doctrines in their work. I find it fascinating when plots are infused with questions of faith and how characters either resolve or struggle with issues related to the beliefs they strive to live by or may not fully understand."

Thomas was now fully engaged and told Richard that he didn't believe there were many new Catholic writers producing the kinds of work he was referring to.

Richard nodded in agreement and said, "Not to change the subject, but this also seems true of the church itself. More than a decade after the Second Vatican Council, the implementation of the Council's teachings in its documents has not been conveyed to the people in the pews with any real clarity. Don't get me wrong, the theology that the Council spoke to is a real gift to the Church. But with regard to the pastoral approach to the results of the Council, there has been plenty of, let's call it, experimentation, with too little effort to explain the faith to the rank and file more clearly. It appears to follow more of an I'm okay, you're okay approach. Yet I don't believe it conveys what the Council documents really mean." Realizing he had strayed a bit from Thomas' original thought, Richard smiled slightly and slowly took a long, slow sip of his coffee.

Impressed by Richard's understanding of both religious and worldly matters, Thomas admitted that he was not as well-read but had recently been trying to broaden the range of his reading from mainly history to other fields, including philosophy and literature. He confided in Richard about his recent struggles to grasp the meaning of his own life, hoping that a foray into philosophical questions that addressed religious questions would better guide his decisions and actions.

Thanks to Norma's attentiveness, the breakfasts arrived just as Thomas completed his thought. Thomas sprinkled pepper on his eggs while Richard slathered butter and syrup on his Belgian waffle. The two men chatted as they ate. Norma stopped by the table again to refill their cups. Then she promptly cleared the table when they finished their meals, asking if either of them needed any more coffee.

Richard and Thomas connected on a level that reflected their growing friendship, and their conversation continued for another fifteen minutes or so before they both decided it was time to move on for the day. Thomas expressed hope that he might run into Richard again sometime for breakfast, to which Richard replied that he was essentially a regular and hoped Thomas would indeed join him again.

## 23.

## *"...slow down. I can't understand you."*

It was 3:00 a.m. when Thomas' phone rang. He opened his eyes and struggled with the covers to get out of bed. Straining to gather the use of his senses, he wondered who was calling at this hour. Had something happened to his mother or his aunt?

As he entered the living room, he picked up the phone beside his large chair. "Hello?" After a moment, Thomas realized that the person speaking rapidly, with emotion in his voice, was Nate. "Nate, slow down. I can't understand you."

On the other end of the line, upon hearing Thomas ask him to slow down, Nate made a conscious effort to speak in a calmer tone. "Thomas, Zack overdosed tonight," Nate said, his voice rising despite his attempt to control it.

"No," spluttered the surprised Klement, standing in his boxer shorts in the living room. The news sent Thomas' heart rate racing. "Nate, what's going on?"

"You won't believe this, man," Nate started, "Zack has been experimenting with drugs, but you already know that, right?"

"Yeah, we've talked about it."

"I guess about a month ago, Zack started using heroin."

"Heroin," exclaimed Thomas.

"Yeah, heroin. No one has been able to get through to him, and I guess he's really fallen into it."

Thomas held the receiver out in front of himself and stared at it as if he couldn't believe what he was hearing. "Aw, come on, Nate, tell me you're screwing with me."

"I wish I could, buddy, but according to some of the guys, Zack shot up earlier this evening and was pretty euphoric at first. However, before long, he got really drowsy and passed out. After a little while, someone tried to check on him, but he was completely out, man. His breathing became very shallow, and finally, someone called an ambulance."

"Where did they take him?"

"South Puget Sound Hospital," Nate replied.

Thomas turned toward his front windows and stared into the darkness. The hospital Nate had mentioned was just a block past the far side of the park. He couldn't believe this was happening. "Nate, thanks for calling me. I'm going to hang up and head to the hospital."

"Sure thing, Thomas. Give me a call when you get back." Thomas listened to the dial tone for a moment, then hung up the phone and went to the bedroom to get dressed.

He stumbled down the stairs of the apartment building and out to the street. The walk through the dark park and another block to reach the hospital took less than ten minutes. At 3:30 a.m., the front desk area of the hospital was surprisingly busy, or so it seemed to Thomas. After speaking with a few people for directions, he made his way to the emergency room entrance. Once there, he checked in at the desk and learned that his buddy Zack Rowland had indeed been admitted. Thomas explained that he was a very close friend. After some verification, they informed him that Zack had been treated but was still unconscious. They finally let Thomas know that Zack was now in the Intensive Care Unit (ICU) and provided him with directions on how to get there.

Ten minutes later, he arrived at the ICU and checked in at the nurses' station. Again, he introduced himself and explained the reason for his visit. The nurse informed him that visiting hours had ended and that he should return in the morning. Thomas rolled his eyes and told them he was the closest thing to family Zack had in the Tacoma area and that he wanted to be there for him. After conferring with another nurse and assessing Klement, they decided to allow him to sit in the room.

It was nearly 6 a.m. Thomas sat watching Zack, who was lying in the hospital bed. Mr. Rowland remained unconscious and connected to machines. A nurse arrived to check on her patient. She informed Thomas that they hoped they were past Zack's respiratory depression, which was the most immediate threat to his life. She continued to explain that they were still concerned and monitoring for a condition known as hypoxia, where insufficient oxygen reaches the brain and other vital organs, potentially causing brain or organ damage. They were also monitoring for possible fluid in the lungs, which could indicate pulmonary complications. Summarizing the situation, she told him that Zack had been treated, and now it was a matter of his regaining consciousness. Thomas thanked her for the information as she moved to another patient's room. Still quite shaken, Thomas sat in a guest chair, bowed his head, and began praying for Zack. After several short prayers, he resumed his vigil in the darkened room.

## 24.

# "... through moments of darkness ..."

The clock in the ICU room now read 9:15 a.m. Zack's condition had not changed much, but as a nurse noted, he wasn't any worse. Thomas made his way to the nurses' station and informed them that he was going to stretch his legs and grab some coffee, but would definitely return. He walked down to the cafeteria, where he bought a scone and a cup of coffee.

While sitting alone at a table and sipping his hot coffee, Thomas, oblivious to his surroundings, continued to reflect on his old friend and what had happened to him. As he lifted the coffee cup to his mouth, Thomas' eyes landed on Father Sinclair standing in line to pay for breakfast. Thomas waved at the priest, successfully catching Father Ron's attention. Once he paid, the priest, smiling broadly, approached and sat down across from Thomas at the table.

"Thomas, it's good to see you," the priest said. He looked more closely at Thomas and added, "I hope everything is alright. Why are you here? You look like you've had a tough time."

Thomas, realizing he probably didn't look his best, replied, "I found out a friend from my university days overdosed on, of all things, heroin last night. He's been unconscious since then. I've been sitting with him, praying he'll pull through with little or no damage."

"Oh, that's terrible to hear, Thomas. So many young people today are being consumed by these awful opioids, stimulants, and depressants. I know many young people who returned from Vietnam grateful to be alive yet hopelessly addicted to various drugs."

The priest and Thomas each took a few bites of their breakfast and sipped their coffee. Thomas then asked the priest, "Why are you here today, Father?"

"Oh, I come to the hospital most days after morning Mass. I'm a chaplain here for a few hours. I bring communion, hear confessions, and offer solace—you know, the standard priest stuff," Father Ron said, drinking more of his coffee.

Then, it occurred to Thomas. "Father, would you be able to do something for my friend Zack?"

"Well, that depends, Thomas. Is Zack a Catholic?"

"No, Father, I don't think he is," Thomas replied.

"That limits what I can do for the young man," the priest reflected. "You know he would need to be Catholic for me to administer the sacrament of the Anointing of the

Sick, although it is allowed under certain circumstances and with his approval." Then Father Ron added, "However, Thomas, I can offer a blessing for him. The purpose of such a blessing would be to pray to the Lord for, in this case, Zack's well-being, recovery, and comfort."

"Father, that would be great if you could do that."

As soon as they disposed of their plates, utensils, and cups, Thomas led the priest upstairs to the Intensive Care Unit. Father Sinclair knew some of the nurses, and after chatting with a couple of them for a minute or two, they allowed him to enter Zack's room with Thomas.

The priest stood silently for a moment, easily identifiable in his black shirt and clerical white collar—the most recognizable symbol of priestly ministry outside of liturgical settings. Then Father raised his hand over the young man in the bed and offered this blessing for Zack in an even, steady, and prayerful voice.

"May the Lord bless you and protect you.

May His face shine upon you and show you grace.

May the Lord show you kindness and grant you His peace.

In your time of need, may you find strength and comfort in the love that surrounds you, both seen and unseen.

May the healing presence of the Almighty touch you, bringing you health in body, mind, and spirit.

And though you walk through moments of darkness, may you feel the light and warmth of God's never-ending care.

We pray this, trusting in the mercy and goodness of the Lord, now and forever.

Amen."

Father Ron made the sign of the cross with his right hand over Zack and offered a final silent prayer before turning to Thomas.

"Thank you, thank you, Father," Thomas said quietly as they stepped out of the room. Father Ron replied that it was his pleasure and that he was grateful for their fortuitous meeting that morning. "Or," as Father added, "maybe it wasn't serendipity." He winked at Thomas and thanked the nurses before saying goodbye. The good priest moved down the hall to carry out his rounds for the day.

## 25.

# "I don't give a damn ..."

Thomas returned to Zack's room. When a nurse entered to check on Zack, Thomas told her he was going to run home, shower, put on fresh clothes, and then come back. As he walked through the park that late morning, Thomas glanced around at the beauty of the setting. He realized he was spending less and less time in these soothing and uplifting surroundings. He needed to rectify that, Klement told himself. After all, the park was a significant factor in his decision to move to the neighborhood in the first place.

After showering and putting on fresh clothes, he called George at the bookstore to share the story from the previous night. He asked if it would be all right to come in later that afternoon so that he could check back on his friend at the hospital. George told Thomas to take as much time as he needed.

As soon as he hung up, the phone rang. It was a nurse from the South Puget Sound Hospital's ICU calling to inform Thomas that Zack was beginning to come around.

He thanked her and left ten minutes later, heading back to the hospital.

When Thomas arrived, he immediately took the elevator to the floor where the ICU was located. One of the nurses he had met earlier that morning guided him into Zack's room. Upon entering, Thomas noticed Zack's eyes open at the sound of the nurse's voice. The nurse explained how patients *transition,* as she described it, through levels of consciousness as they regain awareness of their surroundings.

After the nurse left, Thomas pulled the chair he had used during the night closer to Zack's bedside. The two stared at each other for about a minute. In a slow and labored voice, Zack said, "I think I messed up."

Thomas rested his hand on Zack's shoulder and said in a quiet voice, "Hey, buddy, how are you?" Without waiting for an answer, he continued softly, "I can't begin to tell you how good it is to talk to you this morning. You had me pretty scared last night."

Zack closed his eyes for a moment before saying, "Yeah, it feels good to be somewhere." He glanced around the room and added, "Anywhere, I guess."

Pushing his chair back, Thomas, sensing that his friend would likely get through this ordeal, relaxed and smiled at his buddy.

The two friends, who had not seen each other in over a month, slowly began discussing what had occurred the night before, the different events at the hospital, and Zack's *coming around* about an hour ago. This conversation mainly consisted of Thomas speaking, as Zack had no recollection of being taken to the hospital or of anything else, after having shot up the night before.

Eventually, a nurse returned and informed Thomas that she had a lot of work to do with Mr. Rowland and that it might be best for him to leave for a while. She privately mentioned to Thomas that if everything continued to progress as hoped, the patient would be moved from the ICU to a private room as soon as possible. Of course, everything would depend on the patient's recovery, but she added that he was young and his vitals were encouraging.

Thomas viewed this as even better news. He walked back over to Zack and, once again, placing his hand on his buddy's shoulder, said, "Hang in there. I'll be back later today. You really scared me," his voice trailing off. Turning to the nurse, he thanked her for all the work she and the other nurses had done and mentioned he would return later. With that, he left the room and headed back home.

As he walked through the park once more, he paused to sit on a bench by the pond. The sun shone brightly, and it felt encouraging to bask in its warmth.

As he sat there watching the ducks perform their heads-down, butts-up routine, as he called it, on the surface of the pond, he thought more about Zack. He remembered meeting him when they were both freshmen at Rainier University. Zack was from Sacramento. Of course, Thomas was from, as Zack liked to put it, *Gra-a-ay Land.* Grinning, Zack told Thomas that it didn't sound particularly "inspiring." They quickly became friends and did almost everything together. Over the years at the university, their friendship expanded into a larger circle of friends, including their buddy Nate.

As he reminisced about those good times, another thought intruded: he remembered Bryan. Bryan was Zack's older brother who hadn't gone to college after graduating from high school. Instead, he worked for a while until his number came up in the draft lottery, which led him to join the U.S. Army. Months later, he received orders for Vietnam.

Bryan was *in theatre* in Vietnam for five months when he was killed in a firefight with elements of the Viet Cong (the South Vietnam-based communist guerrillas who fought against U.S. and South Vietnamese regular forces). It was the summer of 1972. The military draft ended in January of the following year.

When Zack returned to campus that fall for his junior year, Thomas remembered how much his friend had changed. He took his brother's death hard, and Zack's attitude toward living shifted in several significant ways. Most noticeably, Zack developed an "I don't give a damn" attitude about life. Reflecting, Thomas recalled how Zack would party harder, drink more, and not study like he had before. It showed, too; he struggled mightily to complete his classwork. He wheedled and cajoled his professors, doing everything he could—short of studying—to earn his diploma. He seemed to pursue anything that would keep him from thinking too much about life. He stayed in Tacoma after graduating to avoid returning to his parents' home in Sacramento, believing the *new* Zack would have been unacceptable to them. He was probably right.

Now what? What could he do to help his old friend? He didn't know, but he would give it a try. He would start later today when he returned to the hospital to check on Zack.

He finally got off the bench and returned to his apartment. His plan was to eat something and then check in at work.

# 26.

# "Then the small bell rang..."

The following day, Thomas woke up around seven and decided to attend the daily morning Mass at Holy Trinity at eight. He arrived ten minutes early and noticed his friend Richard Dart settled in his usual pew, where he often saw him on Sundays. Thomas smiled to himself, noting that he also sat in the same pew, seven rows down on the right side of the church, whenever he came to Mass. He wondered whether it was a *Catholic thing* to sit in the same spot or if everyone who attended any church did the same. He then reconsidered, thinking that maybe it was a *guy thing*, you know, a *creature-of-habit thing*. Then the small bell rang, announcing that Mass was about to begin.

During Mass, he prayed for Minnie, hoping she was okay, and then he wondered where she was. She should have returned to Charlotte's on Sunday, but he hadn't heard from her. He made a mental note to check in on her. Lastly, he prayed for Zack. He felt confused about that situation, but he asked the Lord to watch over his friend and help him recover from the awful events of the last couple of days.

After Mass, Thomas walked toward The Harvester Restaurant, his mind and stomach focused on breakfast.

Susan spotted him walking by Commencement Bay Books and stepped out the front door. "Thomas, I'm so glad I caught you."

Surprised, Thomas walked over to her and asked, "What's up?"

Susan said, "Sharon came in and opened the store this morning, but then she felt pretty sick, so she went home. Sharon said she would be back, saying she just needed to lie down for a bit. I've never been alone in the store before, and the calendar says George isn't coming in because he has an appointment with his lawyer this morning." She looked at Thomas, tilted her head in her sweetest pose, and said, "Please, Thomas, will you work with me this morning so I don't have to be alone in the store in case something comes up that I wouldn't know how to handle?"

Thomas smiled at her and nodded. "Sure, Susan, but only on one condition."

Susan, now excited and a little perplexed, replied, "What?"

"I'd like you to go to The Harvester Restaurant and get me a breakfast roll or scone and a large black coffee. Get something for yourself, too. Here's a twenty." With that, he handed her the money, and after giving him a quick hug, Susan headed for the restaurant.

Thomas entered the bookstore, checked his watch, flipped the sign on the door to open, placed his jacket in the back room, and returned to the front counter.

Susan returned shortly, and Thomas sipped his hot coffee. A little later, Sharon called to check on Susan. To Sharon's surprise, Thomas answered the phone, and they talked about her well-being and some store business. Since Thomas was at the store, Sharon, who wasn't feeling much better, asked if he could cover for her that day. Thomas explained that he had missed a day of work the day before yesterday, and of course, he would hold down the fort. He also urged Sharon to take care of herself and get well. He informed Susan that Sharon had called and that it would just be the two of them until James arrived. The bell on the front door began ringing, and they prepared for the morning wave of customers.

James arrived just before one to start his shift. In the early afternoon, while the three managed calls and customers, Nate entered the store. Susan approached him and asked if she could assist him with anything.

"I'm here to see Tom if he's working," replied Nate.

"Oh," Susan said, "He's upstairs. Would you like me to let him know you're here?"

"No, no, that won't be necessary. I'll go find him, thanks," he said, smiling at Susan. Nate then bounded up the stairs in search of his friend. He found Thomas in the History aisle. They greeted each other, and then Nate said, "Thanks for being there for Zack the other night."

"You would have done the same thing, Nate," Thomas replied.

"Well, I didn't," Nate said. "I called you, and you went to the hospital. I was just shaken by what was happening and didn't have the presence of mind to know what to do. Anyway, I visited him this morning. He's doing much better."

"That's great," Thomas said with a smile.

"Yeah, I spoke with a nurse, and she said there's a program they will enroll Zack in as soon as he's ready. The plan will be to evaluate Zack's physical and mental health. After that, I believe they'll start him on methadone. That's what I heard anyway."

"Isn't that the stuff that's supposed to reduce his cravings for the drug?"

"I think so," Nate said. "The nurse also mentioned that he would receive some counseling, and the program would track his progress."

Thomas asked, "Did you talk to Zack a lot while you were there? Is he coherent? Did you notice any deficiencies?"

"Well, I talked to him. He sounded okay. You know, he knew where he was and all that."

"So, I guess it's up to you and me, Nate, to encourage Zack to stick with the program and not fall back into his old ways. Nate, let me ask you, did Zack use any other drugs that you knew of?"

"Yeah," Nate said with a hint of hesitancy, "I know he did some cocaine. I didn't see him do it myself, but I've heard about it from two different guys since his overdose."

Thomas shook his head and said, "It's so hard to imagine Zack being involved with all this. Yet here he is in a detox program."

"I know it's not good. I feel scared for him," Nate said in a lower voice. Nate shook his head and said, "Well, I just wanted to stop by and give you an update on Zack."

"Thanks, Nate."

As Nate descended the staircase and exited the bookstore, Thomas instinctively exhaled, uncertain whether Zack possessed the mental and spiritual strength for a full recovery.

## 27.

## *"It won't happen ~ period."*

During his afternoon break, while James and Susan were still working and before Susan left for the day, Thomas slipped out and walked across the street to his favorite florist's shop (of course, he had never been to a florist's shop before he had gone there that time for Minnie). He bought a small bouquet of yellow roses for his visit to Cynthia's later in the evening.

When he returned to the store, Susan was ready to go home and thanked Thomas profusely for helping her that morning. He and James closed the store on time, and Thomas rang the intercom at Cynthia's apartment building shortly afterward. He wished he had time to go home, change his clothes, and freshen up a bit, but it was already after nine. Cynthia answered the intercom and buzzed him in. Thomas took the elevator to the fifth floor and knocked on Cynthia's door. When she opened it, Thomas stood there with the small bouquet of yellow roses extended toward her. Surprised by his gesture, she took the flowers from him and welcomed him into the apartment with a faint blush on her face.

Cynthia walked into the kitchen, the scent of fresh flowers filling the air as she gently placed them on the counter. Turning back to Thomas, who had followed her, she whispered, "Thank you," and their lips met in a soft, lingering kiss. Finally stepping back, she said, "I've missed you."

Thomas' eyes brightened with a warm smile. "Your invitation was the highlight of my week," he admitted. Cynthia raised a finger and, with her voice laced with a hint of apprehension, said. "I just need to put the flowers in water. Why don't you go check what's on TV?"

When she finally joined him in the living room, the TV was on, Thomas had flipped through the channels, and browsed the weekly TV Guide magazine. She sat down next to him on the couch. He turned to her and said, "How about Alec Guinness in *The Captain's Paradise*? It's about a ferryboat captain who lives with two different women, one in Morocco and the other in Gibraltar. The movie starts at ten. That's fifteen minutes from now. It lasts only an hour and twenty minutes, so you could have me out of here before midnight."

Cynthia said, "That sounds like a plan. I love Alec Guinness! I'll make some popcorn." She stood up and walked to the kitchen. Ten minutes later, she returned with a large bowl of popcorn. She set the bowl on the coffee table in front of the couch. Then, as if she had forgotten, she asked, "Do you need salt on your popcorn?"

Thomas said, "I have to confess I like it that way."

"Of course you do," Cynthia said with a smile. She grabbed the bowl and returned to the kitchen. She reappeared a minute later with two bowls, handing one directly to Thomas while keeping the other for herself. Then, she sat down and snuggled up against him. The movie started a few minutes later, and they both enjoyed the film. When it ended, Thomas got up to turn off the TV, then returned to the couch, taking Cynthia in his arms and kissing her. She kissed him back. After several minutes, Thomas noticed that Cynthia's breathing had become somewhat labored—at least, that's how it sounded and felt to him. They disengaged for a moment, and in a quiet voice, Thomas asked, "Are you all right?"

Cynthia, appearing slightly embarrassed, said, "You seem to have gotten me a little excited. I told you I missed you." She leaned back against Thomas, allowing him to hold her. After a minute or two, her shortness of breath, as Thomas would have described it, seemed to improve. They sat in the dimly lit living room. It was now after midnight, and Thomas knew Cynthia had to work in the morning.

"Cynthia, are you sure you're okay?" He tried to meet her gaze.

She glanced down before saying, "Thomas, I've wanted to tell you something ever since we met."

Thomas instinctively and ever so slightly tightened his arms around her. He noticed how adorable she looked barefoot in her blue jeans and T-shirt. The weight of her statement confused him.

"Thomas, I don't pretend to know how to tell you this because, yes," she looked up at him, "I think I have fallen in love with you."

Thomas' heart melted. "What, then, is the problem?"

"The issue is that I haven't been entirely truthful with you."

Looking even more puzzled now, Thomas waited.

Cynthia took a deep breath and said, "I haven't told you about my medical condition." Then, with a serious expression, she added, "Thomas, I have a heart condition." For the second time, she lowered her head and leaned into him. With what seemed like courage to Thomas, Cynthia refocused her eyes on his and said, "I have a heart disorder. It seems to run in my family, on my mother's side. I get short of breath too easily. It's technically known as ischemic heart disease." She looked courageously at Thomas and said, "I hate the word disease."

For a few moments, neither of them spoke. Then, tears welled up in Cynthia's eyes as she buried her face in his chest once more.

"Oh, Cynthia, it's okay. Let me hold you." He rubbed her back and held her close. She gripped his shoulders tightly, trying to regain her composure. After a while, Thomas stood up from the couch and got some tissues for Cynthia. They both stared intently at one another.

Then Cynthia said, "Thomas, I thought I had come to understand my situation, what it meant, and what it still means for me." Again, she looked bravely into Thomas' eyes. She continued, "It means I can't get involved with someone to the point of loving them. It can't happen."

Thomas was now at a loss for words. They sat in that room, no longer paying attention to one another, but instead lost in their own thoughts. Finally, Thomas said, "You can't mean what you're saying. It makes no sense."

Cynthia, now recovered from her initial outburst and tension, looked at him with a patience she seemed to have developed over time and said, "Thomas, I don't know how long I'll live. Of course, none of us do, but in my case, there's a reality that people with my condition tend to die younger than, say, a healthy person like yourself. I must follow a specific diet. I take medications. I must manage my high blood pressure. I occasionally experience an irritating, dry cough. I hate it." She paused and began again, "Why do you think I don't walk home from downtown after work? I don't because it leaves me breathless. Yet, they want me to exercise. My whole life has turned into some sort of bad dream, except for the fact that I met you. Still, I would never, could never, ask you to join me in my life. It won't happen – period."

Thomas didn't know what to make of all this. He got up from the couch, walked over to the window, and stared at the trees in the park, shrouded in gloomy darkness. It was now past one. He turned back to Cynthia and said, "I think you're so special. I can't imagine not having you in my life." They moved toward each other and embraced. He held her tightly, and they remained that way, neither wanting the moment to end. A little later, at now close to two, Thomas thought it best to leave so Cynthia could get a couple of hours of sleep before heading to work in the morning.

As Thomas walked home, skirting the edge of the park and noticing that he was the only person on the streets at this hour, he admitted he hadn't expected to hear what Cynthia had to say. Life, meaning, and his recently regained faith were struggling to reconcile with what was happening in his world. This was incredibly difficult. Minnie's situation, Zack and his drug dependency, and now Cynthia with her health issues, weighed heavily on him. Thomas felt anger about it all. What was going on? He decided he didn't like the world he inhabited. The path home seemed filled with questions and shadows.

## 28.

## "I guess I can trust the two of you together."

When Thomas woke up in the morning, he felt heartbroken about the previous evening. He decided to talk with Cynthia again to address their situation as soon as possible. The thought that her life could be cut short was devastating to him.

Thomas was about to head out for breakfast when he remembered he needed to check if Minnie was back from her trip to her friend's place. He called, and Charlotte answered the phone. Thomas asked if Minnie was there. Charlotte told Thomas that Minnie had called her the previous Sunday, mentioning she would be spending a few more days with her friend Vicki. Charlotte noted that Minnie seemed matter-of-fact and indicated she would return soon. Charlotte inquired about how Thomas was doing, and he repeated his concern for Minnie. They talked for a few more minutes before Charlotte suggested he try calling again in the next few days. Thomas thanked her, and they ended the call.

When he left the apartment that morning, he walked through the park. He thought to himself, how could the park be so beautiful while humanity was so messed up?

A couple of days later, still unsettled by Minnie's absence, he called Charlotte again to check if she had returned. To his surprise, Charlotte had news for him. She told him Minnie had called and would be home around dinnertime. She also shared that Minnie planned to go to The Rail for a late shift that evening. Thomas was grateful for the update and thanked Charlotte profusely.

Despite Thomas' concern after learning about Cynthia's heart condition, he felt compelled to see Minnie and discover how she was since their last conversation.

The afternoon and early evening dragged on, with George showing up and ribbing Thomas about the need for more window displays. Thomas stood his ground on the topic, and both grinned and agreed it would be beneficial to involve Sharon in the discussion.

At some point during the evening, Thomas called Cynthia, and they spoke briefly about how she was doing. He asked when they might get together again, and they agreed on the upcoming Friday night. After the call,

Thomas felt somewhat better, not great, but better. In his mind, he reasoned that he was at least doing something instead of nothing.

After closing the bookstore, Thomas walked down the street toward The Rail. He entered and surveyed the room. Noticing that the place was only about half full, he quickly spotted Minnie sitting at a table with whom he assumed, based on her more diminutive stature and long ash-blonde hair, was her new friend Vicki. Thomas knew Minnie was working the late shift, which started at ten, so she still had some time before her scheduled time began. He made his way over to their table.

As he approached, Minnie spotted Thomas. She jumped up from the table and embraced him, kissing him on the cheek as she whispered, "We need to talk," in a tone that sounded more serious than the words implied. Minnie turned to the other woman at the table, saying, "Vicki Prentis, this is Thomas Klement, the man I've been telling you about for the past week."

Thomas nodded and smiled at her. Vicki returned the smile and said, "It's nice to meet you finally."

Thomas took a chair from the table next to theirs and sat down. Minnie also settled back into her seat. Thomas turned to Minnie again and asked, "You've been gone for a while. Is everything okay?" He noticed that Minnie seemed anxious.

She reached across the table and gripped his hands tightly. "I'm okay, Thomas. It's been a hard week."

Thomas noticed that Vicki was watching him, and her evaluating look indicated that she was assessing his words, expressions, and body language.

Minnie said, "I intended to call you tonight during my break to let you know I was back and see if we could get together."

"Yeah, I called Charlotte to check on you, and she mentioned you were coming home and that you'd be here tonight. So, I thought I'd try to catch up with you. I was hoping we could talk. I realize this probably isn't the best time for that, with you starting your shift, but I really wanted to see you at least."

Minnie smiled while maintaining a hold of Thomas' hands as Vicki continued watching them.

"Thomas, I actually need to start working right now. Jake is signaling to me that he needs help. Can we meet tomorrow morning? I really want to talk more with you."

As Thomas listened to Minnie, a sense of unease came over him. This reunion tonight felt awkward, for lack of a better word. He sensed that Minnie was tense, and he couldn't quite understand her friend Vicki. "Of course, Minnie," he said, "We can get together whenever you want. You know that."

"Good," said Minnie, releasing Thomas' hands, standing up, and giving him one last hug. She looked up toward the bar and said, "I've got to get going. I'm really sorry." She glanced nervously at her friend Vicki and said, "I guess I can trust the two of you together." She attempted to laugh.

"We're good, right, Thomas?" Vicki asked flatly.

With that, Minnie glanced at Thomas, then back at Vicki, and, appearing more frustrated than ever, walked over to the bar.

Thomas and Vicki watched as Minnie walked over to the bar and put on an apron. Then, they slowly turned to face each other.

Still trying to gauge Minnie's friend, Thomas asked, "Vicki, are you from Tacoma? I ask because I'm not, and I find that question a nice icebreaker for conversation. I'm from Grayland, a small town near Westport, Washington."

Vicki smiled and replied, "No, no, I'm not from Tacoma either. I grew up in Seattle and graduated from the University of Washington."

He told her that he had a business degree from Rainier University.

She responded, "I graduated from U-Dub with a double major in Women's Studies and Sociology."

Thomas nodded.

"I enrolled in Sociology to explore and question the foundations and biases of women's oppression." Vicki smiled once more and awaited Thomas' response.

"I doubt I would have guessed that in a game of 20 questions," he replied, slightly surprised.

Vicki, disregarding Thomas' attempt at humor, asserted, "Well, Thomas, I take equal rights and legal protections very seriously. That means ensuring equal treatment under the law. Furthermore, I'm a strong advocate for eliminating workplace discrimination and harassment against women."

Thomas wondered if this was just her personality or if she was trying to make some point to him or to any man in general. After all, he had only just met her. He said, "Well, I think I sense where you're coming from, Vicki," as he tried to lighten the conversation once more.

"I think you might be trivializing what I'm saying," Vicki said in a low, focused tone.

"I'm not at all, Vicki. Please don't misconstrue my comments. I was just thinking that we don't really know each other well enough to dive into a serious discussion. I thought we had Minnie as a mutual friend, and I hope any friend of hers would also be a friend of mine." Thomas concluded his thought, his hands open.

Vicki hesitated for a moment but then leaned forward for effect and responded, "You know our friend," she emphasized the word, "was involved with a man who didn't give a damn for her well-being, impregnated her, and walked away."

"Yes, Minnie told me," Thomas replied more seriously.

Now, for whatever reason, Vicki became fully engaged and let Thomas have it. "Listen to me. A woman's right to make decisions about her own body is a fight for her very freedom. Roe v. Wade recognized a woman's right to privacy and the ability to make medical choices. These are fundamental rights. They are human rights," she concluded, her fists clenched on the table.

Thomas noticed her clenched fists and thought she probably didn't realize she was doing it. "Vicki, I'm not sure why you're so worked up right now. I'm not saying what you're discussing isn't important. I'm just saying I don't understand why you seem almost angry with me. You don't know me at all. Just ask me if you want to know how I feel about what you've been saying."

Vicki, a bit taken aback, said, "Alright then, what's your position on Minnie's situation?"

"Minnie's pregnancy, particularly given the circumstances surrounding it, is incredibly sad. Don't get me wrong, I respect the depth of your conviction on this issue." Thomas paused to check if Vicki was still engaged. She was. He took a breath and continued, "I am a Catholic. I come from the Catholic Tradition. That 2,000-year

Tradition teaches that all human life is sacred, from the moment of conception to natural death. For a Catholic, this isn't about control or oppression. It's simply about respecting human life at all stages. No one in the Church is against women making choices regarding their bodies. Is this about Minnie's dignity and freedom? Absolutely. Yet, an abortion also involves the life of the unborn child. In other words, it concerns the human dignity of both the mother and the child. Vicki, I am here to support Minnie in any way I can." He stopped speaking and raised his hands lightly, palms up.

Vicki sat there for a moment, appearing to dislike what she had heard. Then, contemplating her next move, she said impulsively, "Let's see how much you support her when you find out Minnie's already had an abortion about three days ago." She locked her gaze on Thomas and, with the faintest sense of triumph, added, "I think I'm ready to leave. It was nice meeting you, Thomas. I hope someday you gain a better understanding of the modern world." With that, Vicki rose from the table and left the pub.

Thomas sat there, dumbfounded. He closed his eyes. For a moment, there was nothing. Then his ears began to pick up the sounds of the crowd around him and the music from the jukebox. He opened his eyes and scanned the room for Minnie. He saw her taking orders at a large table of people across the room. Thomas looked at her and wondered how she was doing. Then he rose from his chair and walked out of the bar into the night air. He made his way home slowly, as if without direction or purpose.

## 29.

## *"One must endure the dark night..."*

Thomas had not eaten that evening but felt no desire to do so. He moved mechanically around his apartment, hanging up his jacket, turning the kitchen light on and then off again. He walked into the small living room and just stood there as if in a trance. Finally, he sat in his chair and looked out the window toward the park. The sky was dark over the grounds, and the wind stirred the faint outlines of the large trees. With all the lights off in the apartment, the darkness enveloped him, and the only sound he could hear was the ticking of the second hand on the clock on the mantle above the fireplace. For Thomas, the news of Minnie's abortion was another blow to his idea of what the world should be like.

Too many soul-crushing things were happening around him, and Thomas could not process the sorrow he had become aware of over the last few days regarding Zack, Cynthia, and Minnie. He feared that his renewed interest in his childhood faith might not survive the harsh realities of adulthood encircling his life and that of his closest friends.

Thomas continued to stare out the window. Then he glanced at the two-shelf bookcase beneath it. It represented his modest collection of books. After all, as George had told him, he could always take what he wanted home at night and return it the next day. As he gazed at the small collection of books, one stood out. It was a volume his mother had given him when she had moved to Astoria.

It was a copy of *The Collected Works of St. John of the Cross*, a 16th-century Spanish mystic. He remembered how his mother had told him how she had read much of it after his father died in a fishing accident just months before he was born. She had been so distraught by his loss and her fears of being left alone to raise the child from the couple's brief marriage. The poem Thomas remembered his mother telling him about was "The Dark Night of the Soul." When she read it, she was undergoing intense spiritual trials and experiencing the terrible feeling of being abandoned by God.

He got up, retrieved the book, and turned on the light by his chair. He read the poem, which consisted of only eight stanzas, each containing five lines. He also examined some of the commentary provided by St. John. He learned that the *dark night* was a metaphor of sorts for the seemingly divine abandonment of humanity in this world. The poem primarily addresses the hardships and struggles that an individual must endure in their quest for God.

Thomas set the book down and turned off the light. He once again stared out the window into the now thick darkness. He realized that his personal mental anguish regarding Zack's demons and pain, Cynthia's medical fragility, and Minnie's decisions and consequences, in some way, mirrored his own struggles and difficulties in trying to comprehend what God wanted him to understand.

Alas, it certainly seemed as if the world in which Thomas lived was unforgivingly indifferent to the pain his friends were now enduring. Yet the answer he had tried to base his life on—the secular solution—lacked much, including a coherent guide to morality. It possessed a moral relativism that blurred the distinctions between right and wrong, and ideas and answers that inadequately addressed human dignity and worth.

Thrashing around in these thoughts made Thomas' head spin. Outside lay the night, a dark void into which he stared. St. John of the Cross emphasized humanity's ability to find God in the depths of darkness through the soul. In other words, a harrowing transformation of one's soul must occur to align with God's will.

Hadn't he tried to talk to his buddy Zack about the dangers of drugs? Hadn't he told Cynthia that he wanted to be there for her? Hadn't he told Minnie that he would do anything for her? Thomas had done all these things, but to no avail.

He asked himself, "Does this mean that the real question is whether life is simply nothing more than suffering?"

He believed St. John of the Cross would describe it as a journey of faith. The Spaniard would suggest that a person should find the strength to trust deeply in the Almighty when God seems absent or, at the very least, concealed. One must endure the dark night, with God being the only path forward.

Thomas looked again at the darkened sky. He sat there for what felt like an hour, and all he heard was the ticking of the clock's second hand. But in the end, there was no answer, no keen insight, or comfort.

He glanced at the clock. It was past two. Thomas felt exhausted, yet a distinctly different thought crossed his mind. What about his feelings for Minnie and Cynthia?

To this point, Thomas had not really considered his situation. Now, he pondered, delving into the equally never-ending mystery of the human heart. He admitted to having deep affection and complex emotions for both women. But the question arose: How could he honor his powerful feelings for Cynthia and Minnie while staying true to his faith and respecting these extraordinary women?

As three o'clock approached, Thomas, now aware that his night's sleep was lost, decided to write a prayer about his pressing question of the evening. Is life nothing more than suffering? He also chose to write another prayer seeking guidance regarding his feelings for Cynthia and Minnie. Considering the late hour, things truly got out of hand. He determined that both prayers would take the form of poems. This decision stemmed from his experience in the poetry survey class he had surprisingly enjoyed at the university. Since moving to the Wright Park neighborhood a few years ago, he had dabbled in writing poetry and often composed verses while sitting on a bench by the duck pond in the park. He employed a simple, compact rhyming structure, which he would eventually copy onto a small piece of paper, allowing him to carry it in his wallet and pray whenever he wished. Eventually, Thomas would know these prayers by heart.

At 6:00 a.m., Thomas finished the first drafts of his two prayer poems. The sun was rising over the eastern portion of the park, so he made a pot of coffee. He brought a cup of the hot brew into the living room and settled into his chair. After sipping the coffee for a few minutes, he allowed his head to rest against the back of the chair and immediately fell into a deep sleep.

## 30.

## *"... I'm in hell thinking about it."*

After a few hours of sleep, a repetitive noise woke him. Thomas recognized it as knocking on his apartment door. He forced his eyes open and tried to respond, but could only manage an indistinct utterance of hello that didn't come out quite right. Pulling himself up from his chair, he turned toward the hallway and finally managed to say, "I'm coming."

When he reached the door, he unlocked it, turned the doorknob, and opened it to find Minnie standing there. He blinked hard and wrapped his arms around her. They clung to each other tightly for a moment.

Minnie noticed that Thomas looked and seemed a little disheveled. She asked, "Were you sleeping?"

"I fell asleep in the chair."

"Why?"

"It happens."

This clearly was not the best answer Thomas could have come up with to explain his appearance, but he set his face and continued to mentally and physically come to grips with this unexpected situation.

As Thomas' mind slowly cleared from its deep slumber, he put his arm around Minnie's shoulder and guided her into the apartment. They walked into the living room, where Minnie seemed to take charge and led him to the small couch. There, she sat down and invited Thomas to join her. She leaned against him and whispered, "Hold me." Thomas put his arm around her shoulder again, and with her head resting on his chest, they sat in silence as the minutes passed.

During that time, Thomas had the chance to fully awaken and reflect on the beautiful woman he knew had endured so much. My poor Minnie. She felt warm and comforting against him, and he realized just how much he had missed her. Their time together had been brief, exciting, passionate, and, of course, heartbreaking.

Finally, as they both focused on the ticking of the room's clock and their shallow breathing, Minnie said, "Oh, Thomas, I think I've really messed things up again." Before

Thomas could respond, she lightly tapped his chest with a half-formed fist and leaned into him once more. Thomas could hear her sobbing softly. "Come on, Minnie, you don't have to cry. You're with me." He kissed her forehead, and she sat up again.

"Vicki told me that the two of you had a confrontation," Minnie said in almost a whisper.

Thomas nodded.

"Oh, Thomas, I don't know why she did that. I panicked when I saw that you both had left The Rail last night. I didn't know what was happening. Then, a little later, she returned to the pub and told me about the conversation you two had and that she had told you about what I had done."

"I met Vicki while working at The Rail, and I eventually told her my story. She started explaining my rights as a woman and how men, especially David, were oppressing me. I mean, I got really confused. To be blunt, she laid out for me how my life would be ruined. As the reality of the situation sank in, I panicked more. That same day, after I saw you and told you I was pregnant, Vicki called me to discuss it further. She explained that she knew a good doctor who could take care of everything. She made it seem like the right choice. I finally said I'd do it." Minnie's eyes filled with tears, and she burst out weeping.

Regaining control of her emotions and wiping her eyes with the sleeves of her cotton pullover, she said, "Last night

I was beside myself with anger. Vicki had no business talking to you about it. Thomas, you really need to understand that it was so hard trying to figure out what to do. The fact that the baby was David's made me cry every time I thought about it. I mean, he wanted no part of the situation, and I was scared of being a single mother without much education, trying to support myself and a baby."

Both paused, looking at each other with a sense of helplessness. Then, with the incredible courage that Thomas had come to recognize in her, Minnie said, "Thomas, it was my decision, and I made it. Vicki definitely wanted me to do it, too, but for different reasons. However, she didn't make the decision. I did." After another pause, Minnie asked, "How do you feel about it, Thomas?" as she looked directly into his eyes.

Thomas felt himself beginning to tear up. He quickly said, "Minnie, as a man, I really have no idea what you've been experiencing. I mean, yes, I've thought about it all, but the reality of the situation was that it was happening to you," he said, reaching for her hands. He held them firmly and added, "Minnie, I am a Catholic, and you know what I believe, yet I care about you with all my heart."

They stared at each other once more. Then, Minnie rose from the couch, stepped into the center of the small room, and looked out at the park. She continued, "I would give anything not to have ended up in this situation, but now, obviously, there's no turning back or a second chance to rethink it. But on the other hand," Minnie turned and looked directly at Thomas, "I can't get the baby out of my mind. Vicki called it a fetus, but it was a baby, my baby. O God, Thomas, I'm in hell thinking about it."

Thomas stood up from the couch and hugged Minnie. "Come on, if nothing else, I hope you feel safe with me no matter what happens moving forward."

Minnie held Thomas tightly. She spoke in a lower yet determined voice, "I'm feeling a little shaky right now, but I'm not a quitter. You know I want to stand on my own. You know I believe I can write. That's what I want to do. I need to dedicate more time to that goal and focus less on making friends at The Rail."

Thomas leaned over, picked up a tissue, and handed it to Minnie. She replied, "Thanks." Thomas then asked, "Have you eaten yet this morning?"

"No," Minnie answered, still dabbing her eyes and sniffling a bit.

Thomas glanced at her again and noticed that Minnie was struggling, as evidenced by her expression. He said, "How about I scramble some eggs, and we'll have toast with blackberry jam?" She nodded. "I'll start brewing the coffee," Thomas said as he walked into the kitchen.

During breakfast, Minnie conveyed her guilt and how it seemed to cling to her. She shared with Thomas her experiences of growing up in Union and attending a small non-denominational church with her parents. She asked Thomas to tell her more about the Catholic Church, displaying a genuine curiosity.

Thomas shared his Catholic upbringing, discussing his challenges with belief, faith, and church practices. He mentioned that he now attended Holy Trinity, located about half a mile from his apartment.

As Thomas finished washing the dishes and Minnie dried them, he asked her not to disappear again without letting him know where she might be going. He explained how he always seemed to miss her at the moments he most wanted to see her. Thomas reiterated that he was there for her and urged her not to avoid him if something went wrong in her life. He spoke to her about the importance of discovering her true self, not based on what others thought of her, but on who she truly was and what she believed, regardless of everyone else's opinions.

They left the apartment about a quarter to one. Thomas needed to get to work. As they walked together, Minnie took Thomas' hand and said softly but seriously, "You know I love you," before kissing him on the cheek. They then walked the few blocks to the bookstore, where they parted ways—Thomas going inside while Minnie continued toward Charlotte's house.

Once inside the store, Thomas felt intense fatigue deep in his bones.

## 31.

## "...understand what I've been saying."

The day dragged on. To stay awake, Thomas stocked shelves and engaged in other activities that required movement to keep himself from dozing off. He had James working behind the front counter. Later in the day, Thomas told James to "just do it" about a task that needed to be done.

As he turned to perform the task, James asked just loud enough for Thomas to hear, "Are we feeling a bit grumpy today?"

Thomas closed his eyes and then reopened them. He sighed and said to James, "You're right. I'm sorry. I'm just really tired today. I didn't sleep much last night, and I wish it were already 9 o'clock."

James smiled at Thomas and replied, "Hang in there, old-timer. We'll get there."

Closing time finally arrived. They emptied the registers, put the cash in the safe, swept the floors, and completed other last-minute tasks before turning off the lights, setting the alarm, and locking the doors. Thomas apologized once again for being *grumpy,* and they laughed as James headed to his car while Thomas walked up the street toward his apartment.

By nine-thirty, he was settled in his chair—the same one he had slept in the night before—thinking he didn't have the energy to prepare one of his at-best marginal dinners for himself. He compromised by getting up and heading to the kitchen, where he found, peeled, and ate a banana that was nearing the end of its freshness. It tasted fine, and he returned to his chair, wrestling with himself about whether he should just go to bed. He had just decided that going to bed was the better choice when the phone rang.

It was Cynthia. She said, "Hello, Thomas, so you're home from work."

"Hi, Cynthia. Yes, I'm home and sitting in my chair. It's great to hear your voice."

Almost cutting him off, Cynthia said, "Thomas, I really need to talk to you. I've been thinking about this for a while, and I believe we should get together. I mean, I think maybe we should talk tonight. How about you come over to my place?"

At his end of the line, Thomas' eyes widened as he tried to process what Cynthia was asking, and then said, "You want to get together tonight?"

Cynthia rejoined the conversation. "Yes, I think you should come over right now so we can talk."

"Uh, okay. I can do that," Thomas replied, trying to conceal how tired he truly felt.

"Thank you, Thomas. I've been thinking about this all day, and it would mean a lot to me if you could come, if that's alright."

"Not at all. I'll be there in fifteen minutes. Does that sound good?"

"Perfect, see you then."

Cynthia hung up, and as Thomas listened to the dial tone, he stretched his neck from side to side and took a deep breath—both efforts to revive his fading physical strength. After that, he hung up the phone and stood up to get ready. After washing his face and combing his hair, he changed into a clean shirt and pants before heading out the door.

The walk in the night air rejuvenated Thomas, making him somewhat more attentive when he arrived at Cynthia's apartment. She welcomed him and led him to the kitchen, where they sat at the table. Cynthia asked, "Can I get you anything, Thomas?"

"No," Thomas replied with a smile, recalling the banana, "I'm good. I had a little something to eat when I got home."

"All right," said Cynthia, seeming to want to get to the point of their get-together. "Thomas, I want you to understand what I'm dealing with regarding my heart condition. I know we tried to talk about it a little when you were here the other night, but I don't think I provided enough information." She took a deep breath and determinedly began, "Ischemic heart disease is a condition where I have reduced blood flow to my heart. It is caused by the narrowing of the arteries. The less blood flow there is, the less oxygen gets to my heart muscle. Over time, this condition usually leads to further narrowing of the arteries, which in turn reduces blood flow to the heart even more. When this happens, I can experience bouts of angina, which is the medical term for chest pain. If it gets bad enough, it can lead to heart failure. This condition can also lead to an irregular heartbeat or arrhythmia. Any of these issues can obviously be dangerous to my life." Cynthia paused. She wiped one eye with the back of her wrist.

Thomas glanced at her, trying not to appear demoralized by her words, and instead asked, "Are you okay?"

"I am. I know this all sounds terrible, and in many ways, it is, but I really felt I needed to explain my problem in more detail than I did when we last talked." She reached into her sweater pocket and wiped her nose with a tissue. "Thomas, you need to understand all of this because I've kind of led you on for a while, thinking you were handsome, sweet, and caring."

With a smile, Thomas responded, "Yeah, that does sound like me."

"Stop it, Mr. Klement," she said, shaking her head slightly, a trace of a smile showing. Cynthia continued, "Then, I made a mistake I had promised myself not to make some time ago. I promised myself that, due to my heart condition, I wouldn't fall in love with anyone going forward. This was before I knew you, and by allowing myself to be around you, I faltered and fell in love with you." Cynthia looked Thomas in the eyes and said, "You mean so much to me, but because of everything I've been discussing, I need to let you know where I stand regarding the real world." She set her jaw and said, "Thomas, we can never be lovers. We can only be friends." With that, Cynthia stood up from the table, walked to the sink, and turned on the cold water. She reached into the cupboard and grabbed a glass. After filling it, she gulped down nearly half and returned to the table.

Thomas stood up before she could sit down again and opened his arms, inviting her to come to him. She did. They embraced. Despite all the terrible things Cynthia had shared with him in the last few minutes, this moment of true togetherness touched his soul. They finally stepped back from each other, and Thomas said in a measured voice, "So what do you mean when you say we can only be friends?"

"Thomas, you don't really understand how this might play out. There's likely going to be a continued decline in my health. I can't imagine letting you watch me get worse like that. I refuse to let that happen." With that, she took another gulp of water and fixed her gaze on the man in her kitchen.

"But Cynthia, you know I want to be here for you," Thomas said, his voice slightly raised.

Cynthia shook her head. "You don't want a future filled with medical appointments, treatments, likely surgeries, and potential hospitalizations, all while watching me fade away. Those aren't my thoughts for you, period."

Thomas started to speak, but Cynthia cut him off and said, "I want you to see me in a certain light, and it doesn't include any of what I've just explained to you. I'm sorry, Thomas, but what I'm saying is that it's *because* I love you. I've spent many nights reflecting on my life and circumstances. I invited you here tonight because I need you to understand everything I've been discussing. If you care about me the way you claim to, then please understand what I've been saying."

Thomas, now finally defeated and lacking the courage to push the argument any further, said, "Cynthia, just as you've shared your perspective on our relationship, I want you to know that I will always be here for you, even if I can't be as close to you as I'd like."

Both looked at each other, and Cynthia stepped forward again into his welcoming arms, holding him tightly. Thomas whispered in her ear, "Are you willing to describe what kind of relationship we can have moving forward?"

Cynthia smiled and said, "Well, we can always have a movie night if you promise not to chase me around my living room." They both shared a good laugh.

When he arrived home after midnight, Thomas wanted to reflect further on what Cynthia had said. He was troubled by her declaration about how her life would possibly unfold. But by the time he crawled into bed, right as his head hit the pillow, having not slept the previous night and only managing a couple of hours that morning, his body surrendered, and he fell instantly asleep.

## 32.

## *"...my prayer ascends..."*

Throughout the next week, Thomas worked on the drafts of his prayers in poetic form during his spare time, even while at work during lunch or breaks. By the end of the week, he had rewritten and refined each prayer numerous times until he felt satisfied with them. In their final versions, Thomas handwrote the prayers on separate small slips of paper, which he folded and kept in his wallet. With use, he would ultimately commit them to memory. This is how they turned out.

### *Is Life Nothing More Than Suffering?*

In this night, my soul in shadows cast,

whispers to the heavens, vast and deep:

Is the breath of life but suffering vast,

a burden heavy, for the heart to keep?

O Lord Divine, in silent watch, I cry,

through the veil of darkness, seek Thy face.

164

Is there naught but sorrow 'neath Thy sky,
no glimpse of mercy, no tender grace?

For in this pilgrimage, no light I find,
only paths fraught with tears that ever flow.
Is this the lot of mankind, thus designed,
a bitter cup, from which we all must know?

Yet in this dark, a questing soul's refrain,
seeks beyond the shadows, beyond the pain.
O Lord, is life but suffering's chain,
or in this night, does hidden hope remain?

In Thy hands, I place my heart's unsure plea,
trusting Thy wisdom, boundless and divine.
Whether life be joy or suffering's sea,
let Thy will unfold, mingle it with mine.

In this surrender, may I find true rest,
confident that all Thy paths are just and right.
In every trial, in every test,
I seek Thy love, Thy mercy's light.

Thomas knew from his catechesis during his teens and from his mother's constant refrain whenever a trial presented itself in his life that she would always say, "Offer it up." This advice didn't help him understand the *why* of the trial, yet it was about joining his sorrow to Christ's suffering. Now, living with real-world problems on his own, he recognized that he was trying to grasp more of the *bones* of the Church's doctrine. He understood this was not easy. As for his plea to God for wisdom concerning Minnie and Cynthia, his poem was more direct and to the point. Of course, he didn't understand women. He was a man.

### *A Prayer for Wisdom*

In the quiet shadow of this dark, dark night,

I lay before Thee, Lord, my heart's contrite plight.

Let not this plea for clarity and light,

be lost in the vast silence of the night.

In humble submission, my soul does bow,

to trust in Thee, here and now.

Thus, in the night, my prayer ascends,

on Thy wisdom, my heart depends.

## 33.

## *"I mean, we're not kids anymore."*

Later that week, Thomas savored a cup of coffee while gazing out the window of his apartment as the morning sun rose over the expansive park. It was a day off from work, and as he contemplated how to spend it, there was a knock on the door. When he opened it, Thomas greeted his friend Zack. He noticed that although Zack appeared fine, he was noticeably thinner than he had been a few years ago. Despite his slimmer appearance, Zack looked better than when Thomas had last seen him at the hospital after his overdose. They exchanged a handshake and then moved to the kitchen. Thomas asked if Zack would like a cup of coffee, and Zack accepted.

Once Zack settled into a kitchen chair and sipped his hot coffee, he said, "This morning, I stopped by the bookstore hoping to catch you. They told me you had the day off, so I drove over here to see if I could find you."

"Yeah, I slept in a bit this morning, but as you can see, I'm awake and getting ready for the day with some hot coffee." Thomas thought about how great it was to see Zack and then cautiously asked him how he'd been doing.

Zack, now wearing a more serious expression, said, "If you're asking about my issues—he emphasized the word with air quotes—I'm hanging in there. I'm enrolled in a program that's roughly equivalent to AA for drug use. Once a week, I attend a session sponsored by the Tacoma-Pierce County Health Department. It's essentially outpatient treatment, maintenance, and monitoring. You know, Thomas, drug rehab."

"Are you okay with that?" Thomas asked.

Zack smirked at him and said, "Oh yeah, I'm good. I'm as clean as the driven snow."

Thomas filled Zack's coffee cup and asked, "So, what are you doing these days?"

"Funny you should ask," replied Zack. "Well, after the trouble I got into with that drug episode, I lost both of my jobs at the new car dealerships. However, I recently connected with a high-end used car lot that specializes in what you and I would call late-model *muscle cars,* along with the newer, trendy personal luxury coupes. One of my responsibilities is facilitating car lot trades. In other words, I take a car to another dealership that wants it on their lot in exchange for a car we want that's in their inventory. I also have to complete the transfer paperwork, but that usually takes less than half an hour." He paused to let that sink in. Then he continued, "So, that's what I'm up to today. I've got a '75 Dodge Charger out front that I need to take to Seattle, where I'll exchange it for a '74 Chevy Corvette Stingray. I was hoping you'd want to ride with me for company," Zack said with a hopeful smile.

Thomas paused for a moment to think it over. I've got nothing planned for today. Zack's asking me to hang out with him. Why not? "Sure, let's do it," Thomas replied, and they both drained their coffees.

Twenty minutes later, the two friends in the black Charger merged onto Interstate 5, known as I-5 to locals, and drove north. The Charger offered a comfortable, almost luxurious feel, which starkly contrasted with the earlier Chargers that had a 426 Hemi under the hood. Those cars didn't feel comfortable. They felt dangerous.

As they drove into King County, both men felt relaxed, and the conversation turned to local sports. Zack mentioned that he enjoyed watching the Seattle Mariners with Ruppert Jones playing center and right field, along with Julio Cruz at second base. Thomas said he particularly liked Enrique Romo coming out of the bullpen to keep the fledgling M's in some games or to help secure a win in others. They both noted how enjoyable it was to listen to the games, especially at night during the summer. They also discussed the Seattle Seahawks and how, in just their third year of existence, they had developed an exciting offense with the passing duo of Jim Zorn and Steve Largent, and rising stars on defense like cornerback Dave Brown.

In Seattle, as they crossed the Ship Canal bridge on I-5, they could see Husky Stadium to the east, sitting majestically on the shores of Lake Washington. Thomas talked about how Joe Steele, the local boy and star running back at Washington, in his opinion, had turned out to be more of a grinder. Although he was gaining good yardage, he was not as dynamic as Thomas had personally hoped when he signed with the Huskies out of high school. He also loved the play of *Spider* Gaines at wide receiver. On defense, he really enjoyed Nesby Glasgow's performance in the secondary.

They turned west off the freeway, drove to Aurora Ave, and then headed north for another five minutes. Upon arriving at the dealership they were looking for, Zack parked the Charger and went into the office to finalize the exchange. Thomas got out of the car and stretched his legs, admiring all the attractive late-model vehicles on the lot. It took about 45 minutes to complete the transaction. Then, with the keys in hand, Zack returned, and the two of them walked over to admire the white '74 Stingray. Zack told Thomas that this particular one came with the optional RPO L82 engine, which offered 205 horsepower. They climbed into the car, checked out the interior, including all the switches and buttons, and then Zack started the engine, which roared to life. Zack also pointed out that it had a 4-speed transmission and independent rear suspension. Later, Thomas remembered that it felt pretty cool as they returned on Aurora Avenue, heading south. Their road trip took them back through Seattle and then south, with Boeing Airfield on their right as they made their way back to Tacoma.

As they neared the South Center shopping mall, located midway between Seattle and Tacoma just east of the freeway, the conversation—surprisingly, at least to Thomas—took on a philosophical tone. Zack turned down the radio and asked, "Nate tells me you're going to church again, just like during those first couple of years at Rainier. Is that true?" Zack glanced over at Thomas and waited.

Caught off guard by the question, Thomas replied, "Yeah, I go to Holy Trinity, a small Catholic church not far from the bookstore. Why?"

"I'm just surprised. I would have thought you had gotten all that out of your system when you stopped going to church, and we were brought up to speed by the "dialed-in professors" at the university. I mean, we're not kids anymore. What can I say, buddy? Haven't you read any Nietzsche? To be blunt, I'd say hello and welcome to the 20th century, pal. Your idea of the existence of God is, well, a bit medieval, don't you think?"

Thomas, whose jaw had dropped considerably, took a moment to regain his composure and finally said, "I guess I'm just one of those people who believe that the world didn't simply happen or has always existed for no reason. I don't think faith is just wishful thinking," Thomas said. "When I look at the world—at how it holds together, at what the Jewish prophets had to say, at Christ and what the Church has carried through history—it adds up to something. Not a formula. But something that makes sense of everything else."

Zack looked at Thomas once more and said, "Science, politics, and philosophy have all turned their backs on your enchanted view of the world."

Thomas sat there with a slightly stunned expression, wondering how this exchange had begun. Why was Zack asking these questions and making these remarks? Then, out of nowhere, Zack unloaded. "I lost my brother. I looked up to him. He followed all the rules. Where did it get him? He's dead. Why?" Zack took his hands off the wheel, opened his palms, and held them up. Then, returning them to the wheel, he said, "There is no God on which to base reality, one's purpose, or anything else. We are on our own. There is no meaning to all of this. Man, I'm telling you, you blink, and a decade disappears. So, I say enjoy life while you can. You're nearly finished with your 20s. What do you have left, your 30s and maybe your 40s, with your health, and then it's sickness and death? Quite a picture, hey brother."

Thomas stared intently at his friend and said, "I really hope you don't believe that, Zack. I mean that."

Zack briefly gazed at the road before turning up the radio again. As the rock music blared, he pressed down on the Corvette's accelerator, and at one point, as Thomas watched incredulously, the Vette soared well over 100 miles per hour. It took Thomas' loud "Hey, man, slow down" to bring Zack back to some semblance of reality and ease up on the throttle.

They hardly spoke as they passed through Milton and Fife before entering Tacoma's city limits. Once off the freeway, it was a five-minute drive back to the Wright Park neighborhood. As Zack pulled up to the apartment building, Thomas thanked him for the road trip and, in a lower voice, told him, "You can't think like that man, I'd love to talk to you more about your thoughts—maybe just not on the freeway." Zack, to Thomas' disappointment, said nothing. Disheartened, Thomas said, "Take care, Zack," as he got out of the car.

Mr. Rowland waited until Thomas had closed the door on the Vette and then roared away.

## 34.

# "Dust in the Wind."

The next morning, Thomas walked slowly through Wright Park. He crossed the bridge over the duck pond and made his way up the hill toward the conservatory. He was deeply concerned about his friend Zack and uncertain as to what to do. As he approached the beautiful glass structure, he glanced at his watch and saw that he had fifteen minutes before the daily morning Mass at Holy Trinity would begin. Thomas walked toward the church, arriving ten minutes later. A couple of dozen parishioners were in attendance. Father Sinclair said his usual reverent Mass, which included a short daily Mass homily. Thomas offered his Mass for Zack and his growing concerns about him. After the liturgy, Thomas slipped out of the church, acknowledging a few greetings along the way. As he walked, a dark cloud settled over his thoughts. As he had no appetite, instead of going somewhere for breakfast, he headed back toward the park.

Thomas walked briefly into the park before heading home to make a pot of coffee. Sitting in his chair in the living room, he brooded over the Zack situation while sipping from his cup. Thomas noticed that the wind had picked up as he watched the tree branches sway outside his window. Dejected, he ultimately realized he should probably get ready for work.

When he arrived at the bookstore, it was bustling with customers. He immediately began assisting those who had questions. The lively atmosphere of the store helped Thomas forget about Zack and other troubling issues for a surprising amount of time. As the store traffic finally eased late in the afternoon, Thomas felt weak and hungry, having not eaten throughout the day. Rummaging around in the back room, he found a Hershey bar and poured himself a cup of coffee from a pot that James had made a bit earlier. It was still warm. Upon further inspection, Thomas discovered an apple that appeared to have been in the fridge for a few days. It wasn't crisp, but it did help his stomach. He washed it down with the coffee and poured himself a second cup. Opening the chocolate bar, he alternated bites and sips of coffee for another ten minutes. Then he heard James calling for him, as a new customer had a question that James couldn't answer. Thomas walked back out onto the store's main floor and joined in the conversation with James and the customer. After that, the customer count rose again, and he and James answered questions, found books, and rang up customers.

Before Thomas knew it, James mentioned it was time to close the store for the day. Taken aback by the time,

Thomas went through the closing routine with James. After that, they both put on their jackets and left the store, locking the front door behind them. As they turned to head home, Nate suddenly appeared and said, "Hey, I'm glad I caught you."

Thomas said good night to James, then he turned to Nate and asked, "What's up?"

"I'm just in a mood about Zack and wondered if you'd like to grab something to eat and talk about it?"

"Sure, Nate. I've been thinking a lot about Zack today, too."

Nate smiled and suggested, "How about we head to The Deep Harbor Tavern for some of those chicken wings they make?"

Thomas checked the front door one last time and said, "Sounds good. Did you bring your car?"

"Yeah, but I parked closer to the tavern. We can walk there from here, and I'll grab the car when we're done." Thomas was hoping Nate's car was parked right there at the bookstore. He felt tired and hadn't eaten much. He sighed and said, "Okay, let's get going," thinking to himself that maybe the walk would refresh him and that the tavern wasn't too far away.

The two walked about four blocks and entered The Deep Harbor Tavern, where they found a table. The place was crowded, so Nate sat at the table while Thomas placed the order for food at the bar. He ordered chicken wings for Nate and opted for a personal-sized pizza for himself. He returned to the table carrying a pitcher of beer and two glasses. "The New Kid in Town" by the Eagles played on the tavern's sound system. Although Thomas felt tired and hungry, the upbeat atmosphere kept him energized. They each finished a glass of beer by the time their number was called. Nate retrieved the order, and Thomas had his first taste of real food for the day. Minutes later, to the sound of "The First Cut is the Deepest" by Rod Stewart, Thomas finished his second piece of pizza and headed to the bar to buy another pitcher.

Upon returning to the table with the second pitcher, Thomas said to Nate, "I'm sorry, buddy, but I haven't eaten all day. I really needed that pizza." Nate laughed and replied, "You don't have to explain to me that you were hungry. I'm just glad I didn't get my hand too close to your plate. God knows what might have happened."

It was Thomas' turn to laugh. Then, growing serious, he said, "Nate, I'm really stressed about Zack. He stopped by yesterday, and I ended up riding to Seattle with him. He swapped one car from a used car lot out on South Tacoma Way for another from a dealership up on Aurora Ave in Seattle. We had a good talk, not much in the way of substance, but good in the sense that we hadn't talked a lot over the last year or so. It was on the way home that things got a little squirrelly. Zack asked me why I was going to church and why I believed in God. I tried to answer him, but he wasn't interested. At one point, he pushed the Corvette to over 100 mph. I had to shout at him to slow the hell down. I don't mind telling you, it was scary for a moment or two." Thomas paused to let the information he had just shared with Nate sink in.

Nate sat there, slowly shaking his head. Finally, he said, "I had a similar talk with Zack today. He stopped by my place around noon and wanted to know what was going on and if any *parties* were coming up." He took a drink of his beer and continued, "He seemed to be almost angry at different stages of our conversation. I don't know why. We weren't talking about anything in particular and certainly nothing that should have set him off." Nate hesitated for a moment and then, remembering the point he wanted to make, said, "Zack brought you up in the conversation. He told me he couldn't figure you out, which made him crazy. *Crazy* was his word, not mine."

"Yeah, I hear you," Thomas said, twisting his neck side to side in an attempt to relieve tension. "Zack seems to be spiraling. He doesn't seem to care about anything anymore, especially himself."

Nate nodded. "I think you're right, the drug use has taken a toll on him."

Now, both paused and took another drink from their glasses. In the ensuing silence, the sound system played Kansas' "Dust in the Wind." One might say that the conversation and music were sobering, but that was not the case, especially for Thomas. After a couple more slices of pizza, Thomas began to focus on the beer in front of him. He lamented, "I just don't know how to get through to him. I try talking to him, but he doesn't want to hear it."

Nate poured another glass for Thomas. "Well, doing nothing is not an answer. We should talk to a professional, you know, someone who deals with this sort of thing."

"I think you're right, Nate. Our approach isn't enough. We need to do better for Zack."

"I know some people through my parents who I think can help us with contacts for advice on how to approach Zack's situation," said Nate, striking the tabletop with the outer side of his fist.

"That sounds like a plan, Nate. You're so right about getting more professionals involved." Thomas drained the last of his glass.

A group of young women sat at a table on the other side of the tavern, all laughing and singing along to Bonnie Tyler's "It's a Heartache." Only one of them wasn't participating. She instead watched Thomas and another guy, clearly a friend, talking and drinking across the room. Twenty minutes later, when the two men stood up from their table and shook hands, she noticed Thomas looked a bit wobbly and drunk. As they began to make their way out of the tavern, she quickly said goodnight to her friends and followed Thomas and his friend. Outside, she heard the other guy ask, "Are you sure you don't want a ride?" Thomas responded, "No, I'm good. I think walking will help me pull myself together." They both laughed. Then Thomas said, "Thanks again for your update and thoughts on Zack."

"No problem," replied Nate, raising his hand and pointing at Thomas, as he headed toward his car.

Meanwhile, Thomas walked slowly and deliberately toward his apartment a few blocks away, concentrating on getting home without stumbling. Perhaps because he had drunk too much and was making a concerted effort not to trip, he didn't notice that someone was following him, just far enough behind to remain unnoticed but close enough to watch his every move.

## 35.

## "Look at you..."

When Thomas arrived home, he closed the door behind him and turned on the kitchen light. He considered eating something to help soak up some of the beer he had consumed, but the sudden sound of the doorbell interrupted his plans. Surprised, as always, when someone showed up unannounced, he walked to the door and opened it.

He blinked. "Vicki?" he said, his tone disbelieving.

"Hello, Thomas," she said, her voice carrying a hint of amusement. Then, without waiting for an invitation, she stepped into the apartment.

Thomas closed the door behind her. Vicki stood in the hall for a moment and then removed her jacket. Striving to be a gentleman, he took Vicki's jacket and hung it on one of the hooks in the hallway. Then, he followed her as she walked into the living room. She scanned the space and slowly approached the windows, where a stunning evening view of Wright Park welcomed her.

She turned to face Thomas. "This is a nice little place you have here," Vicki said with the faintest hint of a smile.

"Thanks," Thomas replied cautiously. The alcohol clouded his thoughts, making it more difficult for him to process why she was there in the first place. "What can I do for you, Vicki?"

"I saw you walking and decided to follow you. I wanted to tell you something," Vicki said in a softer voice. "I wanted to tell you that I felt bad about leaving you abruptly when we first met at The Rail. I think I was tired, and to be honest, I felt a little intimidated by you. You seemed so confident. I wasn't certain what to make of it. As I'm sure you could tell by our conversation about Minnie, I'm pretty used to getting the final word in discussions like that." She shifted her feet, "I felt slightly off balance by your way of putting things. Frankly, I wasn't sure how to handle you at the time." Vicki tucked some of her long, almost white hair behind one ear.

"Handle me?" Thomas repeated, his brow slightly creasing as he grappled with the excess lager sloshing around in his system.

"You're too self-assured," Vicki continued. "And you challenge people in a way that's… unsettling. I'm used to setting the tone in a conversation, and you," she paused, stepping closer, "you caught me off guard."

Thomas stood by his chair, trying to study her. There seemed to be no trace of the confrontational edge that Vicki had shown at the bar. Instead, her expression and voice were almost inviting. Yet, he felt a hint of uneasiness within his alcohol-compromised thoughts.

"I've thought a lot about you since our conversation," Vicki said, taking another step toward him. "Your, let's say, stubbornness, your faith, your defense of Minnie – it got under my skin. And I didn't like it at all, but…" She reached out and touched his arm lightly. "It also provoked my interest."

Thomas braced himself. "Vicki – "

"Don't worry," she interrupted, lowering her voice to a whisper. "I'm not here to debate the pros and cons of your positions." She moved closer, gently tracing an imaginary line down his arm. "I'm here because I want to understand you. I want to see what's behind that protective covering you seem to wear so well."

They now faced each other squarely, her perfume faint yet provocative. Thomas felt his pulse quicken as she gently tilted her head to gaze at him.

"You seem so confident, Thomas. Yet, I feel there's more to you than the good Catholic boy persona you try to present. I'm here to discover what that might be."

Thomas felt the warmth of her body as she pressed hers against him.

"Vicki, I…" His voice faltered as he searched for words and felt himself slipping toward and challenged by an instinctive, visceral response to Vicki's advance.

"What did you say?" Vicki asked softly, inclining her head again and sliding one hand down the side of Thomas' face. "Do you want to push me away? Do you want to pretend you don't want this?"

Though somewhat hazy, his mind raced to understand what was happening.

"It seems straightforward to me," purred Vicki, opening her mouth slightly while pulling Thomas' face down toward hers, in order to kiss him.

While his body urged him to give in, something held him back. A quiet but persistent voice—call it his conscience—somehow compelled him to stand up straight and say, "I'm sorry, Vicki. I may be a bit drunk—okay, maybe more than a bit—but this can't happen."

Vicki, in total disbelief, stared at Thomas for a moment and then, momentarily regaining control of herself, said, in an agitated voice, "Fine, you let me come into your apartment, and then you push me away - *big man*." The last words were delivered in a mocking tone. But she wasn't finished, "Men are all alike. You think you can have anything you want, whenever you want." She stepped back from Thomas, now her arms flailing as she stamped her feet. She accidentally backed into the large ottoman and ended up sitting on it. From her seated position, she added, "I hate men!" Then she began to sob.

Over the next few minutes, Thomas, wide-eyed, watched as Vicki gradually regained her composure, remaining on the ottoman and facing him. The apartment was now silent, except for some sniffling from Vicki. The living room was mostly dark, with only partial illumination coming from the kitchen light. Thomas switched on the standing floor lamp beside his chair and sat down. He moved a box of tissues from the table next to the chair to the corner of the ottoman.

Vicki used one and then, sizing up Thomas, said, "Look at you. You're drunk. Men do whatever they like without thinking or worrying about the consequences." She pointed an accusing finger at Thomas.

He finally spoke, "You're right, Vicki. I went out with a friend and had too much to drink on an empty stomach, and yes, it gave me a buzz. But I didn't do anything to anyone. I simply walked home." The silence returned. As moments turned into minutes, Thomas realized that the commotion had helped him regain some clarity.

Still seated, Vicki continued to use tissues and collected herself once more.

"Are you okay now?" Thomas asked shortly.

"No," was Vicki's quick response. "Frankly, I'm embarrassed you're seeing me like this."

"I didn't see anything, Vicki. I just don't understand why I seem to provoke such anger in you whenever we see each other."

"Because I disagree with you and your, let's say, worldview. That's why."

She glanced out of the window for a moment before turning her head back toward Thomas. Then, in a low, almost whisper, she said, "I really do hate men," grudgingly showing a small smile.

Thomas did not react to what she said, but sighed and said, "Listen to me. How about if I make a quick pot of coffee? Would you like to have a cup with me? I need to sober up a little more."

In a resigned voice, surprisingly even to herself, Vicki replied, "Sure, why not?"

He made the coffee, and the two drank the hot brew while gazing out the front room windows at the beauty of Wright Park and the Seymour Conservatory, illuminated by some streetlights and the brilliance of a waxing gibbous moon. As they appreciated the view, Thomas spoke to Vicki in a quiet and measured voice about his beliefs. He shared these thoughts quietly and sincerely. Ultimately,

Thomas expressed that from his perspective, both he and she were searching for the same thing – the truth.

When Thomas concluded his thoughts, Vicki sipped from her cup and continued taking in the park's now moonlit majesty. After finishing her coffee, Vicki turned on the ottoman and looked at Thomas. "Thanks for the coffee, and I apologize for whatever happened here tonight. I'm not sure what I thought I would accomplish, but, as I told you, I'm pretty strong-willed."

"No apology necessary. I, too, am sorry for being drunk when you arrived - it's not a great look. Really, I'm sorry."

They both stood up. "Thanks for not giving me a hard time," Vicki said, and to Thomas' great surprise, she gave him a hug.

Afterward, they retrieved her coat from the hallway, and Thomas escorted her to her car, noticing it was parked oddly close to the Deep Harbor Tavern.

## 36.

# "You can't tell anyone about this."

The following morning began on a pounding note. Thomas overslept and felt hungover. He found the aspirin bottle in the medicine cabinet and took a few. After showering, which helped a bit, he made a pot of coffee, ate a classic Washington State apple, and called it breakfast. Greasy eggs didn't seem as appealing that morning. Still reflecting on what had happened the previous evening, he started to feel better after finishing the apple down to the core, getting the coffee circulating, and acknowledging to himself that the aspirin had indeed kicked in. At that point, he was ready for the day.

He arrived at the bookstore around twelve-thirty and began to consider what, if anything, he could offer for the books brought to the store by their owners earlier in the day. The offers included cash or checks for differing amounts. Another option was also available: doubling the value of the offer through in-store credit. About an hour later, Minnie arrived at the front counter to inquire if Thomas was working that day. Susan replied, "Yes," and said she would go get him. When Thomas was informed that an *attractive* woman had requested his presence, he rolled his eyes at Susan, which made her grin. He then exited the back room to find Minnie looking at the new arrivals table.

Minnie said, "Thomas, I hope I'm not interrupting something important."

Thomas waved his hand, indicating she wasn't. He replied, "Hi, Minnie. I planned to catch you after work today, but you're here."

As they came together, Minnie said in a quieter voice, "Is there a chance we can go for a walk or something?" Thomas looked around and saw Susan and Sharon standing together. "Ladies, I'm going for a short walk. I'll be back in a few." Both women smiled and nodded. Thomas and Minnie then left the store.

As they walked past the storefronts toward downtown, Minnie took his hand and said, "I need to share something with you." In a lower voice, Thomas replied, "I'm here."

Minnie began, "Last night at The Rail, Vicki showed up around eleven-thirty. She seemed subdued, and I guessed she wanted to talk. We were pretty slow at that time, so I asked Jake if I could take an extended break to speak with her. He agreed, and Vicki and I sat at a table. Once we settled in, Vicki opened up and talked about her life before coming to Tacoma."

Minnie looked at Thomas directly, saying, "This is for your ears only. You can't tell anyone about this." She paused until Thomas acknowledged that what he might hear, he would share with no one.

Thomas said, raising his shoulders, "Who would I tell?"

Satisfied, she proceeded. "Vicki told me she had experienced a situation similar to mine when she was at the University of Washington. She met a guy there, and they fell in love. She got pregnant, and he ran like hell. He dropped out of U-dub, and, as far as she knows, he ended up attending a university in California. I believe she mentioned Berkeley. Nevertheless, Vicki said the whole experience was a nightmare. Roe v. Wade was decided earlier that year, and she chose to have an abortion." Minnie began to cry. "Thomas, these are awful stories." She clutched his arm tightly. "As a result, Vicki became deeply committed to women's rights issues. I suspect that it was at least in part to rationalize what had happened to her. Vicki said that after that, she really hated men. She said she wanted to show men as the liars and losers they were. Since then, Vicki has been a one-person wrecking crew in that respect. Anyway, I started crying, and then she cried too. I'm not sure what the customers who might have noticed us thought. Given my own experience, her story opened so many wounds. I really felt compassion for her. As we sat there, I tried to offer her some words of comfort, and after a while, she calmed down a bit."

Minnie continued. "Surprisingly, when Vicki regained her composure, she mentioned that she had also learned through different experiences that there might be exceptions to the rule." Minnie turned her face toward Thomas and said, "Actually, she told me you could be one of them. She went on to say that you just might be a good guy." Minnie smiled at Thomas. "I told her I thought you were." She leaned her head on Thomas' shoulder.

Then Minnie stopped, turned to Thomas, and, placing her hands on his chest, said in a low and heartfelt voice, "Now, here is what I really want to tell you. I want you to know that I didn't have my abortion because of the arguments made by Vicki about women's rights." She paused, her eyes welling up, and then pushed through, her hands now in fists. "I didn't know if I could be a working single mother and raise a child, knowing who the father was and his full story. I didn't know if I could live with myself— if I somehow convinced you to marry me—and then left it to you to provide for and claim as your own a child that wasn't yours." She closed her eyes momentarily and then reopened them. "Most importantly, now that I've made the decision and gone through with the abortion, I'm in absolute turmoil over what happened. I wake up every day thinking about the baby. It's not something you can just forget. It's something I'll live with for the rest of my life." She started crying.

Thomas instinctively wrapped his arms around Minnie, holding her tightly. After a minute or two, they resumed walking, with Thomas placing his arm around her shoulder. As they slowly made their way past the Temple Theatre, Minnie shared with Thomas that her current plan was to still make it on her own. She looked up at him, smiling through her slightly reddened eyes, and said, "However, I have learned a lot about life over the last couple of years through my experiences after leaving Union. I hope to incorporate what I've learned into any important future decisions I have to make."

The couple continued to talk for a little while longer before Thomas walked her to The Rail to begin her shift. They embraced one more time before she entered the building. After that, Thomas walked back to Commencement Bay Books, lost in thought.

On the way, Thomas realized how deeply he was affected by what Minnie had told him regarding Vicki's confession about her own experience. It was another sad, sad story of what Thomas believed to be the failure of secular values. It was clear that Vicki's experience had led her to have a low opinion of men in general. He also realized that Vicki hadn't mentioned her visit to his apartment to Minnie. Thomas decided he, too, would refrain from sharing this event with Minnie, believing it wouldn't benefit either of the women. If confronted at some point in the future by Minnie about the incident, he would tell her about it, but he didn't think, based on what had occurred between Minnie and Vicki, that the subject would ever come up. He shook his head and mused on how life can be tricky and challenging to navigate. However, he would include Vicki in the ever-growing list of people he remembered in his Mass intentions. Additionally, hearing Minnie explain her own reasoning was heartbreaking. His thoughts became uneasy as he contemplated his role in the events leading up to Minnie's abortion and the extent to which he thought he might share in the blame.

He was just about to start his self-assessment when he entered the bookstore. James caught his attention as he walked in, waving a piece of paper. Thomas approached the counter, and James handed him a phone message from Cynthia Innes, written in James' barely legible scrawl with her number on it.

## 37.

## "...presented him with challenges."

After being updated on what had happened at the store while he was out for a walk with Minnie, Thomas went to the back room to finish working on the book offers for those who had brought in books from their home collections. He also took a moment to call Cynthia. They exchanged greetings, and Cynthia got right to the point by saying that her previous discussion about health issues was never meant to *scare* him away. They both laughed, and Thomas assured her that he certainly hadn't taken their conversation as a reason to avoid seeing each other again. He shared how busy he had been at the store and updated her on his friend Zack, expressing concern over that situation. However, he did not bring up his recent interactions with Minnie or Vicki.

During the conversation, Cynthia asked Thomas if he was still interested in coming over for a movie night, as they had discussed earlier. Thomas replied that it would be great, and they agreed to get together at her place the following Saturday night.

On that Saturday, Thomas, who had a rare weekend off, arrived at Cynthia's apartment at seven. They embraced, but this time, they kissed each other on the cheek. Thomas brought her a couple of new books he had bought at the store, one was a murder mystery, and the other was a historical romance. They chatted about books and authors in the kitchen while Cynthia poured each of them a glass of iced tea and made popcorn.

The movie began as they sat together on the couch in the living room. It was *North by Northwest*, a spy thriller featuring Cary Grant, Eva Marie Saint, and James Mason. Fast-paced and engrossing, the film lived up to the high standards set by producer and director Alfred Hitchcock. They both agreed it was a terrific movie and discussed it during the viewing and after the closing credits rolled.

During the movie and now after, Thomas became conscious of some *tension* between him and Cynthia. They were both making a concerted effort to establish the *new* relationship they had discussed the last time he saw her. He was acutely aware of how physically drawn to her he was. He had noticed a similar sensation when he walked with Minnie the day before yesterday. Thomas recognized that this was a problem. He understood that he and Minnie had been exceptionally into each other before their breakup, and that unfulfilled longing still lingered. He also knew that he had genuinely developed strong feelings for Cynthia since his separation from Minnie. He didn't believe he had crossed any lines with how the last several months had unfolded, yet each situation presented him with challenges. Minnie had recently endured the harrowing ordeal of deciding on and then having an abortion. He had witnessed how fragile her psyche was during their walk a few days ago. The last time he and Cynthia were together, she laid bare her soul to him about her physical condition and the resulting dilemma it presented regarding life, love, and men.

Cynthia swung her feet onto the couch and pressed them against Thomas' leg. "What are you thinking about over there?"

Thomas placed his hand on her feet and replied, "I'm thinking that this is tough, Cynthia." He flashed a small smile and added, "Don't get me wrong, I completely understand where you're coming from - I just don't like it."

"I'm struggling myself, Mr. Klement," she said as she pressed her toes deeper into Thomas' leg.

The conversation shifted back to the movie, with Cynthia describing Cary Grant as drop-dead handsome and expressing her enjoyment of all his films. Thomas told Cynthia how much he looked forward to another movie night and more of that delicious popcorn.

Then, there was a silence in the room, and both felt a bit awkward. Thomas rubbed her feet for a moment before saying, "Well, it's after eleven. Maybe I should think about getting out of your hair." Cynthia closed her eyes briefly and sighed. They were both definitely laboring with their new relationship.

Thomas broke the uncomfortable silence by rising from the couch and gathering the popcorn bowls and glasses. He carried them to the kitchen and placed them in the sink. Cynthia followed him. Thomas said, "As I mentioned, it's late. I go to the early Mass on Sunday mornings, so I think I'll head home."

Cynthia leaned against him as he wrapped his arms around her.

Trying to sound cheerful, Thomas said, "We'll figure this out as we go. I'm glad you've come into my life, Innes."

"Well, I agree with you, but if you really want to know, I'm not entirely happy with what I've created." They smiled tiredly and kissed each other on the cheek before saying goodnight.

As Thomas walked along the edge of the park, he tried to sort out the situation. By the time he reached his apartment, he was no closer to understanding how he and Cynthia would resolve their feelings.

As he got ready for bed and before turning off the bedside lamp, he read his "Prayer for Wisdom" regarding Cynthia and Minnie very slowly and prayerfully.

## 38.

## *"...you threw me a lifeline..."*

After Mass had ended the following morning, Thomas decided to go downstairs and greet Richard Dart. He found Richard at his usual table, and they shook hands. Thomas joined him after pouring himself a coffee and grabbing a donut. Their conversation flowed into a discussion about Pope John Paul II, who had been elected by the College of Cardinals the previous year following the untimely death of Pope John Paul I. Richard was a big fan of the Pole and argued that he would achieve great things as the Roman Pontiff. While Thomas didn't know as much about the pope as Richard did, he also held high hopes for his papacy. If Thomas learned nothing else, he discovered that Richard Dart was extraordinarily well-read and knowledgeable about nearly all topics. This morning, Richard was very excited about John Paul II's first encyclical letter, *Redemptor Hominis* (*The Redeemer of Man*), published just weeks earlier. It effectively outlined the plans for his papacy, and Richard wanted Thomas to promise to take the time to read it. Thomas agreed to Richard's request, and the two enjoyed their coffee, talking for the better part of an hour.

During that time, Father Ron stopped by the table briefly to greet them before heading upstairs to prepare for the final Mass of the day. Finally, Thomas looked at his watch and noticed the morning was passing by. He told Richard that he needed to go to work at the bookstore and, after finishing the last of his coffee, made his way out of the basement and down the street toward Commencement Bay Books.

Since it was Sunday, the store was open from eleven to five. Thomas arrived with fifteen minutes to spare. To his surprise, the entire crew was present. George looked up and said, "Thomas, I'm glad you made it. I want to talk to everyone before the store opens." Thomas walked over to the counter, and George began, "Today I have some very good news," he paused, "I also have some bad news." This, of course, piqued everyone's interest. George slowly turned to Sharon and said, "I want to congratulate Sharon on her time with our little bookstore. She has accepted an offer to be a *bigshot* curator at the Rainier University Library."

A moment of silence followed as the news sank in, and soon everyone started clapping, congratulating, and giving Sharon hugs. Sharon then expressed to the crew how much she loved working at the bookstore and how deeply she would miss everyone.

Looking at the clock and eager to open the door for business, George mentioned he had one more thing to tell them. "With Sharon leaving, I'll need everyone to step up and be prepared to work extra hours until I decide how I want to proceed with staffing the store and other matters. Oh, and one more thing, Thomas, I need you to cover Sharon's shift and also close the store, at least for a while. I apologize, but everyone will need to pitch in. I'll be here too, though I'm not certain what my schedule will look like just yet, but we'll work it out. Thank you."

With that, George walked to the front of the store and unlocked the door. The store was open for business. Susan and James continued chatting with Sharon while George motioned for Thomas to join him in his office. George asked Thomas to close the door behind him.

"It's hard news that we're losing Sharon," George lamented. "She was a huge help with the store's accounting, business forms, and tax filings."

"Yeah, she was great with the paperwork," Thomas agreed.

George raised his eyes and, peering over the top of his glasses, asked, "Will you be able to take on these responsibilities moving forward?"

Thomas smiled at George's uneasy body language and said, "I'm good with about 90% of it. For the other 10%, I'll check with Sharon before she leaves. She'll bring me up to speed. I don't see a problem."

"Good, good," George repeated. "That was a concern of mine. You've made me feel calmer about it." He glanced at some notes he had taken from his briefcase. "Once again, Thomas, are you okay with opening and closing for a while?" He looked at Thomas to gauge his reaction.

"Like I said earlier, when you announced Sharon was leaving, I'm happy to help, George. I still owe you for giving me my job in the first place. I was pretty much lost at that time, but you threw me a lifeline. I haven't forgotten."

George smiled widely and said, "I promise you, Thomas, if you can help me get through this, I'll make it worth your while. Just between you and me, I have some things to handle in the next couple of months, and Sharon's news kind of messed up my plans."

"Like I said, we're good," replied Thomas.

With that, the two shook hands, and Thomas stepped out onto the main floor, noticing the number of customers who had entered the store since he had spoken to George. A nearby customer asked him, "Do you have a clean copy of Milton's *Paradise Lost*, preferably a version in simpler English?" Thomas smiled and replied, "Poetry, let's start there and see what we might discover."

## 39.

# *"...chaos, with all its attendant fury."*

That evening, alone in his apartment, Thomas prepared a simple meal and washed it down with tap water. After eating, he stayed seated at the small kitchen table. His mind drifted, prompting him to reflect on his life. Approaching thirty, he wondered what he had to show for it. Not much, he concluded. A sense of futility settled over him. He vividly recalled that after graduating from Rainier University, he was overwhelmed by a sense of...angst. The thought of a conventional nine-to-five job in Seattle repelled him. It surprised everyone who knew him, including himself, that he moved to the quiet Wright Park neighborhood and decided against owning a car. He remembered that his original plan was simply to go with the flow of events in his life. In his mind, that approach was failing spectacularly. Minnie had endured a traumatic abortion that now seemed to haunt her life. Cynthia, through no fault of her own, had to face a life-threatening disease and its impact on her personal life. His friend Zack had become a stranger he hardly recognized anymore due to drugs and a hollow worldview. All these factors, combined with his feelings of aimlessness and lack of direction, left him despondent.

Thomas realized that as life's problems pressed in on him, the modern secular approaches to dealing with them left him wanting. It was true that he was rediscovering the principles of the faith he had practiced since his youth. Yet even this made him wonder how he could practically apply his religious beliefs to a world that the so-called *enlightened* insisted was purely existential and therefore lacking any objective truth.

Thomas moved to the living room and tried to watch some television, but nothing caught his interest. So, he turned off the TV, straightened up the apartment, did the dishes, and decided to call it a night. He had to reset his alarm for 7:00 a.m. With a sigh, he prepared for a 9-to-9 shift the next day, uncertain how long this arrangement would last. George had been vague about the things he needed to address. Thomas recalled that George had mentioned the term *possibly months* instead of weeks. It had sounded easy to agree to help George when he had asked, but the reality was beginning to feel somewhat like a sentence. He turned off the bedside lamp and, despite his exhaustion, fell into a restless and troubled sleep.

Thomas had a disturbing dream at some point in the early morning hours. It was his ocean beach dream, yet it wasn't. It had been transformed. In this version of the dream, it was late afternoon. A completely disordered wave thrashed its way up the beach. When the wave advanced as far as it could, there was no silence, as in his dream of the dawn wave, but one of chaos and all its attendant fury. The relentless wind howled and crashed while the ocean's water churned. The clamor was intense. Then, the next wave roared and rumbled over the retreating one as if the former had never existed, sweeping up the beach and into the continuous maelstrom.

Thomas awoke drenched in sweat, feeling as if he had fought to maintain his position on the turbulent shore in his dream for far longer than his strength would allow. He removed the blanket covering his sheets and lay there, staring at the ceiling and wondering what had just happened. The clock on the side table read 4:00 a.m. Thomas rubbed his head and eyes, trying to drift back to sleep. At around 4:45, he told himself, *enough,* and climbed out of bed. He moved to his big chair in the living room and flopped down. After another half-hour of sleeplessness, he got up and took a shower. By 5:30, he was brewing coffee and frying an egg with toast. As he sipped his second cup of coffee after breakfast, the disorder of his world pressed in on him.

At 6:45, as the sun rose, Thomas put on his jacket and headed to the park. Once there, he meandered through the tall trees that formed a lofty canopy overhead, providing him a slight sense of solace. He walked around the conservatory. Finally, he crossed the bridge over the pond, sat on a bench, and observed the ducks.

Traces of his dream lingered, fostering a persistent unease that felt both irrational and inescapable.

Then he realized there was still time to attend morning Mass at Holy Trinity, so he got up from the bench and walked quickly to the church. Before the liturgy began, Thomas prayed to the Lord for insight into his unsettling dream. Did it mean anything? Thomas mused that his dawn dream, which he had often experienced since moving away from the ocean, reminded him of how much he loved walking on the beach at sunrise. Those memories of the beach were powerful—just him and all of God's creation. However, his dream last night brought back memories of many afternoons spent on that same beach when the winds would whip up quickly and howl, and the ocean made jarring and dissonant sounds. Yes, he remembered days like that, but last night's dream—really a nightmare—only seemed to add to the pile of difficulties and crises he was already carrying around in his head. It seemed as though everything happening in his life was, to some degree, overwhelming him. As he knelt there, he buried his forehead against his folded hands and prayed, "Dear Lord, help me."

## 40.

## "We've lost a sense of God,..."

As Mass was about to begin, Thomas' thoughts were clouded by his disturbing dream and the trials of his friends. The new *temporary* work schedule required his presence at the store from opening until closing, what, six or seven days a week? But this morning, thankfully, before walking in the park and going to Mass, George had called and offered him a slight reprieve, telling Thomas that he would open the store before heading to an early afternoon appointment. Amid the sacred silence of the Mass, Thomas' heart was heavy with an ever-growing list of petitions, which he laid bare before the Lord, pleading for divine intervention.

As the Mass concluded and the small group of daily congregants began to file out, Thomas lingered near the back of the church, looking toward the altar and the Crucifix on the wall behind it. When he finally stepped outside and started descending the steps, he found Father Sinclair standing alone in front of the church.

"Thomas," Father said warmly. "You look deep in thought."

"I am," Thomas admitted. "Father, do you have a minute? There's something I've been trying to make sense of... the way I see the world."

Father Ron raised his eyebrows and smiled. "I do have some time this morning. I am not going to the hospital until eleven or so. Do you want to continue this over coffee in the rectory?"

Thomas nodded, grateful.

The rectory was a small house just next door. While Father brewed the coffee, they exchanged small talk—about the weather, parish news, the Mariners' chances this year. Then they settled into a pair of deep wood and leather chairs across from an unlit fireplace. The aroma of coffee hung in the air, warm and grounding.

Thomas took a sip and exhaled. "Father, I feel like everything I believed in growing up is unraveling. Attending Mass with my mother and what I learned in my church catechism classes gave me great hope and a strong foundation to work through my problems. But while I was in college, the basic message was that secularism had replaced all that religious foolishness. I was taught that reason alone could resolve the world's problems. Religion, especially in public life, should be set aside. And that's what I did. I have kept it separate."

He hesitated, then added, "Secularism puts man at the center of everything. That's where I get stuck. Everything feels... off."

Father Ron leaned back in his chair. "We might need a little more time for this discussion," he joked. They both smiled.

"Thomas, you're not wrong. We've lost a sense of God in our culture today. It's been happening slowly, over centuries, but now it's everywhere. Secular thought tells us we don't need God. And if there's no God, then there is no sin — at least, not in the way we used to understand it."

He set his cup down, his tone tightening.

"And when sin, or moral clarity, disappears, things start to shift. What was once unthinkable becomes acceptable. Acts like abortion — once seen as tragic — become defended, even celebrated. Eventually, the only real sins are those that offend not God, but man. And that," he said quietly, "is a dangerous path to go down."

He paused before continuing. "You even see it creeping into the Church. We talk a lot about mercy these days — and rightly so — but sometimes the hard truths get lost. Fewer people go to confession – a lot fewer. The commandments? For many, they're now background noise. That worries me."

Thomas nodded, feeling the weight of what Father had said. Then something inside him broke open.

"I have a friend who had an abortion. Another is using drugs. And still another — through no fault of her own — has a life-threatening genetic condition. I don't know how to help them, or even how to think clearly about what they're going through. I feel helpless."

Father Ron studied him, sensing how deeply Thomas cared. "That's the thing, Thomas. Secularism loosens all the anchors. From the pill to no-fault divorce, we've redefined relationships, simplified and watered-down responsibility. Even conscience now means doing what *you believe* to be right, not what *is* right. And the fallout? Broken families, lost young people, suffering that feels random and cruel."

He stood up and refilled their cups.

Thomas accepted the refill with a nod. "Thanks, Father. I try to sort these things out on my own at night. But it's not the same as talking to someone like you."

"I'm glad you came," Father said, settling back into his chair. "Now, about your friend with the illness — suffering is one of the hardest things for anyone to understand. People ask, If God exists, why does He allow it? And I don't blame them."

Thomas leaned forward. "That's exactly what I want to know. I need something solid I can hold onto."

Father Ron pointed at him gently. "Then you should talk to Richard Dart. He wrote something a few years ago — a reflection on suffering in the Old Testament. It's worth reading."

Thomas raised an eyebrow. "What about your take?"

Father smiled. "Well, here's mine. The Church teaches that when we suffer — and choose to offer that suffering in union with Christ's — it becomes part of something bigger. It's not wasted. It draws us closer to Christ, who also suffered. And somehow, in God's mysterious way, it can help others too."

He paused, "It's called Redemptive Suffering. Suffering exists because of our brokenness, but that doesn't mean it's meaningless. It can open us to grace. It can shape us in love. And yes, it can even become redemptive."

He sat back and folded his hands. "Between Original Sin, Job's story in the Old Testament, and our redemption through the Suffering Christ is the answer you're seeking. I would start your quest by talking to Richard. He has a good way of putting things."

"Thank you, Father. I'll do just that," Thomas replied, feeling satisfied that he had asked Father the questions in the first place.

Their conversation drifted to Father Sinclair's future at Holy Trinity and his thoughts about his eventual retirement. When the coffee ran out, they decided to meet again for another discussion. They both enjoyed themselves, and Thomas left, hoping their next conversation would happen sooner rather than later.

## 41.

## *"Maybe you could give me some advice."*

Thomas greeted James, who had been waiting outside the store. Klement unlocked the front door, and both entered. It was another twelve-hour day, Thomas thought to himself as he slowly walked over to the front counter. James turned on some of the store lights, and the two of them began discussing how many boxes of books needed to be broken down by category for shelving and who would handle which sections. James was also putting in a twelve-hour shift today because Susan had some appointments. Although Thomas felt tired, he was in a relatively good mood, all things considered.

He had spoken with Cynthia the day before, and they had arranged another movie night for later in the week. She had been feeling better and was in a cheerful mood. They discussed some new construction on the opposite side of the park from where they both lived, Thomas' work schedule, and her office stories. The call lasted about three-quarters of an hour and was satisfying for both when they finally hung up.

Nate had stopped by the store the day before to talk about Zack. According to him, the people he met with to discuss options for Zack were friendly and open to working out a plan to help his friend. Nate told Thomas they were going to meet in about a week to finalize the details. Now, as he explained to Thomas, all he needed to do was convince Zack to go with him and assure him that it was in his best interests. Thomas asked a few questions and apologized for not being able to help with Zack because of his hectic work schedule.

Thomas decided he needed to talk to George as soon as an opportunity presented itself to check on how he was doing. Thomas had become concerned about George's behavior at the store. There was also a noticeable secretiveness about what he did during the day when he had to leave the store for an hour or two or more. Thomas was starting to wonder why George had not hired someone to replace Sharon after her departure. Yes, it was a good time to sit down with George to see what was going on.

With the long hours and short staffing, the days at the store became less enjoyable. They felt more like work and less interesting. The extra four hours a day and the lack of days off—unless arranged with George—were beginning to take a toll.

Thomas thought about Minnie. He had seen her two or three times since their last serious talk when they had gone for a walk together. Those encounters had been brief at The Rail while she was working. He decided to try to see her there again after work. And, since Tuesday nights business-wise this time of year were usually slow, he hoped she might have more time to chat. Then he considered that she might be off today, but quickly dismissed that idea and reassured himself that he would go to the pub tonight and hope to see her there.

Thomas arrived at The Rail around nine-thirty. He noted that he was right about the less-than-full house. Now, was Minnie here? He took a seat at the end of the bar, as was his habit. Shortly after, a young lady arrived and asked if he wanted to place an order. Thomas ordered his usual fish and chips and a pint of lager. The Heidelberg arrived before the chips, and he sipped the beer while looking around the room. A minute later, he saw Minnie taking an order from a table in the corner. As she finished,

Thomas waved at her, and she noticed him. She came right over and expressed how pleased she was to see him. They chatted for a moment, but then she had to return to the kitchen. She returned shortly and asked Thomas to sit at a table she was pointing to. By then, his fish and chips had arrived, and she helped him move his dinner to the table. Then he sat down, and she joined him.

"I'm on my break now," said Minnie as she reached out to take his hand.

Thomas' face lit up, and he replied, "That's great. How have you been?"

"I've been okay. Like you, I've been putting in a lot of hours. As they say, work takes your mind off things."

Thomas nodded in agreement. In a tone slightly more serious, he asked, "So, for real, how are you doing?"

"As well as can be expected, I guess."

Thomas noticed that Minnie had appeared so vibrant and carefree, not all that long ago. Now, she bore the marks of worldly experience, though her beauty remained undiminished.

As Thomas stared at her, Minnie said, "Oh, Thomas, I wanted to tell you that rather than running around having a good time and meeting new friends, I've started spending more time at Charlotte's house, enjoying her beautiful view of the bay, and I've been writing some short stories." She waited for his reaction.

Thomas sat up and leaned forward slightly. "Minnie, that's great!"

She could tell immediately that he was genuinely pleased. "It was hard at first, but since I had done it when I was younger, I remembered some of the techniques and practices I used to construct my stories. It still works."

"Minnie, I would really love to read some of them if you'd let me."

"Oh, Thomas, I thought about you wanting to read my stories, and it freaked me out, I must admit."

They both laughed. "But if you really want to, I've already decided that if you asked, I would say yes." Minnie blushed and said, "Maybe you could give me some advice."

"I can't wait to read them," grinned Thomas.

"Well, if you really mean it, I can bring them by the bookstore tomorrow on my way to work."

"That would be perfect," Thomas replied.

"Oh, and Thomas," she pointed at him, "You be nice to me after you've read them. This is really nerve-wracking."

They both laughed once more.

By now, Thomas had finished his meal, and Minnie glanced at the clock on the wall and said, "My break time is over, and then some. I'm so glad you stopped by. I don't get to see you much since you've practically moved into the bookstore. When will that change?"

"Soon, I hope. I'm going to talk to my boss about it. I'll let you know."

They got up from the table and embraced. In a softer voice, Minnie said, "I really miss you, Thomas." As they released each other, Minnie gave Thomas a kiss, and he didn't stop her.

Staying true to her word, the next day, Minnie delivered a packet containing ten of her short stories, with lengths varying from as little as six pages for one to a few stories nearing thirty pages each. Thomas was not there, having gone to the bank with the daily deposit.

That night, Thomas took the packet home with him, sat down in his chair, and started reading. The stories were captivating. It took him three nights to read all of them. As he finished the last story, he leaned back and said to himself, "Minnie has real talent. Those stories were excellent and truly compelling. I can't wait to talk to her about them." Then, he glanced back at the packet of stories and wondered, "Does she know she's that good?"

The next day at the store, James asked Thomas when George would be in. "I don't know," Thomas replied, "but I'm going to give him a call to check on him." James nodded and went upstairs. Thomas frowned and wondered, "What on earth is going on with George?"

As he dialed George's number, Thomas caught a glimpse of Minnie walking in front of the store. After reaching the door, she stepped inside. He hung up the phone before finishing dialing. "Hi, Minnie," Thomas said.

She smiled and cautiously approached him. "Hello, Thomas. I wanted to check if you had a chance to look over any of my stories."

"I did, Ms. Cadieux." He paused.

She halted just before the counter.

He smiled. "Of course, I read the stories. "Minnie," he paused again for effect, then continued, "They were terrific, wonderful. It's as if you've been writing short stories for years."

"Oh, Thomas. You're not making fun of me, are you?" She tilted her head slightly, looking almost anxious."

"Minnie, I loved them." She stepped closer to him.

They discussed the stories for about ten minutes, and then the store became busy. Excited, Minnie said she had to leave but wanted to arrange a time for a more in-depth discussion.

As Minnie walked outside and down the sidewalk in front of the store, Thomas, who was watching her every step, saw her say *yes* to herself, accompanied by a triumphant little shake of her fist.

## 42.

## *"Please enlighten me."*

When Thomas arrived at his apartment that night, he felt a quiet sense of satisfaction. Seeing Minnie and having a brief conversation with her about her short stories lifted his spirits and reminded him of their time together. He genuinely meant what he told Minnie about how much he admired her writing prowess.

After standing in front of the refrigerator *grazing* for a couple of minutes and calling it dinner, Thomas settled into his chair. He sorted through Minnie's stories, placing his favorites on top of the pile. He returned them all to her original packet and set it on the kitchen table before heading to bed.

The next day, he took the stories with him to work and planned to reread them over the next week or so during his lunch break in the back room.

After locking up the store that evening, Thomas went to Cynthia's for movie night. They watched *Please Don't Eat the Daisies*, starring Doris Day and David Niven. The lighthearted and entertaining romantic comedy had them both laughing throughout the night. To Thomas, Niven was a true talent.

Despite the laughter, an underlying discontent lingered between the two movie watchers. After the show ended, they engaged in small talk, each aware of the unresolved tension in their relationship. Cynthia glanced at the clock. It was almost one, and she asked Thomas when he had to be at work in the morning.

Thomas replied, "Nine."

Cynthia reluctantly urged him to be on his way. They parted with an unsatisfactory embrace.

On his walk home, Thomas reminded himself once again that he needed to maintain respect for Cynthia and Minnie while searching for the key to solve his puzzle.

Later that night, before heading to bed, he pulled out his slightly crumpled piece of paper with his prayer of discernment regarding both women and prayed it. At the end of the prayer, Thomas read a short prayer from a holy card he had picked up at church the previous Sunday. It read, "Trust that God has a plan for your life and your relationships. Surrender your worries to Him and have faith that He will guide you on the right path."

Two days later, Thomas found himself crawling around in the Philosophy Section of Commencement Bay Books, trying to alphabetize some recently acquired used tomes by author. Why, he wondered, does it seem like all the books I personally have to shelve or re-shelve always end up on the bottom shelf of the bookcase? He had not yet completed this half-serious thought when a customer interrupted him. He looked up and immediately recognized Richard Dart staring down at him. Thomas said, "Hello, Richard," as he stood up from kneeling. Richard had been in the Religion Section when he noticed his younger friend from Holy Trinity on his hands and knees in the next aisle, so he walked over to say hello.

After exchanging pleasantries, the two men walked to the railing overlooking the main floor and gazed at the endless rows of shelves filled with thousands of books. It was a sight that only *bookers,* as Thomas referred to them, could truly appreciate.

Thomas recalled that Father Sinclair had suggested he speak to Richard about the concept of suffering. "Richard," Thomas began, "Father Ron mentioned that you are the person I should ask about the issue of suffering. You know, how can a good God allow terrible things to happen?"

Richard paused to think. "Thomas, I've wrestled with that question for years, and yes, I've written about what the Old Testament has had to say about it. It is, how should I put it, a fascinating topic."

"Do you have any time to explain things to the guy you just found crawling around on the floor?" Richard chuckled and replied, "Sure, Thomas. When would be good for you?" "Well, I don't know your schedule, but mine is a mess. I'd really appreciate it if you could talk to me now or at another time here at the store."

"Now, works for me. I'm just out stretching my legs and looking at old books."

Thomas said, "Great. Let me tell Susan and James that I'm going to have my lunch in the back room, and we can head there now if you're up for it?"

"Let's do it," replied the respected Mr. Dart.

Thomas shared his lunch plans with Susan and James, and then he and Richard disappeared into the back room. Thomas offered and poured a cup of coffee for both himself and Richard. They sat at the lunch table, one on each side, and began their conversation.

Thomas said, "Richard, Father Ron asked me to speak with you about my question regarding why there is suffering. Please enlighten me."

Richard, who had a certain reticence and restraint about things in general, seemed almost eager by his standards to engage with the younger man's question. "Well, Thomas, as I mentioned, it's an absorbing subject. In modern times, the character Ivan Karamazov posed the question most famously in Dostoevsky's *The Brothers Karamazov*. I'm summarizing now. If God is real and made this world, then presumably He shaped it with intention and purpose. In that case, isn't He ultimately responsible for all that occurs in it? Why, then, does He allow so much pain and evil?" Richard paused, allowing Thomas to take in what he had just said.

Then, resuming, he said, "The question itself, the why of evil and suffering, at least for our purposes, traces back to the Old Testament in the Bible, most notably to the story of Job and the trials he faced. In the story, we know how this very prosperous and devout man of God loses everything: his family, wealth, and health. Then Job falls to the ground and says to God, I'm paraphrasing again, but I think I'm very close, Naked I came from my mother's womb, and naked I will return. The Lord has given, and the Lord has taken away, blessed be the name of the Lord (see Job 1:21)."

"Although Job's story spans over forty chapters, the core explanation of suffering is found in those two verses. The essence of Job's message is not one of resignation. Instead, it reflects an act of trust. Job understands that everything he ever possessed, including his family, health, and wealth, were gifts bestowed upon him by God. These same gifts could also be taken from him at any moment. Job responds with faith. He humbly accepts what has happened and entrusts his life to God's providence. Job recognizes God as the essence of his existence. He owes his life and being to God. Furthermore, he believes that God will not abandon him. This is not blind faith on his part. It is a faith that grapples with the reality of suffering while holding onto God's mercy and goodness. True faith is trusting in God despite life's trials."

Richard took a breath and continued. "In the book's dramatic conclusion, near the end of his trial, Job asks God, *Why?* Job's misery demonstrates that although God permits suffering and evil, He is not the cause of it. Ultimately, it points to God's respect for the integrity of human freedom to choose."

"Regarding natural evil, such as earthquakes, floods, fires, and other calamities, God suggests that some aspects of creation are beyond human understanding. While natural evil is allowed, it serves a purpose greater than our comprehension, one that requires trust in God's ultimate goodness and plan."

Richard smiled and said, "While studying the subject, I ended up memorizing a few passages near the end of the Job narrative. I wanted to understand what this story meant and how it applied to Job or any of us, for that matter. At first, Job thought that all the terrible things happening to him were the result of some sin he had committed, believing that he was being punished for it. However, with his finite comprehension, he tells God that he does not believe he has committed any sin. Regarding this statement, God eventually answers Job *out of the storm…* (Job 38:1a) and speaks with him. This transcendent meeting allows God to explain to Job how little he understands about the things he discusses. Later, after God enlightens him, Job acknowledges his lack of wisdom concerning evil and suffering. He states, *I have spoken but did not understand; things too wonderful for me, which I did not know* (Job 42:3b). It is then that Job gains sudden insight. *By hearsay, I had heard you, but now my eyes have seen you* (Job 42:5b). At this point, Job is not referring to a vision of God per se but perhaps to the knowledge or practical wisdom acquired from his encounter with God. He learns that God cannot be held accountable. God's ways are far beyond man's capacity to comprehend. Job now understands that he needs God. Through Job's special encounter with God, the Almighty gives himself to Job. In other words, God's presence becomes the solution to Job's problem. Job learns that he must place his trust in God in all his life experiences."

Richard paused again.

Thomas finished his last sip of coffee.

Richard said, "In summary, the Book of Job remains the best exploration of the problem of suffering until the incarnation of the Son of God in the person of Jesus Christ. Then, through Christ's passion and death on the Cross, Jesus brought about the salvation of humanity. In doing so, the Lord provided us with a much fuller and more insightful view of suffering and its meaning. Of course, the Church teaches that we can participate in Christ's redemptive work by uniting our sufferings with His Passion. All suffering will ultimately be transformed and find meaning in the light of eternal life."

Thomas jotted down a few more notes for himself and thanked Richard for his explanation. Before finishing their conversation, Richard shared one last thought: "Christ grants us grace (his favor, his love, the influence of the Holy Spirit) to bear our individual crosses in life. This grace fosters endurance, or perhaps you could say strength and fortitude. St. Peter tells us, *Rejoice to the extent that you share in the sufferings of Christ, so that when his glory is revealed, you may also rejoice exultantly* (1 Peter 4:13). St. Paul states, *I have been crucified with Christ...* (Galatians 2:20). To be like Jesus is to be shaped by the Cross." With that, Richard concluded his summary of the research he had done and waited for Thomas to finish scribbling down the last of his notes.

"Some of those Bible quotes might not be 100% accurate, but they're real close," Richard added.

"Richard, I can't thank you enough for your thoughts and that wonderful overview."

Richard paused briefly and said, "It's interesting that you would mention *thoughts*. If you're looking for a unique perspective on Christianity, suffering, and its significance, I suggest reading Blaise Pascal's work, *Pensées* (Thoughts). He was a man who lived in 17th-century France and truly understood the nature of suffering. Yes, that's what I would recommend you read."

Thomas said, "*Pensées*, I've heard of that. In fact, I think we have two or three copies in the store. Richard, you've really impressed me with your knowledge of the subject."

"It was my pleasure. I'm glad I looked into the topic before, or I wouldn't have been much help, would I?"

They both laughed.

The two men retraced their steps to the store's second level, where they found the copies of *Pensées* that Thomas had recalled. Richard examined them and said, "Go with this one."

Thomas thanked Richard once again and then had another thought. "Richard, would you have time to look at some short stories a friend of mine wrote? I'd really appreciate your feedback on them, like whether they are, I don't know, worthy of being published."

Richard replied, "Sure, that's what I do. I read. Do you need them back right away?"

"No, there's no rush at all. I'll get them for you." Thomas went downstairs to the back room and retrieved the packet of short stories. He returned and handed the packet to Richard. "Thanks again for your time, Richard."

Richard simply smiled and walked out the door.

## 43.

# *"It has been a grueling ordeal."*

Then there was George. Old Mr. Renko had been as mysterious and secretive as anyone could imagine over the past month or so. After Richard Dart left the store, George arrived unannounced and settled into his office. A little over an hour later, Thomas entered the room and asked

George if they could talk. Looking up from the papers he was reading, Renko sighed with an expression of resignation and, with a wave of his arm, invited Thomas to join him. Thomas, somewhat warily, closed the door behind him and slid into the chair in front of his employer's desk. George looked haggard.

"George, are you okay?" Thomas asked, his voice tinged with trepidation.

"Between you and me, Thomas, no. I'm not okay. Ever since I got my diagnosis and Sharon left, it's been really tough."

"What diagnosis?" Thomas asked, his gaze lifting to meet that of his boss, mentor, and friend.

"I will tell you, Thomas, but you must not share it with anyone else. Promise me."

"I won't, George, I promise."

"My doctor told me I have prostate cancer."

Thomas was left speechless and just stared at Renko.

"That's how I took the news, Thomas. I just stared at that doctor. He told me I was old, and it was common for a man my age to develop it. I asked him what could be done. He said there were several options for how to proceed. We could watch and wait to see how it progressed. He could remove the prostate through surgery. But then, the doctor quickly added, because of your age, surgery was a riskier proposition and may lead to all kinds of urinary problems. However, he mentioned a third option that he believed would be the best for me. That option was radiation therapy. He explained that I would receive doses of radiation for several weeks without the risks and side effects associated with surgery. I've been undergoing radiation treatments for the past six weeks. I must tell you, Thomas, I feel incredibly exhausted after each session. I often must go home and rest for hours. This fatigue has been overwhelming. It has been a grueling ordeal. Hopefully, once I finish the treatments in a couple of weeks, I can regain my vitality, which is completely absent today."

Looking at George now, after hearing him share his story, Thomas noticed a hollowness etched into the old man's face. In light of what he had just heard, it was clear that George had lost weight. He looked gaunt. With heartfelt sympathy, Thomas said, "Oh, George, I'm so sorry to hear what you've been going through."

"Thank you, Thomas." George shook his head and repeated, "Remember, you said you wouldn't tell anyone."

"I did, and I won't," Thomas assured him.

The room was silent for a moment until George spoke up, saying, "Anyway, I'm nearing the end of my treatments, and I hope to recover well enough to spend more time at the store. However, I realize I can't ask the three of you to continue with the demanding work schedule I've imposed on you. So, I will tell you that I've hired a couple of new staff." He paused to gauge Thomas' reaction.

Thomas was still stunned by George's revelation about his predicament, and his expression did not change when Renko announced hiring new staff.

George pressed on, "Here's what I've done. I've hired a young man named Dwight Newman. He'll help us provide some time off for Susan and James."

Now, gathering himself, Thomas was able to reengage and said, "That is good news, George.

"I've also hired a woman, Linda Stuart, who has significant experience in the book-selling business. There is one caveat: I had to offer her the day manager job to get her to agree. She wouldn't accept my offer if it involved night hours. I thought it was worth it to give you some time off. You will now have some days off again, and you'll have the mornings off, but you'll still need to be my night manager for now." Now, George was worried about how Thomas might react.

Thomas smiled and said, "George, it's great to look forward to getting my mornings back and having some days off. Yet I'm more concerned about your health. Is there anything I can do for you?"

George's eyes softened. "Thomas, you've been my best hire, and you're my friend. Just be a friend and help me through this trial I'm facing." With that, George quickly wiped one eye with the sleeve of his shirt.

The two men continued their conversation. Thomas learned that the new hires were scheduled to start working the next day, and once everyone was up to speed, the staffing schedule would revert to normal.

George suggested that Thomas sleep in a little the next day, as he would be coming in to inform the staff about the new hires. Thomas expressed his gratitude.

The news about George was sobering. Thomas hoped that old man Renko would survive his treatments and recover well. Thomas thought the latest hires were a blessing. He really needed the time off.

## 44.

# *"...a pathway...in the silence of our souls"*

Thomas carried the copy of *Pensées* he had purchased earlier in the day as he walked home that night. He also had three other books with him that he had *borrowed* for the evening. They focused on Blaise Pascal and his writings. After grabbing something to eat, he returned to the living room, removed some papers that had *accumulated* on the oversized ottoman in front of him, settled into his chair, and browsed through the three books he needed to return to the store the next day.

By the end of the evening, Thomas discovered that Pascal had been a child prodigy educated by his father. He was an intellectual and a polymath who, in addition to his contributions to scientific study and significant advancements in mathematics and probability theory, also invented what became known as the mechanical "Pascaline" calculator. These achievements alone formed a remarkable body of work. Despite all his achievements, his contributions to theology, philosophy, and literature remained his most enduring legacy. Surprisingly, Thomas discovered that Pascal completed all this work in a remarkably short life, passing away in 1662 at just 39 years old.

As the night deepened, Thomas filled page after page with notes on a white paper tablet as one revelation followed another in Pascal's biography. He couldn't mark up the books he was reading because, of course, they belonged to George and the bookstore. When he finished perusing the last of the books about Pascal, the clock read 3:05 a.m. Fatigued but enriched, he laid down his pen as weariness settled over him like a shroud. He stretched, got up from his chair, and surrendered to his need for sleep.

The next day, Thomas arrived at the bookstore around ten-thirty, following George's advice to sleep in. He returned the books he had borrowed to the shelves and learned from Susan that George had been in when the store opened and had shared his announcement about his new hires. Renko introduced the new staff and presented the improved schedule for the next couple of weeks before taking his leave. No one was more excited than Thomas when he realized he had three days off starting the next day. Klement, who was utterly exhausted, couldn't wait.

When Thomas returned to his apartment that night, he decided he would not tackle the *Pensées* until he was well-rested. Completely exhausted, he quickly fell asleep.

Thomas woke up close to eight, feeling wonderfully rested. He calculated that he had slept for nearly nine hours.

After a light breakfast, he grabbed his copy of *Pensées* and walked to the park, where he settled on a bench overlooking the duck pond and began reading.

Thomas plunged into Pascal's thoughts, wishing for another cup of coffee but telling himself he should earn it. Pascal had died before he could write his great apologetic work. After his death, his sister collected his notes or fragments and published them posthumously.

Thomas read the book for nearly three hours before realizing he truly needed the cup of coffee he had considered earlier. While reading *Pensées*, he annotated parts of the book, underlining and circling sections and jotting down notes in the margins. He recorded a few thoughts on a smaller tablet he had brought, which fit snugly into his jacket pocket. He gathered the book, pen, and notepad, stood up, stretched his legs, and walked over to The Harvester Restaurant. There, he enjoyed the cup of coffee he had been thinking about, accompanied by a scone. While sipping the coffee, with one generous refill, Thomas reflected on what he had read. After finishing, he returned to his apartment.

Thomas resumed his reading as the hours slipped away. He read all afternoon, marking up the book, jotting down notes in the margins, and writing separate thoughts on a larger tablet of paper. He took a quick break for a sandwich and an apple before returning to his book. Time flew by once more. It was after ten when he finished the *Pensées*. He hadn't spoken to anyone that day. He had immersed himself in Pascal's book, hoping to gain insight into his own life's questions and a deeper understanding of his religious faith. Rubbing his eyes, he headed for the bedroom.

The next morning, Thomas gathered his notes and the now marked-up copy of *Pensées*, placing them on the large ottoman. He tore the pages from the tablet one by one and sorted them into thematic stacks, including the contents of the smaller tablet. Using a felt-tipped marker, he added theme-based headings for each pile and arranged the stacks in a preliminary order. Then, he reviewed the book, utilizing underlined passages and margin notes, and created new notes to place on their corresponding stacks. This process consumed most of the morning, after which he paused to grab something to eat.

Thomas sifted through the first stack of notes labeled Original Sin. The phrase had sounded abstract to him all his life – too old, too weighty. However, reading Pascal had changed all that. Suddenly, it wasn't about ancient transgressions or theological conjecture. No, it was about what he saw in himself. According to Church teaching, we were made in the image of God. Nonetheless, something in us had clearly broken. Pascal put it plainly without embellishment: we are a paradox – capable of greatness yet drawn constantly toward wretchedness. Original Sin wasn't just a doctrine. It was a mirror. We inherited a flaw, not of our own choosing. We focus on ourselves. We have a blindness to what matters most.

The tension between the concepts of greatness and wretchedness explains so much: why do we build cathedrals and yet make war?

And then there was suffering itself. The Frenchman didn't offer a way around it – he knelt beside it. In one of his *thoughts,* specifically "The Mystery of Jesus," he wrote of Christ's agony in the garden and of his sorrow unto death. Thomas could hardly read it without catching his breath. Jesus didn't explain suffering away – He entered it. Embraced it. Transformed it.

It was here that Thomas began to understand what the Church meant by *offering it up.* St. Paul had spoken of this mystery. It meant joining one's suffering to Christ's, making it part of something larger, something redemptive, for the salvation of the world.

Pascal believed God was hidden from man, not absent. He thought we should look inward. For Pascal, a pathway to the Almighty would be found in the silence of our souls. In that silence, Thomas stopped analyzing and overthinking things. Something stirred within him—not certainty, but presence.

For Thomas, this reflected Pascal's faith-based explanation of humanity's ultimate purpose and hope. It helped to clarify the world and the suffering within it. It contrasted with the often bleak outlook of the purely secular existential perspective prevalent in the mid-to-late 20th century. Pascal believed that living a meaningful life required humility, acknowledgment of one's limitations, and dependence on God's divine grace.

A feeling of hope, with perhaps even a dash of confidence, washed over Thomas. After nearly thirty years of life, he felt as if he had discovered a pathway. He knew this trail would still be full of questions and challenges, yet it would lead to meaning in his life. He was sure of it. He was elated, yet suddenly drained. He grabbed his jacket and walked to The Rail. He checked and found that Minnie was not working that night. He had wanted to share his newfound hope with her. However, Thomas didn't allow himself to feel downcast by the news that she was not there. Instead, he ordered a burger with fries and a beer. The meal revived his spirits. His exploration of Pascal's work and what he had learned allowed him to truly relax for the first time in what felt like an eternity. He quickly said a mental prayer, thanking God for letting him experience Blaise Pascal's extraordinary book of thoughts.

## 45.

# *"...his image fades away..."*

Back home that evening and into the late morning of the following day, after another good night's sleep, Thomas continued to process what he had learned from his now favorite 17th-century Frenchman. He concluded that Pascal's perspective, framework, and method of applying his thoughts to the world's reality notably resonated with his own ongoing, yet undeveloped, reflections. Viewed through Pascal's lens, the part-time philosopher and theologian directly confronted life's big questions and presented a compelling argument—at least for Thomas—about why life was the way it was and how to approach it.

That afternoon at the bookstore, while working with the new guy, Dwight, Thomas discovered a devotional work filled with spiritual writings and prayers among the boxes of used books the store had purchased from customers. It was written by his new best friend, Monsieur Pascal. He promptly walked to the front counter and bought the volume for himself.

During a slow stretch that evening, while waiting to close the store for the day, Thomas thumbed through his new book and came across an extended prayer titled "Prayer to Ask God for the Proper Use of Sickness." The prayer was quite lengthy, spanning a dozen pages. Cynthia entered his thoughts, and he resolved to read the entire prayer that night. If he found that it aligned with Cynthia's situation, he would share it with her. Later, in the solitude of his living room, Thomas read and studied Pascal's "Prayer to Ask God for the Proper Use of Sickness."

When he finished the prayer, Thomas quickly jotted down some notes. He understood clearly that Pascal encouraged those who recited the prayer to view illness as a means of spiritual growth rather than merely a physical affliction. The prayer emphasized the opportunity for believers to detach themselves from worldly problems and focus on the virtues of patience and humility, seeking God's grace to endure suffering. Ultimately, the prayer advocated for viewing illness in a redemptive light, aligning with the Church's teaching of uniting one's suffering with Christ's own suffering. In summary, the prayer fostered a spirit of surrender to the Lord and a commitment to do His will.

The next morning, he took the slim volume to the park and read the prayer again while sitting on a bench under a tree at the foot of the hill leading up to the Conservatory. The morning sun shone brightly, sparkling against the great glass structure sitting atop the higher ground. This time, Thomas pulled out a small ballpoint pen from his jacket pocket and marked some passages in the prayer that struck a chord with him. He added a few notes in the margin and decided to try to meet up with Cynthia.

Later that day at the bookstore, Thomas called her, and they exchanged greetings. Each shared what they had been up to over the past week or so, and then Thomas suggested they get together. Cynthia proposed another movie night at her place.

Thomas accepted her invitation, and two nights later, he arrived at her door at nine-thirty sharp. Upon entering her apartment, he noticed that Ms. Innes looked particularly attractive. The way she twisted her long, dark hair and pinned it up on top of her head always caught his attention. It gave her a distinct charm that Thomas clearly appreciated. Cynthia broke his fixation on her hair by asking, "How have you been, Thomas?"

"Well, I'm finally starting to recover from those crazy hours I worked until about a week ago."

"I've missed you," Cynthia said with an enigmatic smile and a look Thomas could only describe to himself as slightly alluring. Caught off guard, he felt it was apparent and tried to recover as best he could.

"Likewise," Thomas replied, inwardly shaking his head and wishing he had said something more meaningful.

She stared at him for a moment, sighed, and then kissed him on the cheek. "I'll go make the popcorn."

Feeling a bit lost, Thomas gathered himself and said, in a smaller-than-expected voice, "No, let me make it tonight," seizing the opportunity to regain his composure. Without waiting for a response, he headed to the kitchen.

When he returned to the living room with two bowls of white popcorn, customized to their tastes (plain for Cynthia), she had already turned on the TV and was sitting on the couch. Thomas sat down and placed the bowls side by side on the coffee table. He laid a kitchen towel between them and watched Cynthia as she used the remote to find the right channel for the movie.

They chose a British film from 1966, *Blow-Up*, starring David Hemmings, Vanessa Redgrave, and Sarah Miles. It centered on a successful photographer in London who, while taking photographs in a park, later discovers that his photos may contain evidence of foul play, specifically murder. The rest of the film showcased Hemmings enlarging photographs to uncover what they might reveal. In fact, his photos suggested the possibility of a body, so he later returns to the park to find it. He goes back to his studio and flat to call the police, only to discover that someone has stolen all his photos and film. Again, he returns to the park, this time to see that the body had also been removed. With the photos, film, and body gone, there is no way to prove anything.

In the final scene, Hemmings watches a troupe of mimes play a game of tennis. At one point, the mimes look at him and gesture for him to return a tennis shot that has landed near him. Hemmings pretends to pick up the imaginary tennis ball and throws it back. They resume their soundless game. Moments later, as Hemmings continues to watch the mimes, he begins to hear the ball being volleyed back and forth by the players. Then, as he stands there, listening to the sound of the ball, his image fades away from the screen, leaving only a shot of the grass where he had been standing. The movie ends.

Both Thomas and Cynthia found the movie to be *different,* to say the least. They speculated about what the film was supposed to mean. Was the absence of a solution to the crime intended to suggest something? Did it reflect the uncertainty of life? The meaning seemed to be left to the viewer's imagination. Thomas added that it seemed a bit Camus-like to him, as he reflected on his college days of reading existential authors about the absurdity of life.

Thomas gathered the bowls and the towel and returned them to the kitchen. When he got back to the living room, he noticed that Cynthia had turned off the TV and swung her legs up onto the couch. Thomas sat down beside her feet. They chatted for a while, and then Thomas began rubbing her feet. She said, "Oh, that feels wonderful, don't stop," closing her eyes in contentment.

Thomas smiled and obliged. As they sat there, with Thomas rubbing Cynthia's feet, he quietly began to share his thoughts about his newfound author, Blaise Pascal. He provided her with an overview of what he had learned from the theological philosopher and what it meant to him. Still enjoying the foot rub, Cynthia listened intently, her face reflecting curiosity and contemplation. Thomas then turned to the prayer that Pascal had written about the proper use of sickness and attempted to explain it to her.

Surprisingly, at least to Thomas, at the end of his detailed explanation of the prayer, Cynthia made an uncertain face and conveyed to Thomas that some of his explanation still eluded her. They continued to discuss the topic, exchanging thoughts. Twenty minutes later, Cynthia finally said, "Thomas, I think maybe I need to read the prayer for myself," with the slightest hint of frustration in her voice.

Thomas quickly agreed, apologizing for not bringing a copy of the prayer with him. He mentioned that he would make a copy at work and bring it the next time he visited. He reluctantly released her feet and stood up to leave. "It's well past midnight again. I should be going. I know you have to get up earlier than I do."

Cynthia stood, wrapped her arms around Thomas' neck, and jokingly said, "You're right. You shouldn't keep me up so late on a work night." She rested her head against his chest, and the two embraced for a moment, the silence betraying their unspoken arrangement.

Thomas finally sighed and walked toward the door. "I'll give you a call when I make that copy of that prayer."

She presented him with a tired smile, and the two said goodnight.

## 46.

## "Oh, brother . . ."

In the back room of Commencement Bay Books, Thomas used the store copier to reproduce the prayer he wanted to share with Cynthia. George arrived, and he and Thomas had a good conversation about how things were going at the store with the new hires. They then discussed store business, including maintenance needs for the aging building. A little while later, as George began sharing jokes he had heard over the years, James walked in and mentioned he could use some help with an influx of customers. Both men headed out onto the sales floor to assist shoppers. Thomas was quietly pleased to see George looking cheerful and interacting with the patrons. The older man's voice seemed lighter than usual and even somewhat buoyant. Thomas hoped that perhaps George was turning a corner in his ongoing struggle with his cancer.

After closing the store and returning to the apartment that night, Thomas received a phone call from his mother. He had spoken to her the previous week during their regular phone chat, but this time, she couldn't wait for him to call. "Hi, Mom, what's up?" He didn't waste any time wondering why she was reaching out.

"Thomas, I wanted to let you know that your aunt has taken a turn for the worse. I'm doing everything I can to keep her comfortable, but to be blunt, I don't know how much longer she has, and I wanted you to be aware."

"I'm really sorry to hear that, Mom. Is there anything you'd like me to do?"

"Well, of course, I want you to pray for her. She's been through so much."

"Do you want me to come down there?" Thomas asked with sincerity.

"No, I don't think that's necessary. You would only add to the confusion that's already happening, with nurses and friends coming and going. I just wanted you to know what's happening. She needs your prayers now."

"Oh, Mom, I feel so bad for her. How are you holding up?"

"Oh, I'm doing alright. I mean, I'm glad I can be here for her. It's hard to watch her suffer."

"Mom, I promise to pray for Aunt Carol as well as for you. You are the best gift a sister or son could ever have."

"Oh, Thomas, thank you." Over the phone line, Thomas heard his mother begin to cry.

They talked for a few more minutes and exchanged a final "I love you" before the call ended.

Thomas could only think about what a saint his mother was. He and Aunt Carol were truly blessed to have her in their lives. He went to the bedroom and found his rosary in a drawer. He made the sign of the cross with the crucifix and recited the five sorrowful mysteries of the rosary for Aunt Carol, along with a heartfelt prayer for his courageous mother.

As he finished his prayers, there was a knock on the door. It was after ten. Thomas, puzzled, walked to the door and opened it. There stood Minnie Cadieux. He smiled, pleased to see her, and invited her in.

She entered with a grace that seemed both unusual and warm. "I was hoping to find you here. I know it isn't easy for us to see each other with our schedules," she repeated an oft-repeated fact. She smiled and quickly kissed him on the cheek.

"You're absolutely right about connecting with you, Minnie. It's definitely a challenge," he said as he took her jacket and hung it on a coat hook in the hallway.

As they moved into the living room, Minnie said, "I heard you came to The Rail a while back and asked for me." Then, with a look that could stop any man in his tracks, Minnie asked, "Did you miss me?"

"I did. I wanted to tell you about a book I read, and, of course, I wanted to see you." As those words escaped his lips, he mentally recognized and acknowledged his dilemma with Minnie and Cynthia.

"I miss you, too, Thomas. So, I decided to take a chance and see if I could catch you here tonight. Is that alright?"

"Of course, please have a seat. Can I get you anything?"

"No, I'm fine. I just want to catch up and spend some time with you."

"Let's do it." He gestured toward the couch, and Minnie settled in. Thomas sat in his chair.

"Tell me about this book," Minnie asked.

"Honestly, it felt much more significant on the day I stopped by after finishing it, and I was so worked up about it. Maybe now, after a couple of days…" He smiled and tilted his head. "It was a book by a 17th-century French part-time theologian and philosopher named Blaise Pascal. I mean, the book was incredibly important to several philosophical and theological topics that have kind of been haunting me, but as I say it out loud and reflect on it, maybe it doesn't sound like I had to rush out to the pub." Thomas threw his arms up in embarrassment. They both laughed.

Then Minnie, in a more serious tone, remarked, "No, it was important to you then, and you chose to share it with me. I truly value that." She leaned a bit forward on the couch, and they both felt a sense of connection with one another.

Minnie finally broke the spell and said, "My world is kind of a mess, Thomas. I can't explain it right now, mainly because I'm still working through so many things." She paused and rubbed her forehead. Then, with a slightly forced smile, she said, "I don't know, I just wanted to spend some time with you."

Thomas, not really knowing what to make of Minnie's mental uncertainty, replied in a now equally indeterminate voice. "Yes, let's talk."

For the next hour, the two spoke about their lives. Thomas shared his struggles with questions about his philosophy of life, while she opened up, to some degree, about the personal demons she faced related to her time with David Street, her abortion, and the baby.

Thomas noted that she did not discuss the future beyond vague references to figuring it out in due time.

Finally, Minnie said, "Hey, it's getting late. I should head home." Thomas quickly grabbed her jacket and walked her out to Charlotte's car. Thomas was so caught up in being with Minnie that he forgot to tell her he planned to track down Richard Dart to see if he had read her stories and what he thought of them.

As he walked back into his apartment, Thomas felt a sense of incompleteness about his relationship with Minnie. He remembered how excited he had been to share his *Pascal experience* with her the night he had gone to The Rail almost a week earlier. Then, he considered his feelings for Cynthia and his desire to support her. Thomas couldn't shake the weight of his unresolved emotions for both Minnie and Cynthia. The complexity and intensity of his feelings stirred a renewed unease within him. "Oh, brother," he muttered. After moodily standing in front of the living room window, gazing out over the darkened park, he retreated to his bedroom. He took a quick shower before bed to help sort through everything happening in his life. Just before turning off the light next to the bed, his final act was to read, for what now seemed for the umpteenth time, his

"Prayer for Wisdom" concerning those two remarkable women.

## 47.

## *"...a path not taken. A life not lived."*

No sooner had he fallen into a deep sleep than the phone rang. He forced his eyes open, turned, dropped his feet to the floor, and unsteadily made his way to the living room, where he strained to focus his mind and picked up the receiver. Standing in the darkness, he recognized Nate's voice on the other end of the line. It had to be bad news, he thought.

"Tom, I'm sorry, but I knew you'd want to know."

"What is it, Nate?" Thomas replied, already sensing that the news must be about Zack.

"I received a call from a friend. He told me that Zack had overdosed again on heroin."

A silence settled between them, and Thomas asked, "Where is he, Nate?"

"He's at South Puget Sound Hospital, just like last time."

"Do you have any other information?"

"No, but like I said, I knew you'd want to know."

"Thanks, I'll go find out what's going on."

"Let me know, Tom," Nate replied. "I'm sorry I had to be the one to tell you."

"Thanks, Nate," Thomas said before he hung up.

Thomas stood in the now gloomy living room, gazing out at the silent trees in the park and rubbing his eyes.

Thirty minutes later, he stood at the hospital front desk, attempting to find Zack.

Thomas was directed to the Intensive Care Unit (ICU), where he eventually spoke with a nurse in a small waiting room. He explained his relationship with Zack, noting that the patient had no immediate family in the area. She hinted at Zack's condition and told Thomas to sit in the waiting room, assuring him she would return shortly with an update.

Thomas took a seat and observed a stream of anxious visitors arriving at the ICU, each bringing with them a new wave of grief and anguish. For Thomas, it served as a reminder of the world's inherent cruelty. Everyone was under immense stress. This made Thomas reflect on his thesis that the world was fundamentally one of suffering.

Being in the ICU at this time of night, he felt like he was living in an amplified version of his argument.

Over an hour later, the original nurse he had spoken to returned and signaled for him to come to the desk. The woman, her face reflecting the weariness of countless nights amidst this relentless parade of suffering, informed Thomas that Zack had indeed overdosed on heroin. She also mentioned that he had come around some in the last hour, but there were many potential issues they would need to monitor over the next few hours and days to evaluate Zack's physical and mental status. She strongly advised Thomas to go home, get some sleep, and return in the morning. She noted that she would leave messages for the morning shift, informing them that Thomas would be back and that they should update him. Thomas thanked her and chose to follow her advice, going home to get some rest.

The next day, after nearly an hour at the hospital, Thomas briefly spoke with a doctor in the ICU. The doctor informed Thomas that stabilizing Zack's vital functions was the top priority. During this process, Zack would be evaluated for responsiveness, breathing patterns, and basic neurological functions. Once that was completed, he would undergo neurological tests to check for signs of brain damage.

Thomas didn't feel good about what the doctor was telling him. What he heard seemed much more serious than during his last visit with Zack. Thomas thanked the doctor and said he would contact Zack's parents to pass along the news. He also mentioned that he would check back the next day.

Back at his apartment, Thomas called Nate to share the grim news. Nate wanted to jot it down since he intended to contact Zack's parents with the unfortunate update. Thomas thanked Nate, explaining that he had to leave for work soon and would have only had a minute to speak with Zack's parents. After hanging up, Thomas quickly prepared a sandwich to eat before heading out for his night shift at the bookstore.

The next morning, Thomas visited Zack in the hospital, and the initial wave of what would become sad news emerged. A CAT scan indicated potential issues stemming from Zack's overdose. Thomas felt disheartened. Once again, he shared the news with Nate Wilson, but this time, Nate had already learned about it after visiting Zack and receiving the information from a nurse a few hours before Thomas arrived.

They commiserated over the developing prognosis that Zack would likely suffer some degree of brain damage from the experience. The extent of the damage and its consequent impact on Zack would unfold over the coming weeks and months. Thomas and Nate also discussed whether they had done enough to support Zack before the incident occurred. Nate mentioned that he thought the counseling he had arranged for Zack, with a little more time, might have made a difference. Thomas expressed a wish to redo the day he had traveled to Seattle and back with Zack. The answer came quickly to both of them—they hadn't done enough. Now, Zack's fate was out of their hands, and the outcome remained uncertain.

Thomas attended daily Mass the following morning, offering heartfelt prayers for Zack's health and well-being. The prayers seemed to hang there in the stillness of the nave and sanctuary of the church. Once again, there had been a crisis, a painful failure, and overall a disaster.

While coming to terms with the possibility of a friend facing impairment, he found his mind drifting back to thoughts of Minnie and Cynthia. He now realized that the more he contemplated these two women, the clearer it became to him that if only one of these situations, Minnie's pregnancy or Cynthia's health, had been presented to him, he would embrace it wholeheartedly. Life happens; deal with it. That much he had learned.

Thomas thought more about both women. I loved Minnie from the moment I met her, but when things got complicated, like having her over to my apartment, I needed to avoid letting the situation devolve into circumstances that could threaten our relationship. After it happened, I became too protective of my feelings and potential self-interests. Hell, even then, when I found out who Minnie was with, why didn't I confront her and David Street right then? Why didn't I stand up and let them both know where I stood? Who knows, she might have chosen me. Thomas rolled his neck from side to side as stiffness settled between his shoulder blades. And what about Cynthia—was I scared of her situation once I learned about it? Looking back, why didn't I just not take no for an answer instead of giving in to her firm yet, in my mind, misguided notions of independence and going it alone?

Now, both women were constantly on his mind. Each represented a path not taken and a life not lived. As he tried to silence his inner conversation, Thomas knew one thing for sure: he needed to be completely honest with himself and both women, and to be truthful to them in every way.

## 48.

## "So you're happy?"

The next evening, Thomas' phone rang. It was his mother informing him that his aunt had finally succumbed to the ravages of Parkinson's disease and died earlier that day. They spoke for about twenty minutes about their love for her and shared memories of the times they had together. His mother mentioned that she had already made arrangements for her sister's funeral Mass and burial. Thomas said he would take the train down to Astoria the day before the funeral.

A couple of days later, Thomas arrived at his aunt's house. It was chaotic. His mother worked to prepare everything for the next morning's Mass and the subsequent burial at the cemetery, while also cleaning the house for the wake. Thomas helped where he could, primarily being assigned tasks such as lifting, pushing, and carrying items from one place to another. That evening, he and his mother attended the rosary service for his aunt at the funeral home. The Our Fathers and Hail Marys echoed in the dim light, each bead of the rosary slipping through their fingers like time itself fading away.

After the Mass and graveside blessing the following day, Thomas returned to the house to find himself among strangers—faces that had known his aunt and mother in a way he never would. Then, in the evening, he helped his mother clean up after everyone had left. Restoring order to the house by tidying up and rearranging things, wrapped up around midnight.

The next morning, while sitting at the kitchen table with coffee and some leftovers from the previous day, Thomas finally chatted with his mother.

"How are you holding up, Mom?"

"I'm just glad everything seemed to go well yesterday," his mother replied, taking a large sip of coffee.

"Well, what happens now, Mom, now that Aunt Carol is gone?"

His mother poured a splash of cream into her coffee and stirred it slowly, as if the motion might somehow bring clarity to her thoughts. "Well, Carol left me the house. Looking back, it's funny, Thomas, how life works out. Carol had no children, and I only had you. I got married young and never remarried after your father's death. She waited and then was struck by that dreadful disease. I mean, life never seems to go how you think it will. There's always one surprise after another." She paused, reflecting on what she had just said. "So, given that, I suppose I will live right here. Over the years, I've grown accustomed to the house and, for that matter, Astoria. It's a beautiful city. I have a job here at Pacific Northwest Bell. I've also made many good friends. I honestly can't imagine myself in another situation."

With a slight grin on his face, Thomas said, "So you're happy?" "Yes," she replied, her own smile mirroring her son's. "Well, if you mean it, and I can't imagine why you wouldn't, I'm very happy for you." Thomas reached across the table, his hands encircling hers with a tenderness that came from years of shared understanding. "Are you sure you'll be alright living here in Aunt Carol's house by yourself?"

She smiled at her son and, squeezing his hands, said, "Yes," pausing with a mischievous twinkle in her eye, "As long as you come to visit me more often than you do now."

Slightly embarrassed, Thomas replied sincerely, "I will, Mom."

They spent the next two hours talking. The rest of the day unfolded through a series of small, shared tasks: running errands, preparing dinner, and settling into the comfortable rhythms of companionship that only a mother and son could share. Memories flooded back from their time in Grayland. They enjoyed a nice dinner together and continued their seemingly never-ending conversation in the living room until nearly eleven.

While they talked, Thomas reflected on how his mother had raised him alone during his childhood. He silently thanked God for the greatest gift a son could ever receive.

In the morning, he began the journey back to Tacoma, his heart filled with the enduring love he and his mother had always shared.

## 49.

## "...and to you, I owe everything."

Upon his return to the city overlooking Commencement Bay on Puget Sound, Thomas began to think once more about his immediate circle of friends, all of whom were grappling with some form of ordeal in their lives. He thought of Minnie—her name evoked a deep sigh from within him. How many tears had she shed while wrestling with the decision to abort her baby? Then he considered Cynthia and, as she put it, her likely advancing condition. He couldn't help but admire her strength of character and will. He reflected on the plight of his friend Zack, whose mental faculties were now imprisoned by a folly of his own making. Then there was George. Thomas pondered what it would feel like to be in his position, with the very real specter of cancer looming over his life. He contemplated the loss of his aunt and the suffering she had endured. Finally, he even tossed into the cauldron of his melancholy the disaster of his life strategy, which he had so carefully constructed at the end of his university days, seeking secular solutions to life's challenges. He now saw it for what it was: an edifice built on sand. It had collapsed under the weight of human suffering. What remained? Only faith. Only the rediscovery of something eternal. His Pascal experience had instilled in him the hope that he could rebuild his life on the firmer foundation of the good news of Jesus Christ, which had been preserved for two millennia by the Church.

The next day, Thomas carried his mental cache of personal issues with him to Sunday Mass. He knelt in *his* pew and poured out his heart in prayer. Once again, the profound impact of discovering Pascal's writings came to mind, and he thanked God for it. As he concluded his prayers and petitions to the Lord, the soft ring of the sanctuary bell announced the arrival of the priest and accompanying altar servers, marking the beginning of the Mass.

The Mass proceeded from the greeting to the penitential rite, followed by the day's readings, including the proclamation of the Gospel, and finally, the homily. Father Sinclair was striving to nourish and strengthen the worshipping community in the pews, as he often did by explaining the day's readings from the Old and New Testaments. Thomas thought it wasn't Father Ron's fault that the kid from Grayland wasn't feeling *it* this morning. It was simply a reality.

After the homily, the Mass entered its Eucharistic phase, where the singular Sacrifice of Christ on the Cross is *made present* to everyone in attendance. Father Sinclair prepared the gifts of water and wine. Then he said, "Pray, brethren, that our sacrifice may be acceptable to God, the Almighty Father." Thomas, standing, heard, as he had at every Mass, the words *our sacrifice*. Yet this time, he paused, grasping that the priest was saying that he, too, through Christ, was offering himself to God the Father. The Sacrifice of the Mass is not a new sacrifice but the making present of Christ's once-and-for-all eternal sacrifice on Calvary. It allows believers to unite with Christ's offering of himself to the Father and receive the graces that flow from it. Thomas realized that this understanding constituted the reason he was there. Thomas Klement was truly participating in the greatest and most perfect gift to God the Father.

Thomas could hear and feel his heart beating. Father Sinclair continued with the prescribed prayers. Then, the old priest raised the host and recited the words of consecration spoken by the Lord at the Last Supper. "Take this, all of you, and eat it, for this is my body which will be given up for you." While holding the host aloft, the bells rang three times. All the parishioners gazed at what was now the body of Christ under the appearance of the host.

As the bells finished ringing, a deep and profound silence enveloped the nave and sanctuary of the church. Thomas had experienced this silence during Mass countless times in his life, but today, this morning, it struck him to the heart like never before. It was the same silence he had felt on certain early mornings at the ocean beach when the waves reached their apex on the sand and lingered there for a sacred moment. He recognized it—the same feeling as if the entire world had paused for a split second. It was incredible, as if heaven and earth had touched. He stopped breathing. Thomas had unraveled the mystery of his ocean mornings. The same sacred sense of presence that had stilled each ocean wave as it broke onto the beach now stilled his heart. Then, the priest broke the silence by finishing the words of the consecration, this time with the chalice in his hands, concluding with "Do this in memory of me."

While this was happening, Thomas felt weak, as if he were in a trance. He then heard the priest's words: "Let us proclaim the mystery of faith." Everyone responded, including Thomas, with the words, "When we eat this

Bread and drink this Cup, we proclaim your Death, O Lord, until you come again." By the end of the response, he had begun to pull himself together. The priest then recited several prayers. Thomas, with his eyes fixed on the crucified image of Jesus on the Cross hanging on the wall behind and above the altar, inwardly prayed words that came directly from his soul.

"Lord God Almighty,

I offer you through your Son, our Lord Jesus Christ,
my life, my joys, my sorrows,
my sufferings, my prayers and petitions,
my praise and adoration.

All that I am, I lay before you.
For you have made me from nothing,
and to you, I owe everything.

May I be conformed to your Son,
our Lord Jesus Christ,
that I may become the person You created me to be.

I thank you, O Lord, for this moment, this grace,

when heaven and earth come together,

and the veil between them is lifted,

and in every Mass, everywhere, every day,

you make yourself present to us,

and you fulfill your promise to be with us,

   *...until the end of the age* (Matt 28:20).


All glory, all honor, all praise,

be yours, now and forever.

Amen."


Like the riddle of the ocean's dawn wave, Thomas remained in a trance-like state until he heard Father Ron pronounce the words, "Through him, with him, in him, in the unity of the Holy Spirit, all glory and honor is yours, almighty Father, forever and ever." Thomas and everyone else responded, "Amen" (So be it).

The Mass continued, culminating in the reception of Communion. Once those receiving the grace of the body and blood of Our Lord Jesus Christ had partaken of the Blessed Sacrament, the Concluding Rites were performed.

Then Father Ron said the prayers leading to the dismissal: "The Mass is ended; go in peace to love and serve the Lord." The response was, "Thanks be to God," or as Thomas remembered from the Latin Mass he grew up with, "Deo Gratias."

Thomas was exhausted. As the congregation began to file out of the church, he stayed behind, kneeling once more and burying his forehead into the back of his hands. When he finally felt steady enough to rise from the pew, Thomas looked around and realized he was the last one left.

That morning, coffee and donuts didn't appeal to him, so he wandered the neighborhood streets, ultimately finding himself at Wright Park. He made his way along a path that led him to his favorite bench by the duck pond. There, he sat for a long time, slowly trying to make sense of his experience and what had transpired at Mass that morning.

## 50.

# *"He closed his eyes and listened to his heart."*

After work that evening, Thomas sat in his chair with the flat, wide arms, sipping a nearly cold cup of coffee as he reflected on his inner life and the lessons he had learned that day.

In what he could only describe as an epiphany, Thomas' lifelong recurrent ocean dream, the wisdom and insight of Blaise Pascal, the inexplicable grace he experienced during the transcendent moment of the Holy Sacrifice of the Mass, and Christ's promise to be with mankind *"always, to the end of the age,"* all united to lead him to realize that he must voluntarily surrender and entrust his life to the Lord. True, he had been taught this since his days in faith formation in Aberdeen. Yet, he felt that his experience at Mass that day had granted him the grace to firmly say to himself, "Lord, you are the rock upon which I stand. You are the source and summit of all my hope." A circuitous path had led him to that conclusion, but he had arrived there, nonetheless. It felt good. It felt right. Of course, this did not mean life would become easier or necessarily happier. However, it did mean that, no matter what was happening, he would strive to make decisions and choices guided by the words of Christ, as well as the tradition and teachings of the enduring witness of the Church.

Thomas remembered from the Gospel of John when Jesus said to those following him, "I am the living bread that came down from heaven: whoever eats this bread will live forever, and the bread that I will give you is my flesh for the life of the world" (John 6:51). This teaching was too hard for many of Christ's followers, and they left him to return to their former lives. Then, when Jesus asked the twelve if they wanted to leave him as well, Peter responded, "Master, to whom shall we go?" (John 68b). Peter's thoughts resonated with Thomas. He had experimented with modern secular reasoning and teaching, only to return to what had been passed down through generations within the tradition of the Church.

Regarding his purpose in life, a question he had always stumbled over until this point now lay before him with utter simplicity. It had always been there, yet he had somehow failed to recognize and accept it. His purpose was as clear as the old Baltimore Catechism he had learned in grade school stated: "God made me to know him, love him, and serve him in this world."

Thomas' final thought of the evening came down to the realization that he could no longer live with the situation he had allowed to develop in his heart and soul regarding

Minnie and Cynthia. He needed to walk the walk, not just talk the talk, about his newfound and strengthened personal convictions. Although he didn't believe he had intentionally created his dilemma, it needed to be addressed. Before rising from his chair and heading to bed, he looked out over the expanse of the now-darkened park. He closed his eyes and listened to his heart.

## 51.

## *"The silence...was deafening."*

The next day, Thomas, now filled with new determination, called Cynthia from the bookstore. He asked if they could meet up because he had things on his mind that he wanted to share with her. Cynthia replied, "Sure, how about after you get off work? You can come over here."

Thomas quickly accepted and went directly to Cynthia's after he closed the store. Arriving at her door, they exchanged greetings and moved to the living room. Cynthia sat on the couch. Thomas did not sit but instead walked over and looked out the front windows at the park, where the dark shapes of trees with their branches swaying in the wind were visible. He thought that not even the darkness of the park could provide him with refuge. He continued making small talk, trying to build up the nerve to say what he wanted. He noticed how great Cynthia looked, and at that moment, the slightly forced, casual conversation slowed and then came to an end. Still tense, Thomas glanced at Cynthia and said, "I might as well tell you that I have, for lack of a better term, a confession to make."

Cynthia, somewhat surprised by Thomas' seriousness, sat up straighter on the couch and wondered what was on his mind. She maintained a calm demeanor and noticed that Thomas appeared unusually uneasy. Thomas realized the moment had come to speak, yet suddenly, he wished there was a way to postpone it. He felt the weight of what he was about to say, but now there was no turning back. He took a quick breath in, and as he exhaled, he began, "Cynthia, before we started seeing each other, there was someone else. I had been in another relationship. Her name is Minnie Cadieux, and she's from a small town up on Hood Canal." He hesitated momentarily, unsure how to describe his relationship with Minnie. "I met her one night at The Rail, where she works as a waitress. We dated. I believe we had strong feelings for each other. I know I did for her. At one point, we had a disagreement that I would call a misunderstanding. In fact, I'm not sure what to label it because it became blown out of proportion. Anyway, because of that, she left me. Not long after, Minnie got involved with another guy. They were together for a while, but different and more serious circumstances ended their relationship a few months later."

"After Minnie and I broke up, you and I started seeing each other. A short time after you and I got together, Minnie stopped seeing the guy she was with. She came to me, and we developed a renewed friendship. We don't go on dates or anything like that. It is, I don't know, more conversational." Thomas took a deeper breath and said, "However, over the last few months, I've found myself thinking of her more and more." He paused, noticing how still Cynthia had become. He also observed that there wasn't much change in her expression.

"Listen to me, Cynthia. I think about you all the time, too. I don't know how the situation turned out this way, but it's why I decided I needed to tell you, and tell Minnie, about what's been going on. And by that, I mean I'm not trying to take advantage of either of you. You have to know that's not the case. Am I in the wrong for allowing the appearance of something inappropriate to continue? Yes, in my mind, I am, and I'm trying to correct that starting tonight. I'm sorry if any of what I've said makes you think less of me. If it does, then I suppose I deserve it. But

Cynthia, I swear I never thought I was taking advantage of you during this time." He shook his head and looked at her. "Anyway, you both deserve my honesty." Thomas didn't know what to do next. He stood there awkwardly, putting his hand in his front pocket, then taking it out. He rubbed his jaw, all the while waiting for Cynthia to react. The silence in the room was deafening.

Finally, after what felt like an eternity, Cynthia spoke, "I don't know what to say to all of that, Thomas." There was no accusation in her voice. "I'm truly at a loss for words."

Thomas had no idea what to expect from Cynthia. To him, she seemed withdrawn and contemplative. Thomas asked, "Is there anything else you want to know about what I've just shared with you?"

Silence followed.

Thomas finally ended the silence, saying, "All of a sudden, I feel like a real jerk."

Cynthia appeared thoughtful but replied, "You should, Mr. Klement." She closed her eyes and exhaled from her slightly puffed cheeks.

"Please, Cynthia, I'm speaking from my heart. Don't ask me to leave." Thomas' expression was faltering.

For her part, Cynthia seemed somewhat distant from the immediate conversation and was acting more introspectively. She then turned her head toward Thomas, noticing that he was struggling mightily after telling his story. Cynthia couldn't watch Thomas suffer any longer and said, "Maybe I need some time to process what you just told me," giving him a chance to regain his footing.

Thomas marveled at Cynthia's undeniable strength and had never felt so uncomfortable. Upon hearing Cynthia's words, he readily accepted and replied, "Sure, of course, I will give you space. I just want you to tell me you will allow me to return so I can talk to you again about this." His face and body language almost implored her to agree with him.

Cynthia got up from the couch. Thomas thought she might pull away from their close proximity. Instead, she stood there and, in a small voice, said, "Alright, Thomas. Let's try that."

Thomas instinctively moved closer to her. She permitted him to give her a remorseful embrace.

On his way back to his apartment, Thomas reflected and clearly recognized that his failure to inform Cynthia about Minnie earlier was just wrong. Yet she had been the one to establish the rules for their relationship, stating how they could never be together. He sighed. One thing was certain to him. He couldn't keep convincing himself that it was somehow acceptable to have feelings for two different women without addressing the issue outwardly rather than in his mind. He felt like a real loser. He shook his head.

## 52

# *" . . . our other conversation is not over."*

Thomas called Minnie the next morning and arranged to meet her for a walk in the park before noon. While waiting for Minnie, who was always a bit late, Thomas sat by the duck pond, where he reflected once again on his conversation with Cynthia the previous evening. In hindsight, he wished he could have presented his confession in a clearer and possibly more understandable manner and tone to her. He shook his head and looked up to see Minnie approaching.

They exchanged smiles and greetings before Thomas suggested walking through the park to enjoy the sights and sounds. So, they strolled along a path toward the other end of the park. Upon arriving there, they turned and began retracing their steps.

As they continued walking, Thomas announced he had something to say to her.

"That reminds me, Thomas," Minnie said, "I've got something to tell you, too." She smiled, looked at him, noticed unrest in his eyes, and asked, "Is something wrong?"

Thomas, starting to feel like he had the night before, said, "No, no, I just have something to tell you that I should have shared a while ago."

Minnie's eyes widened with surprise as she searched his face and said, "Well, talk to me, Klement."

Thomas immediately felt the same uncomfortable emotions as the previous evening when speaking to Cynthia. He faintly shuddered and chose to continue with what he was going to say. "Minnie," he said more forcefully than he had intended, "I want to tell you that when we split up and after you started seeing David Street, I started seeing a woman who had come into the bookstore a few times." Her name is Cynthia Innes. She's a bookkeeper for a stationery store downtown. We watched movies together at her place, and I developed strong feelings for her during that time.

Upon hearing this, Minnie stopped in her tracks and, with a piercing gaze, asked, "Did you sleep with her?"

Thomas, caught a bit off-guard, also halted, shook his head slowly, and said sincerely, "No, Minnie, I did not."

Minnie visibly struggled with what Thomas had told her. She seemed to be trying to better understand the situation in order to address it. "Tell me more about this, Cynthia," said Minnie, her mind now wholly focused on Thomas' words and body language.

"I'm not sure what you want me to say," he said, looking slightly surprised.

They started walking again, slowly.

Thomas turned to Minnie and said, "You wanted no part of me and were with another guy."

Minnie shot him a challenging look.

Thomas made a mental note that Minnie was a bit more unpredictable than Cynthia. It was then that Thomas spotted a familiar face approaching them. "Richard, what are you doing at the park?"

Richard's face crinkled with a smile, and he answered, "Just enjoying the day like the two of you."

Thomas looked at Minnie and then turned to his older friend. "Richard, I want you to meet my friend Minnie Cadieux."

Richard reached out and shook Minnie's hand warmly. "This isn't, by any chance, the same Minnie Cadieux who has authored some excellent short stories I've been reading, is it?" Minnie looked at Thomas, then blushed, caught off guard by the revelation and praise.

Richard noticed her blush and said, "Ms. Cadieux, that's exceptional writing. I was hoping to see your friend here again to tell him that I loved your work and have shared it with a couple of small publishers I know. Both expressed interest in potentially including some of the stories in a monthly journal. One of them mentioned including one or more in a mixed collection of short stories, if you would be interested."

"You're kidding!" Minnie exclaimed, her voice suddenly filled with excitement. Still exuberant, she turned back to Thomas and said, "I didn't realize you were going to share my stories with anyone."

Thomas, watching her, felt a surge of enthusiasm at her joy. He smiled and said, "I should have asked you first, I guess, but the stories were fantastic, and I asked Richard, who has some connections in the publishing world, whether your work could be worth considering. I haven't seen Mr. Dart since then, pointing at Richard, but as far as I can tell, it seems that he has good news on that front."

Minnie's eyes lit up. "Oh, I don't know what to say. I'm really excited about the possibility," she said, looking back again at Thomas.

Richard smiled at both of them and said, "Well, that's great to hear. Is there any chance we could go over some possibilities and details, maybe over a cup of coffee?"

Thomas glanced at Minnie, who was now caught up in the good news. "Richard, I have to get to work, but I'm guessing Minnie will have a few extra minutes to talk to you."

Minnie nodded with delight.

The three discussed the short stories for a few more minutes, and then Thomas said he had to go. As Thomas began to walk away, Minnie caught his eye and said, "Shoot, I didn't get to share my news," her expression filled with regret. Then, refocusing, she added, "Oh, and believe me, our other conversation is not over." She gave him a glance that seemed pretty intense to him. He acknowledged her and made his way up the hill in the direction of the conservatory, on his way to the bookstore, while Richard and Minnie walked to a café across the street from the park.

## 53.

## "...but I'm telling you now..."

At the bookstore that night, near closing time, Thomas attempted to assess how his conversations with Cynthia and Minnie had gone. He felt that neither discussion seemed satisfactory. Cynthia seemed to have turned inward in her reaction, and they had agreed to talk about it later.

Minnie's reaction had been more animated, yet because of Richard's appearance, the conversation felt incomplete and indeed, as Minnie had put it, unfinished.

He didn't go to The Rail after work because even if Minnie was there, she would be working, and continuing their conversation under those circumstances seemed pointless. That night at the apartment, Thomas had a quick bite to eat. While he was cleaning the kitchen, the phone rang. He dried his hands with the dish towel and answered it. It was Cynthia, and she sounded distressed.

In a strained and faltering voice, he heard, "Thomas, I'm not sure how to ask you this, but could you come over?"

"Cynthia, of course, I can come over. What's wrong?"

"Thomas, I'm having a bit of an episode with my heart. I need your help."

Thomas replied, "I'm on my way right now."

Cynthia started to say thank you, but she heard Thomas hang up the phone.

Thomas grabbed his jacket and rang the door buzzer to Cynthia's building in less than five minutes. She buzzed him in. Moments later, after a brief ride in the elevator to the fifth floor, he found himself knocking on her door.

Cynthia opened the door. Her hair, which Thomas had enjoyed so much when he saw it in a ponytail flaring from the top of her head, was now unkempt and hanging loosely below her shoulders. She was barefoot, wearing a loose-fitting white cotton nightgown. Additionally, she looked pale and fragile. After Thomas entered and she closed the door, she walked directly to the bedroom. Her movements were slow and uncertain. Once there, she crawled into the unmade bed and propped herself up on her pillows in an attempt to ease her shortness of breath.

"Thank you so much for coming over, Thomas," Cynthia almost wheezed at him. "I didn't know what to do, and I knew you were just five minutes away." Her eyes were dark. "Thomas, I'm scared." Then she began to cough.

"Let me call an ambulance. Let me take you to the hospital," Thomas said with much concern.

"No, I don't believe that will be necessary," replied Cynthia in a little stronger voice.

Standing beside the bed, Thomas exclaimed, "Then what can I do?" His voice was filled with helplessness. "Just tell me what to do."

"I need you to get me my nitroglycerin tablets. They're in the bathroom medicine cabinet on the middle shelf. Oh, and a glass of water."

Thomas hurried to the bathroom, grabbed the medicine, and filled the glass by the sink with water. He examined the medicine and noted that the nitroglycerin was intended for use in acute chest pain episodes. He returned to the bedroom, offering Cynthia the medicine and water. After she swallowed the pills, she adjusted her pillows and said, "Thank you, Thomas. Let me hold your hand. I could have gotten the medicine myself and taken it, but I've only used this medicine a few times before, and it scares me. The doctor says it's quite powerful. That's why I wanted you here first."

"Are you sure you don't want me to call an ambulance?" Thomas' voice was filled with anxiety.

With a labored yet steady voice, Cynthia said, "No. I've been here before. This will pass. Please stay. Stay with me, Thomas."

Moved by her plea, Thomas nodded in agreement, pulled a chair from the other side of the room, placed it next to the bed, and sat down. She offered her hand, and Thomas held it with both of his. Cynthia was still short of breath, pressing her free hand to her chest. After a while, she mentioned that she felt dizzy. She said this was one of the side effects of the medicine. As the night continued, she appeared increasingly fatigued. Once again, she quietly told Thomas that she was still short of breath.

He wanted to call an ambulance, but each time he suggested it, Cynthia squeezed his hand and assured him it would be all right. He only left the room once to get Cynthia some more water. After a while, her dizziness turned to nausea, which eventually passed. By 3 a.m.,

Cynthia had calmed down, was much less short of breath, and the pain in her chest had eased. Cynthia told Thomas he could go home, but he refused. After that, she fell asleep and finally looked peaceful.

Thomas let go of her hand and walked over to a larger chair in the corner of the bedroom. From there, he watched her, and eventually, he, too, fell asleep.

When Thomas woke up, he noticed that Cynthia's bedside clock read seven-thirty. He got up and moved back to the chair next to the bed. As he looked at her, she greeted him with a soft "Good morning." After they chatted for a few minutes, he helped her up and put her robe on her. Then, he led her to the bathroom. When she came out, Thomas had moved to the couch in the living room, where she joined him.

Cynthia sat beside Thomas and cuddled up to him. Thomas wrapped his arm around her. They remained silent for a long time. Finally, Cynthia said, "I can't thank you enough for coming over here."

Thomas said softly, "Stop it. You know how I feel about you. I would do anything for you."

"I don't really experience these episodes very often. They began a couple of years ago. I have to be cautious because using the medication too frequently over time can lead to tolerance, making it less effective. The issue with it is that it causes headaches, and I also get dizzy spells from it."

"Do you want me to make you some breakfast?" Thomas asked her.

"No, Thomas, you've done more than enough. I'm sure you have things to do. All I did was keep you up all night."

"That's not true, Cynthia. I actually slept for a couple of hours after you fell asleep. And I'm not going anywhere until I'm comfortable you're coming around and feeling better."

Without responding, Cynthia rested her head on his chest once more. About half an hour later, she sat up again and rubbed her eyes. After a minute or two, in a soft but controlled voice, she said, "Thomas, I need to tell you something. It's about what you mentioned the other day, you know, when you first told me about this, Minnie." She paused and immediately perceived Thomas' discomfort. "I was, of course, taken aback. However, I've since had some time to think it over and realized I needed to be honest with you." She stopped briefly and unconsciously lowered her gaze. "Thomas, I've been in your position before."

Thomas, unsure of where she was heading with her words, perked up.

Cynthia continued, "What I mean is that I, too, have had a relationship with someone for whom I had strong feelings. His name is Eric. The relationship was not unlike ours. I fell for him, and then, similar to our situation, I decided it couldn't continue because of my heart issues. He took it pretty hard. We haven't seen each other in a while. When you shared your story, I wasn't sure if I should share mine, so I suggested we talk again later. I'm sorry I didn't tell you then, but I'm telling you now, and yes, as it seemed for you when speaking of this Minnie person, it is uncomfortable." Cynthia rolled her eyes, feeling awkward and embarrassed.

Initially, Thomas didn't know what to say. Seeing she was distressed, he simply stated, "So you still have feelings for Eric."

"Yes, I suppose so," Cynthia said, nodding toward Thomas. "But I also have feelings for you." Again, he could see through her body language and facial expressions how difficult this conversation had become for Ms. Innes.

"Well, I'll be," replied Thomas, a faint smile crossing his face.

"Oh, stop that," Cynthia said, beginning to blush. Thomas' attempt to diffuse the tense conversation seemed to do the trick. She relaxed.

Cynthia turned her back into the corner of the couch and, in a familiar act, put her feet up against Thomas' thigh. He placed his hand on her knee. They remained seated, silent, now aware of each other's past, yet both

283

understanding their strong feelings for each other. The room was quiet now with only the faint sound of the morning traffic outside. Both reflected and intermittently gazed at each other, wondering what the future held in store.

## 54.

## *"... perhaps it was good enough."*

When he returned to his apartment after the harrowing night at Cynthia's, Thomas brewed a pot of coffee, scrambled some eggs, and made toast. As he ate his breakfast and sipped coffee in preparation for work, he decided to call Minnie to share what had happened with Cynthia and see if they could get together to finish their conversation.

The phone rang at Charlotte's home. After three rings, Charlotte answered, "Hello." Thomas identified himself. Charlotte replied that she recognized his voice and that his identification was unnecessary. After exchanging pleasantries, he asked if he could speak with Minnie. On the other end of the line, Charlotte suppressed a chuckle but then, laughing a little, said, "Thomas, you have the worst timing I've ever known. My dear cousin, Ms. Cadieux, left for Union this morning. She told me she was visiting her parents and would return later in the week."

Thomas couldn't believe it either. He remembered Minnie telling him at the park the day before that she had something she wanted to share. Charlotte and Thomas talked a little longer before ending the call. He thought about Minnie, shook his head, and said, "This is so Minnie."

He cleared the kitchen table and placed the dishes, utensils, and pan in the sink. Then he walked toward the living room with a refilled cup of coffee. He glanced at the calendar on the wall and did a double-take. He didn't have to work today. George had changed the schedule a couple of days ago, and with everything going on, he had forgotten.

He cleaned up the apartment a bit and then took a couple of loads of laundry to the local laundromat in a drawstring bag. While watching his clothes swirl through the wash cycle and then tumble in the dryer, Thomas thought about Zack and wondered how he was doing. Upon his return to the apartment, he called Nate at his father's shop. Someone answered the phone and then passed it to Nate.

"Nate, this is Tom. Sorry to bother you at work, but do you have the address for the facility where Zack is staying? I have the day off and was hoping to visit him if possible." Nate said, "Sure," and provided the address. They agreed to talk later and ended the call.

Thomas left his apartment and angled across the park in order to catch the bus at "I" Street and Division. From there, he rode west, getting off a block before the bus reached Point Defiance Park. He walked to the street address about a quarter of a mile away and entered the facility. Thomas spoke to the front desk staff, who gave him directions to Zack's room.

When he entered the room, he saw his university buddy sitting in a chair, seemingly watching television. Thomas approached him, and Zack, seeing him, nodded. Thomas hugged him and took a seat across from Zack in a folding chair.

Over the next couple of hours, Thomas was updated on his buddy's recent activities by a helpful intern. He learned that, as the intern described, Zack had suffered communication deficits. Consequently, much of his time was devoted to speech therapy. He also received physical therapy for his motor control and coordination issues. Sadly, Thomas came to terms with the reality that Zack was in the process of relearning basic skills, such as dressing, feeding, and bathing.

While he was there, Thomas helped Zack into a wheelchair and took him to his physical therapy session. He observed the activities during the session, and when it ended, he returned Zack to his room. The two friends communicated as best they could until it began to get dark. Thomas told Zack he had to leave to catch the bus, but would return soon to visit him.

During Thomas' bus ride back to the Stadium District and his Wright Park neighborhood, he was deeply affected by what had happened to his friend because of the overdose. He wanted to know how quickly and how much Zack could recover. Earlier in the day, he had spoken privately to the intern in the hall. He learned there was no real way to know how his friend's situation would evolve over time, but realistically, one shouldn't get their hopes too high. In other words, a complete recovery was unlikely.

As he got off the bus across from the park and walked toward his apartment, he vowed to create a schedule to visit and support Zack as much as he could. At the very least, Thomas thought he could be there for him.

Making his way along the edge of the park, he realized he hadn't eaten lunch or dinner. He walked past his apartment and found his way to The Deep Harbor Tavern. There, he ordered that killer personal pizza they served. As he enjoyed the meal and washed it down with his favorite beer, he remembered all the good times he and Zack had shared together at Rainier University.

After finishing the pizza, Thomas headed home but took a detour and ended up at the bookstore. He went inside and said hi to James and the new guy, Dwight Newman. Before leaving, he wandered into the back room, where he was surprised to see the photocopy of Pascal's prayer for the proper use of sickness that he had made for Cynthia a while back. He had forgotten he had left it there. He picked it up, walked out onto the main floor, said goodnight to the guys, and headed to his apartment.

Finally, back at home, Thomas settled into his chair. The previous night, spent with Cynthia and the mentally exhausting experience with Zack, had left him feeling flat. He reflected on Pascal and his views on suffering as an unavoidable aspect of life. Suffering existed everywhere in the world, and that wouldn't change. And then he recalled that Pascal also believed suffering was, in some significant ways, a gift. He reached into his pocket and pulled out the folded copy of the prayer. Sighing, he contemplated going to bed.

Then Thomas remembered how Cynthia, whom he regarded as much wiser than himself, had struggled to grasp his explanation of Pascal's prayer. It was probably his inelegant presentation that confused her. However, as he gazed more intently at the prayer, an idea struck him:

perhaps, just perhaps, he could refine it. Maybe he could make the essence of the prayer more straightforward and human, which might resonate with Cynthia's heart in a way that the twelve pages of theology or his rudimentary presentation skills could not.

Over the next two days, he focused on making the lengthy prayer more comprehensible. His plan was to transform the prayer into a poem, much like he had done with other texts. In this case, with Pascal's assistance, he aimed to explore the concept of turning pain into something meaningful. Pascal's prayer acknowledged human frailty and vulnerability. It also perceived suffering as a divine instrument, an opportunity for reflection, a surrender to God's will, and a path to purification. He thought to himself that he was beginning to get pretty good at this poetry thing. Thomas settled on a simple, structured rhyming scheme. He then devoted every waking moment, both at home and during downtime at work, to the task. In the end, this was the product:

*The Proper Use of Sickness*

With humble heart, I seek Thy grace,
to find in suffering Thy Holy Face.
Teach me to use this pain I feel,

as a tool to shape my soul, to heal.

Not with despair, but with your grace,

to find in pain a sacred place.

In every ache, in every tear,

let me feel your presence near.

Let not this suffering be in vain,

please let it cleanse like gentle rain.

Refine my heart, my spirit pure,

in Thy great love, let me endure.

Help me to bear this Cross I hold,

with patience, courage, and a heart made bold.

May every moment of distress,

draw me to your tenderness.

In shadows deep, where pain resides,

I lift my heart, my spirit cries,

Grant me, O Lord, the strength to wear,

this weight of illness, this Cross I bear.


Thomas read the poem several times and felt it wasn't perfect, but perhaps it was good enough. Now, he needed to share it with Cynthia. He knew his poem wouldn't be mistaken for real poetry—of that, he was sure. Thomas simply hoped Cynthia might find some measure of solace, insight, and strength in Blaise Pascal's theological writings through the poetic interpretation of the *night manager* at Commencement Bay Books.

## 55.

## "...attempting to confront age and time..."

George called his night manager the following morning and inquired as to what he was doing. Thomas replied, "Nothing important," and asked, "What can I do for you?"

"That is good to hear," said George in a voice that was all business. "Can you come in early today? I need to talk to you. Maybe you can see your way clear to be here by eleven?"

Thomas was surprised but replied, "Sure, George, I'll be there." George thanked him and hung up. Thomas stared at the receiver for a moment, feeling uneasy. Is he okay?

At the stroke of eleven, Thomas walked through the store's front door to be greeted by the ever-ready smiles of Susan and the new day manager, Linda Stuart. They asked him why he had arrived two hours early. He smiled and replied, "I just can't get enough of this place."

Linda said, "George told me to tell you when you showed up to go see him in his office."

"Was he in a good mood?" Thomas asked.

"He seemed alright," Linda offered.

"Okay, I'll head back there." Thomas turned and made his way to George's office. The door was slightly ajar, and Thomas knocked on the frame a few times, saying, "Knock, knock."

"Is that you, Thomas? Come in, come in."

Thomas noticed that, even after 40 years of living in America, George's voice still retained an old-world charm.

Thomas opened the door, and there sat Renko. George smiled, and Thomas could tell it had been a while since he had undergone radiation treatment. He seemed more vibrant than before.

George gestured with his hand, saying, "Have a seat, Mr. Klement."

Thomas settled into the chair across from him and asked, "What can I do for you?"

A smile spread across George's face as he replied, "Today, it's what I can do for you."

Thomas tilted his head slightly, trying to make sense of George's words.

At this point, George's expression softened. He looked at Thomas and said in a slow, deliberate voice, "Thomas Klement, I have an offer to make to you. But first, as your generation would say, you need to understand where I'm coming from." He paused for effect. "I barely escaped from Central Europe before the Germans overran Czechoslovakia and then most of Europe. I arrived in this country with nothing. I worked many thankless jobs while saving as much as I could. When I purchased the building that has housed Commencement Bay Books for the past 35 years, I vowed to turn it into my dream bookstore. It was nothing but work, 18 hours a day. I slept here in this office, and I loved every minute of it. It took five years to assemble all the elements of my ideas with the reality of the space and the book inventory, and to this day, it still has the same look and feel as I envisioned back then. I couldn't be prouder of it." Again, George paused, and this time, it seemed as if he wiped a tear from his eye with his sleeve.

His speech and fervor deeply moved Thomas. He focused intently on "Old Mr. Renko," as everyone affectionately referred to him, to see where he was going with this speech.

It was then that George took a deep breath and, seemingly filled with frustration, continued. "Thomas, I don't know how to tell you this." For the third time, he paused.

Thomas suddenly feared that George would say that, due to his age and medical situation, he was either going to sell the bookstore or had already done so. He looked intently at George.

"I've decided it's time to consider retirement." He raised his chin proudly, attempting to confront age and time defiantly, albeit weakly.

Thomas experienced a sinking feeling in his heart.

"Oh, I'm just going to say this and get it over with. Thomas, I need a succession plan for myself." Haltingly, he finished his thought. "Thomas, you have been like the son I never had. I never married. The store was my family. I want to give you the store as a gift," he then quickly added, "a gift with conditions." He looked at Thomas.

Thomas realized that his own mouth was hanging open. He quickly shut it and stared at George again, unsure of what to say.

Meanwhile, George had regained his composure, and his voice was steadier as he began to explain what he meant by a *gift with conditions*. He started by discussing how he had saved a substantial amount of money over the years from the business's net revenues. He wanted to continue working for as long as he could and take a small percentage of the profits. When he eventually retired, Thomas would assume full ownership of the store.

George discussed the store's legacy and how it should be preserved. He wanted the store to continue focusing on specific genres and independent authors while steering clear of placing too much emphasis on commercial bestsellers. He repeatedly emphasized his desire for the store to serve as a cultural and community hub. Yes, there would be financial considerations. With George's assistance, they would establish a *financial buffer* to ensure the smooth management of the bookstore's operations. George also had much to say about the taxes on the *gift* that would need to be addressed.

Finally, he articulated his primary wish: an exit strategy that would allow him to help co-manage and advise Thomas on various operational aspects. In other words, while relinquishing ownership, he wanted to remain involved with the store until he either left or passed away. "Thomas, I am fully confident that if you wish, you can make the store successful for the foreseeable future."

As George spoke, Thomas sat, listening in shock. Throughout the past week, he had reflected on his life and felt overwhelmed by the personal epiphany he experienced at Mass. This realization led him to commit to being completely honest and to becoming the best man he could be for Minnie and Cynthia, no matter the cost.

Now this. Was George saying what he thought he was saying? Was it possible? Thomas returned to reality when George asked, "Well, are you interested? What do you think of my offer?"

"George, say no more. Of course, I'm interested in the store. I'm overwhelmed by what you're saying." Thomas replied, "George, are you sure?"

"I've never been more sure in my life. Thomas, we make a great team now and will continue for as long as I can stay upright." They both laughed.

"Well, if this is all true, and you mean what you say, I'm all in."

"Oh, Thomas, this is wonderful. I've been working with my lawyer on the idea and all the necessary paperwork, and we will need to review everything, but I am fully and completely committed to it."

George rose from his chair and extended his hand. Thomas stood, and they shook on it.

# *56.*

# *"Who does that?"*

After meeting with George for over an hour, they agreed to take a break and would continue reviewing the paperwork over the next few days. Thomas picked up a sandwich from The Harvester Restaurant, returned to the store, and began his shift.

He was beside himself. No matter what he did during the day, he saw everything in a different light. The whole situation was mind-boggling. Was he no longer going to be the night manager, or did this mean he would become the day and night manager?

As evening approached, he remembered his intention to call Cynthia about the poem. They spoke and agreed that Thomas should do his usual routine and stop by after work.

When the workday ended, Thomas went home, changed his clothes, grabbed the copy of Pascal's prayer and his poem version of it, and walked over to Cynthia's apartment. Upon his arrival, Thomas noticed that she looked much better than she had a few nights ago. Her signature ponytail was back, and she wore a relaxed smile. Thomas held onto his poem until Cynthia led him to the living room, where they stood looking at each other, unsure of where to start.

Cynthia, ever gracious, began the conversation by thanking him once more for being there in her time of need. Thomas expressed how worried he had been at that time, as he was deeply concerned about her well-being. This exchange conveniently led Thomas to the topic he wanted to discuss that evening.

Thomas looked at her seriously and said, "Cynthia, do you remember me talking to you about Blaise Pascal, specifically the 12-page prayer he wrote on the proper use of sickness?"

She nodded, leaning slightly forward on the couch where she had just sat down.

"Well, I remember giving a pretty awful presentation on the topic, hoping it might spark your interest in the prayer due to your heart issues. I also didn't have the prayer with me to show you. Anyway, I made a copy of the prayer, and here it is." He pulled out the folded, stapled twelve-page prayer and handed it to her.

Cynthia took it from him, unfolded it, and began to flip through its pages slowly.

Thomas, observing her, spoke up. "You can see that it's quite lengthy and I guess complex. When I originally read it, I thought of you and hoped it might pique your interest.

After my poor attempt to present the ideas to you, you asked if you could read it yourself. We agreed that it was a good plan. So, there it is. After making the photocopy, I took it home, reviewed it once more, and came up with the idea of transforming the 12 pages of writing into a short poem."

He gave Cynthia a wide-eyed look and said, "Don't, don't you dare laugh at me. I won't have it." He smiled. Cynthia started to laugh softly.

"Alright, enough of that," Thomas said. "I really worked hard on the poem. I want you to know that I truly care about you, and I want you to be well."

Cynthia asked, "Am I allowed to see it?"

Feeling a slight twinge of trepidation, he handed her the single piece of paper containing the handwritten rhyme. Cynthia accepted the offering and, this time, settled back on the couch, swinging her feet up onto it. There, she began to read the poem.

Uncertain of what to do as silence enveloped the room, Thomas wandered back to the window and gazed out at his favorite park. Minutes drifted by.

Thomas turned toward Cynthia when he heard her folding the paper.

Cynthia urged him to join her. "It's a beautiful poem, Thomas."

Thomas sat down beside her on the couch.

"This is beautifully written. I can tell it comes from your heart. You did this for me?" she asked, not seeking acknowledgment. "I didn't know you were a poet, Thomas."

"I took an introductory poetry class at Rainier University," he said, slightly shrinking back into his corner of the couch. I've found that sometimes it's easier to grasp what's being said when I reduce it to a simple rhyming poem. It has worked for me in the past, and I thought it might work for you, also."

"Well, it is very meaningful. I want to read it a few more times, but honestly, Thomas, it's such a wonderful gesture. Thank you." She got up on her knees on the couch and leaned over toward Thomas, put her arms around his neck, and kissed him on his lips.

Once again, a silent pause enveloped the room as each contemplated their puzzling relationship. Then, Cynthia sat back in her corner again, this time stretching her legs across the couch and playfully nudging him with her toes. "So, Mr. Klement, have you told this Minnie person you love her yet?" She gave him another mischievous push with her toes.

Strangely feeling somewhat relaxed, Thomas rolled his eyes and said, "I met with Minnie and told her about you, but then a friend of mine interrupted us, and we were unable to finish the conversation. She's been at her parents' home up on Hood Canal for most of this week. I've been waiting for her to return."

"How did she react to the idea of you having feelings for me?" Cynthia asked, a mischievous grin playing on her face. Thomas slightly returned her grin and replied, "Well, she definitely seemed a bit more intense in her response to what I said compared to your lack of reaction."

"You know, Thomas," Cynthia mused, "I go and fall in love with Erik and then you, and then I mess everything up by telling both of you that it can't be. I'm all screwed up. Yet, I'm of Scottish ancestry. We are made of sterner stuff. I will get through this. Like I said, I've been through this before. However, you were so sweet and special the other night when I was struggling. I don't know if I will ever get over that."

"Anytime, Cynthia - no matter the circumstance."

She slowly nodded, recognizing his sincerity. She recalled the poem he had written for her. Who does that? Cynthia closed her eyes for a moment. I can handle this. Then she exhaled and said, "I'm definitely interested in hearing how your next conversation with her goes." She raised her knees, pulling her feet away from Thomas' leg. Cynthia sat there, turning these thoughts over in her mind, then sighed, raised her hands, and asked, "Should we watch a movie?"

Thomas smiled as the tension finally eased. "You choose the movie, and I'll pop the corn."

## 57.

## "...no matter the outcome."

A few days later, Minnie phoned Thomas. She told him she had checked at the bookstore for him, only to find out it was his day off. Thomas had been reviewing some papers related to the store that George had given him the day before. The papers were spread out on the ottoman in front of him. They mostly involved taxes and finances, so Thomas was pleased on many levels to hear from Minnie and set aside the mind-numbing paperwork for a while.

It was a beautiful day, and the two decided to meet at the Botanical Conservatory in the park. Minnie would take a few extra minutes to arrive, so Thomas strolled through the park alone for a while. It was then that he began to think deeply about Minnie. Once again, she had left town only to return. His heart began to race. He realized he felt pretty nervous. What would she say? Was Minnie going to tell him something he didn't want to hear? As he pondered this, he recalled that her voice had sounded somewhat matter-of-fact during the phone call. Had Richard set her up with a publishing deal, or maybe a lead on a job, possibly somewhere outside Tacoma? Was she going to announce that she was leaving?

As his head continued to spin, Thomas saw Minnie approaching the crest of the hill toward the Conservatory. He waved, and they arrived at the front doors of the large glass structure at the same time. They embraced, and he held the door for her as they entered the building. They walked past the pond, where the koi swam in graceful arcs, and ventured deeper into the indoor gardens. The flagstone and dirt path revealed a lush abundance of greenery, with tropical plants arching overhead against the glass panes. They proceeded until they reached a small bench, slightly set back from the path, which offered some privacy. Thomas and Minnie sat down.

"How have you been?" Thomas asked, all his worries and questions swirling in his mind. Minnie turned to him, her expression unreadable to him.

"Thomas, I'm sorry for not letting you know in advance that I was visiting my parents last week, but what you mentioned about that other woman and all the excitement Richard brought really threw me off balance, I suppose."

"No, no, that's okay," Thomas said. "You're here, and that's what matters. So, is that what you wanted to share with me? I know you visited your parents because Charlotte told me when I tried to call you the next morning after we ran into Richard. Of course, I just missed you, as seems to be the case with us…"

"Thomas," Minnie interrupted, "it was not the visit I wanted to tell you about, but I wish I had. What I wanted to say was much more important to me."

Thomas felt uneasy as she spoke those words.

"First, though," Minnie said, looking as serious as one could imagine. "I want to share with you what happened to me after the abortion."

Thomas, very surprised, didn't know what to expect next.

Minnie continued, "I told you I couldn't get the terrible experience out of my mind." The botanical gardens, quiet to begin with, became silent. "I couldn't come to terms with what I had done. I would lie in bed at night, staring at that dark, dark ceiling, and cry my eyes out. During those times, I thought of all sorts of good and bad things about my life." She turned her head toward Thomas, who had been staring straight ahead until that moment. "One thing that stuck with me was you, Thomas. You were always there for me during that living hell. You didn't tell me what to do. You were kind to me. You were just there for me."

Minnie paused and looked at Thomas before continuing, "I thought about it a lot—the situation where Vicki told you about my abortion. It made me reflect on what you told Vicki about your faith, and I agree with everything you said. I also remembered that you mentioned your church, Holy Trinity, so I went there and met Father Ron. He told me he knew you. He is such a wonderful man. We talked in generalities at first, and then I had many questions for him. In the end, I shared everything with him. There were several things I didn't understand, but Father Ron was incredibly patient and caring. Over the past several months, we met twice a week, and he really helped me come to terms with everything that happened during that terrible time. It went so well that I asked him if he could help teach me about the faith, and that wonderful old priest said, 'Of course.' So we continued to meet twice weekly for what he referred to as private instruction." Minnie waited for a moment to gauge Thomas' reaction.

Thomas remained silent but attentive. Minnie again spoke, "Thomas, I'm going to be baptized."

Instinctively, Thomas wrapped his arms around her and held her close. Minnie's eyes brimmed with tears as she sniffled.

"Minnie, I'm at a loss for words," whispered Thomas. "I had no idea."

"I'm so excited for this to happen," replied Minnie. "It's exactly what I need to do to come to terms with everything that has occurred. You need to know, Thomas, that I will always have a place in my heart for that baby."

Thomas quietly nodded in approval while they embraced on the bench, the silence stretching out for what seemed like an eternity.

Eventually, they got up and left the conservatory. Thomas asked her whether everything had gone well with Richard and her short stories.

She said, "After calming down from my excitement about Richard's news, I agreed to let him be my *unofficial* agent. He believed that with my approval, the stories would be published, likely later in the fall or no later than after the first of the year."

A bit further along the path, Minnie said, "We need to finish our conversation about this, Cynthia."

Thomas said, "Yeah, okay, let's do that. But before we go there, I have something more to share with you about Cynthia." Minnie's nose twitched.

"That night, after we last spoke, I received a call from Cynthia saying she was in physical distress. She asked me to come to her apartment, and I did. She has a heart condition, and I ended up sitting in a chair watching her endure some pretty awful pain. As I mentioned, I tried to contact you the next morning, but you had already left for Union. Cynthia takes nitroglycerin when she experiences severe chest pain, and the side effects scare her. It really wasn't easy to watch."

He glanced at Minnie. She looked back at him. "She was scared, Minnie. I told her I would be there for her in any way I could."

Minnie took this in, processed it briefly, and replied, "That sounds like you, Thomas." After considering her words, she continued, "Thomas, you told me you had strong feelings for this woman."

"Yes," Thomas replied. "Minnie, I still had strong feelings for you, but you had left me." He lowered his head and, in a soft and uneasy voice, added, "I was crushed and heartbroken to see you with Street."

"I left you because I was embarrassed," revealed Minnie. Then, looking Thomas straight in the eye, she said in a heartfelt voice, "I know this sounds unbelievable, but when you stopped us from making love, I felt like a complete fool. I don't know what I was thinking. The best way to describe it is to say I wasn't thinking at all. I initially got together with Street to make you feel bad and want me. It was a big mistake. I did everything wrong. It strains credulity that I managed to commit all the terrible and horrible things I did." Minnie hesitated, then stopped walking and turned to face Thomas. She grasped his arms and said, "All I know is that I loved you. I love you now more than I did before." And, looking into his eyes, she said, "I want you to love me. Thomas, I want to start a family with you. I don't know how else to express this to you. I'm a broken woman who has had an abortion, and I feel so guilty about it." Her eyes filled with tears.

Thomas said, "Don't cry. It pains me greatly to understand the part I played in what happened to you." He paused, a look of torment crossing his face. "This ordeal you endured is my fault." Then he stepped forward and embraced her. "My self-preservation and pride kept me from doing what I should have when I found out you were with David Street. I should have fought for you right then and there. My insecurities and pride held me back. I gave up on the woman I loved. I acted pitifully. Later, when I finally figured out who I wanted to be when I grew up," his voice rising with self-contempt, "I knew I had to tell you and Cynthia where I stood, no matter the outcome. I love you, Minnie. I've always loved you."

The two then embraced, holding each other as if there were no tomorrow. "Oh God, Minnie, can this really be happening?"

"Just hold me, Thomas Klement. I want to share your name."

With that, they kissed, taking the first step on a path they would walk together, come what may.

## 58.

## "...the riddle of the waves..."

It was the summer of 1985. Thomas Klement had become the owner of Commencement Bay Books. The gift, *with conditions,* had unfolded just as George had hoped. Despite the rise of large bookstores like Barnes & Noble and Borders, which focused solely on new titles, this respected mid-sized contender offered used books alongside a solid selection of new stock. The Tacoma bookstore reminded many in the Northwest of a smaller version of the well-known Powell's Books in Portland, a two-hour drive to the south.

During these five or so years of ownership change, the store remained the same, with only the staff experiencing some alterations. James had been promoted to *Night Manager,* filling big shoes, as Thomas liked to joke. Susan, who had worked the day shift, married and moved on with her life. Linda Stuart, George's last hire, left after a couple of years with no hard feelings to pursue other interests. Dwight Newman continued to work at the store alongside James on the night shift. Mary Hogan, a new employee and

Thomas' first hire, worked during the day and turned out to be, as George described her, *an absolute dynamo.*

In George's mind, the idea of extending the life of his beloved store worked out perfectly. During the first year, he devoted himself to working with Thomas on the transition. However, after that effort, George recognized that it was going to succeed and decided to, as he put it, *sort of retire.* He embraced his semi-retirement like a fish taking to water. He still came in most days, but his attitude shifted, and he became nothing if not Mr. Wonderful to the staff and customers. From that point on, during the spring and summer, George, though looking frailer as the years passed, could be found sitting in the back room, having relinquished his office to Thomas, wandering around the store, or sitting at a table outside at the restaurant next to the bookstore, listening to Seattle Mariners baseball broadcasts on a transistor radio that Klement had purchased for him complete with an earphone jack and earpiece. Thomas held a surprise 80th birthday party for him at the store. There was even an article in the Tacoma paper lauding George and the bookstore as a landmark and contribution to the city's civic and historical culture. As George reflected on his life, he realized he couldn't have been happier.

Regarding Thomas' friend Zack, his parents finally persuaded him to return to Sacramento to live with them.

They undertook the effort to see how much of Zack's old life could be salvaged. Thomas always remembered Zack while offering his prayers to the Lord before Mass, with a special intention for his parents, who had to bear the loss of one son in the Vietnam War and the struggles that their other son was enduring.

Nate remained a close friend, although he now spent most of his time with a nurse he had met at Zack's original rehabilitation center—a woman with whom he intended to build a life.

Vicki Prentis, conflicted, fierce, and indomitable, returned to Seattle, where, as the last anyone had heard, she was fighting battles for the National Organization for Women (NOW)—advocating for issues such as reproductive rights, equal pay, and the ongoing struggle over the legal status of the Equal Rights Amendment (ERA). Although passionate about her cause, Vicki adopted a less aggressive approach toward men during their *discussions,* having learned that not all men were the enemy.

Holy Trinity Catholic Church continued to meet the needs of the small Catholic community on the edge of downtown Tacoma. When Father Sinclair retired in 1982, he was allowed to remain at the church and live in the rectory. He continued to act as the chaplain for the sick and suffering in the parish and at the South Puget Sound hospital. He would say Mass as needed for the new pastor,

Father Brendan. Father Ron was also a devoted confessor, sitting in the confessional, ready to offer grace to contrite souls seeking reconciliation with God. It goes without saying that Father Ron also spent time on Sunday mornings in the basement of Holy Trinity, sharing thoughts and opinions on everything in the world with Richard Dart while enjoying a cup of coffee and perhaps a donut. Father Ron meant the world to Thomas for his pastoral work with Minnie during her "Dark Night of the Soul."

Richard Dart continued to follow the papacy of Pope John Paul II while writing articles about the pontiff and other church-related topics for the archdiocesan newspaper. He also told Thomas that the key to longevity was to walk three miles a day, which he did.

The Wright Park neighborhood remained an oasis at the edge of the downtown business district. Tacoma's once vibrant downtown had never recovered from the construction of the Tacoma Mall in the city's South End in the mid-1960s. The large anchor retail stores moving to the Tacoma Mall from the downtown core were the death knell for the downtown retail experience. Despite the efforts of future mayors and city councils who came and went, promising a revival of the glory days of the old downtown core, they never succeeded in recreating it to any meaningful degree.

*********

Alice Klement sat in a folding beach chair, with the sand dunes behind her, gazing out at the water as the sun climbed over the stretch of shoreline in front of Grayland. The sun during early August was nearly always ideal for relaxing on the beach.

She recalled the decades she had lived here, meeting her husband and then raising their son single-handedly after his soul-crushing death. Although the loss of Thomas' father was the most devastating event in her life, not to mention the painful loss of her sister, her memories were primarily fond as she reflected on the past.

Then, her daughter-in-law, Minnie, walked over and sat down on another beach chair beside her, accompanied by Alice's granddaughter, Gracie. "Look at the little darling. She's really enjoying the beach," Grandma said with a smile.

"She loves the sand between her toes," Minnie offered, smiling. "Have you recovered from volunteering to walk your granddaughter around in the middle of the night until she finally fell asleep?"

Alice smiled and said, "Oh, she's an angel. Trust me, when they are your own, you love them and do whatever is necessary for their well-being. As a grandparent, you just love them and enjoy them and marvel at the mystery of God's plan."

The two women continued to chat. "It was so kind of you and Thomas to invite me on your vacation," Alice said.

Minnie replied, "When we decided to take this vacation and come here, Thomas immediately thought of inviting you. He said this place held too many memories for both of you not to visit."

"He's right. Grayland carries so much of our past," sighed Alice. At that point, she stared at the water, and so many memories came back to her.

Meanwhile, while her mother-in-law gazed at the water, Minnie reflected on the last five years. Looking back, she remembered that when she and Thomas had finally *gotten over themselves* and admitted their love for each other, things moved quickly. Most importantly, she was baptized into the faith and the Church, which had become so important to her. Then they were married at Holy Trinity by her and Thomas' favorite priest, Father Ron. Next, they moved into Thomas' apartment. She became pregnant. By the time she had the baby, they needed to find a house because the apartment had quickly become too small. Fortunately, the home they found was still in the neighborhood. Although it didn't have a view of the water or the park, it did have three bedrooms and two bathrooms. It was only 1,800 square feet, but it worked for them. Then they purchased a car, and it was totally worth it, despite Thomas' protests to the contrary. Most amusingly, she remembered when Thomas had to obtain his driver's license. Minnie shook her head slowly and smiled. She remembered he felt embarrassed about his age, but he had marched right into the Department of Motor Vehicles among all the sixteen-year-olds. While he may not have been at the top of the class that day, he managed to pass his test.

Minnie smiled to herself and then reengaged with Alice. "Thomas works crazy long hours at the store, but I know he loves it. I still manage to write a short story or two each year. It's good for my sanity. That dear Mr. Dart still handles the agent's work of getting those stories into journals or collected works for me. Every dollar helps us. And, lest I forget, God bless George Renko. Without him, I'm not sure your son would be as happy as he is today with his choice of profession. If you know him, and you certainly do, you know it could not have worked out better for him."

"How's Cynthia Innes?" Alice asked, curious.

"Actually, she's a sweetheart. As you know, she and I became friends. We spend time together. She's had a rough go of it. I've told you how insanely jealous I was of her back then, but it's hard not to like Cynthia once you get to know her."

Minnie pushed some sand around Gracie's feet. The young Klement girl giggled. Then, glancing back at Alice, she said, "About a year ago, Cynthia ran into her old boyfriend, Erik. I think his last name is Grove." She paused, considering whether she was correct. "Anyway, as I understand it, she told Erik that, over time, she had decided not to keep him at arm's length. Cynthia told him that she was ready to explore what they might discover about themselves together if he was still interested. Health-wise, she's been doing pretty well. Her doctor says that if things worsen, there is a good chance they will be able to perform a new procedure on her. I forgot what it's called. Anyway, she told me she would be ready if and when that time came. I have to give her credit. Cynthia is really brave."

Alice looked down toward the ocean and saw Thomas and Blaise at the water's edge. Thomas animatedly gestured towards Blaise while talking. Blaise, for his part, watched his father intently while dancing in and out of the surf. Alice said, "What could a father possibly be saying to a four-year-old that requires such energy and enthusiasm?"

Looking at *her boys,* as Minnie called them, she said, "I'm almost positive Thomas is sharing with Blaise what he would call the riddle of the waves. As Thomas would say, it is never too early to teach your children the faith."

The three Klement women smiled, including little Gracie.

*The End*

316

## Acknowledgments

Once again, like my previous novel, *North Pacific*, I would like to thank Mary Smith and William Randolph Parrett for taking the time to read, review, ask questions, and offer suggestions to improve the storyline of this book.

I also appreciatively acknowledge the assistance of ChatGPT, whose thoughtful prompts and literary insights helped shape the characters, themes, and language of *In Pascal's Shadow*. Any mistakes are, of course, my own.

Much of the story takes place in Tacoma's "North End." The text mentions various buildings, businesses, institutions, and locations across the city. Some sites are given fake names, and others are entirely created from the author's imagination. It is a work of fiction. No characters in the story are based on real people.

Finally, I would also like to thank my wife, Becky, for editing the book and taking on the thankless task of preparing the manuscript for publication. I am forever grateful.